The Tree Bride

ALSO BY BHARATI MUKHERJEE

Darkness

The Tiger's Daughter

The Holder of the World

Leave It to Me

Jasmine

Wife

The Middleman and Other Stories

Days and Nights in Calcutta (with Clark Blaise)

The Sorrow and the Terror (with Clark Blaise)

Desirable Daughters

The Tree Bride

A Novel

BHARATI MUKHERJEE

NEW YORK

Library of Congress Cataloging-in-Publication Data

Mukherjee, Bharati.
    The tree bride / Bharati Mukherjee.—1st ed.
        p. cm.
    ISBN 1-4013-0058-8
    1. East Indian American women—Fiction. 2. India—Emigration and
immigration—Fiction. 3. Women revolutionaries—Fiction. 4. Arranged
marriage—Fiction. 5. Calcutta (India)—Fiction. 6. Women immigrants—Fiction. 7. Women—India—Fiction. 8. Married women—Fiction. 9. Sisters—Fiction. I. Title.
    PR9499.3.M77T74 2004
    813'.54—dc22
                        2004042507

Hyperion books are available for special promotions and premiums. For
details contact Michael Rentas, Manager, Inventory and Premium Sales,
Hyperion, 77 West 66th Street, 11th floor, New York, New York 10023-
6298, or call 212-456-0133.

FIRST EDITION

10 9 8 7 6 5 4 3 2 1

For Quinn Xi Anand Blaise

All kings must see hell at least once.

Hence you have for a little while

been subjected to this great sorrow.

MAHABHARATA, CHAPTER XCVII
CHAKRAVARTHI V. NARASIMHAN, TRANSLATOR

Part One

Prologue

Abbas Sattar Hai: I pray we do not meet him again.

Bish and I were standing on the back porch of my house in Upper Haight on a warm, November, California night. My daughter must have been the size of a half-corpuscle. I wouldn't even know of her existence for another two months.

Rabi, our fifteen-year-old, came running out of his front bedroom asking, "Did you hear that?" Voices and scuffling on the sidewalk at three o'clock in the morning, he said, then the *slap-slap* of running sandals. We told him no, we hadn't heard a thing. We were worried that he'd heard us.

And that's all I remember, until I found myself in the backyard under a shower of glowing splinters and balls of flaming tar that had been my home. My hair was singed off, my face and arms pitted by embers. Poor Bish lay beside me, his cotton pajamas burned into his skin and his feet transformed into blackened blocks from having carried me over the coals and flames that had been the back stairs and the lower deck. Rabi, the first one down, had leaped over the deck and railing. He was unhurt, but he was moaning and shivering in the heat.

Our lives will not be safe until Abbas Sattar Hai is apprehended.

When I was a very small child back in Kolkata, my paternal great-grandmother told me a very strange, very moving story about life-before-birth. Call it the Hindu version of the stork legend. Between incarnations, she said, the individual soul wanders in a dreamless state, like a seed between plantings, in the windy realm of *vayumandala,* waiting for its allotted time to reinhabit a living body. When the time arrives, it slips through a seam in the fetal skull and begins its phase of deep dreaming. The bodies it has previously inhabited have perished, but the soul persists. Fire cannot burn it, nor water drown it. It dreams of its past tenancies. It remembers the terrors and triumphs of its many lives on earth and links them together with the logic of dreams.

That was a typical nighttime Calcutta—sorry, Kolkata—story told by a great-grandmother to a wide-eyed six-year-old. The story held for me the same vibrancy that comic books do for Americans. It still does. My daughter floats inside me, projecting dream-stories fashioned from lives lived and imagined.

There was one lesson that my great-grandmother, a widow who couldn't read or write her own name but who'd memorized many tales and Sanskrit prayers, insisted on teaching us through the stories she told. The cosmos is created, sustained, destroyed, and re-created over and over again, but only one town on earth is spared during the period of cosmic dissolution. She named the town: Kashi. From my parents and my two older sisters, I knew Kashi by its secular name, Varanasi, the old British Benares. But my great-grandmother set me straight. Kashi, she explained, is both the City of Light and the City of Liberating Cremation. The god Shiva carries Kashi on the prongs of his trident. When the cosmos chars into total blackness, Kashi glows because Shiva created it as a sacred space where to die is to be saved. She intended to die in Kashi, she insisted.

And that always led her to tell more stories about Kashi that made death sound like a blessed event.

As it happened, when I was nine years old my great-grandmother died of congestive heart failure in our house in Kolkata. I begged my parents to cremate her in Kashi. "Kashi exists only in our minds," my father explained. "You can be sure that she died in Kashi and not upstairs in her bed."

1

had only one requirement for any doctor who would be poking around down there (well, two): that she be Indian.

My old ob-gyn had pulled out of our health plan, but gave me two names, one of them American, the other "V. Khanna." Veena or Vibhuti? I wondered, which goes to show that nothing in this world is as simple as it looks. Also, that there are no coincidences in the universe. My imagined Indian doctor turned out to be a sturdy, well-conditioned older woman with blondish-white hair and gray-green eyes.

I've become attentive to framed degrees on doctors' walls, the eloquent medley of their mute accomplishment. V. Khanna's was particularly impressive. On my first visit, I took in the framed degrees, the diplomas and photos on the walls. The same efficient-looking white woman appeared in front of the Taj Mahal, posed on the Great Wall, and tending patients in tents and makeshift build-

7

ings. I wondered if I had barged into the wrong office, or, at the very least, a joint practice.

The first degree read: *Victoria Alexandria Treadwell, B.A. English, University of Alberta.* Five years after that, Miss Victoria A. Treadwell received a Ph.D. in History from the University of British Columbia. A decade later, Victoria Treadwell-Percy earned a medical degree from the University of Edinburgh. And fifteen years ago, Doctor-Doctor Treadwell-Percy disappeared altogether and in her place emerged V. Treadwell-Khanna, ob-gyn at Stanford University Medical Center. Other plaques celebrated an F.R.C.S. (London), a medal from Beijing, another from New Delhi, and the Bay Area Doctor of the Year Award for her discovery of the Khanna Factor in AIDS transmission. She was also cited for her work on "appropriate contraception" in socially conservative Third World cultures.

She was all business on that first visit. She drew blood, listened in, smiled, and confirmed what my home-testing kit had told me. Tara, old girl, you've got company. I'd aged twenty years in the past six months. I covered my stubbly, second-growth hair with a shawl. The fire-borne sparks and ashes had freckled my face with a myriad of tiny black pits; some will never heal. Even on Haight Street, when I'm pushing Bish in his wheelchair, I'm the one they stare at. *Poor thing,* I hear. But on that first visit, Dr. Khanna didn't appear curious, didn't ask, and I didn't tell.

On my second visit a few weeks later, Dr. Khanna acknowledged the public "me" I've learned to deny. She merely said, "Well! I'm honored to meet you!" and left it at that. That's Tara Bhattacharjee, B.A. (English Honours), Calcutta University, and, after a twenty-year gap, Tara Chatterjee, M.A. (English), San Francisco State University. I can't put the rest of the story on the wall. Like Dr. Khanna, I have pictures and clippings, but unlike her, they're the things I hide. Let's just say I'm in recovery from celebrity. I'm alert to the squint of passersby, the smirk and the cupped-hand whisper into another's ear (*Isn't that? Didn't she? Wasn't she?*). I am, I did, and I was. For a few months I had been a "People." *In a Flash—An Immigrant Dream Goes Up in Smoke.* Subheading: *Indian Mafia Targets Silicon Superstar.* And finally, *Bomb's Secret Disclosure: The Kinky Sex Life of an Immigrant Wife.* In the racier tabloids I was, briefly, the "Rani of Rivoli Street" and "The Brahmin Bombshell." The small burns have left black pockmarks. My hair has grown back straighter, with white strands. And the Indian Mafia, led by Mr. Abbas Sattar Hai, is still out there. I carry my talisman, Jack Sidhu's card, and Jack's on my speed dial—Sgt. Jasbir Singh Sidhu, Ethnic Squad, SFPD—in case Mr. Hai chooses to show up again.

Victoria Khanna confirmed the expected, and the obscure. A rubella shot just in case, and please, my dear, forgo the nightly wine. I may be holding up, but my genes are old and feeble. Her accent is as mangled as mine, clipped and clear, a bit English and Scottish, American and Canadian. She asked some questions: parental health (poor, I said); mine (no lasting effects); teenage son's (he divulges on a need-to-know basis); husband's (good days and bad, ten steps forward, eight steps back; still in physiotherapy). She called him Dr. Chatterjee, indicating that she knew a little more about him, or us, than she'd let on. She said, "You've had . . . let me see, malaria, hepatitis, typhoid, meningitis— rather typical of a tropical childhood, isn't it? Tests will probably confirm exposure to tuberculosis and polio, but you threw them off. Strong girl. They like to say whatever doesn't kill you makes you stronger, don't they? Don't believe it. At least it gives you antibodies. You've got an allele for cystic fibrosis. No problem, unless the father has one too."

I interrupted to say that sixteen years ago I conceived a child with the same man. Rabi's got issues, maybe even genetic issues, but no cystic fibrosis.

"Blood tests are like big thick novels, aren't they?" she mused. "They can tell us more than we need to know. The history of the race for instance. Out of Africa, into San Francisco."

More like a haiku, I think. One drop is a hemo-synecdoche of the world.

She continued: "Thank God for recessiveness. Elevated recessives are quite common among long-term inbreds." She seemed to smile. "Bengali brahmins for example."

Well, thank God I now have a name for it. Long-term inbreds—I felt myself blushing. We've been practicing communal incest for five thousand years. Except for my oldest sister, who married a Punjabi, no relative of mine or Bish's has ever married outside our caste and community. When I think of my older relatives, I remember the litany of their health complaints. Arthritis Auntie, Uncle Insulin, Cousin-We-Don't-Talk-About. We all get headaches. My mother is in the final stages of Parkinson's. We were taught to think of disease as the special badge of our refinement, a price to pay for the privilege of birth in Calcutta high society. All the same, Dr. Khanna was clearly better informed on the medical histories of Bengalis than my first ob-gyn in Palo Alto, when I'd been pregnant with Rabi. For her, Indians were exotic, uncomplicated, baby-producing machines, uncorrupted by PCBs and other impurities of American life.

"Marriage inside a very confined community is high risk after a few hundred generations," she continued. "Genes drift, like the continents. You can shuffle the same deck of genes only a few hundred times before the advantage of randomness is lost. Bengali brahmins have been at it a long time." She studied my files.

"Parkinson's, like your mother's, is possible, along with migraines and bouts of depression. Breast cancer? Not likely. Alzheimer's? Probably not."

An X-ray, an MRI, a scan, a pressure-sleeve, a stethoscope told her what was inside and building, what she suspected but couldn't see, what had once appeared but now is hiding. Forty years ago, in the upper-left-hand corner of my mental map of the world, in northern Alberta, the girl known as Victoria Alexandria Treadwell had been, like me, an English major, *ma semblable, ma soeur*. Like me, she saw blood and genes in narrative terms, tragedies averted or waiting to happen.

She said, "It is very fortunate that you came to me, Mrs. Chatterjee." I must have looked alarmed. "Not for medical reasons," she quickly assured me. "You're fine, take normal precautions and the baby will be healthy. You are slightly elevated in age, but these days who isn't? Do you believe in destiny, Mrs. Chatterjee?"

I let it pass. Who doesn't in my family? Some cultural habits never die.

2

ish Unbound needs a tether. Even in a wheelchair, with numbed feet and hands, Bish Unbound taps out formulas and calls up Internet articles. Now that he's liberated from running the day-to-day of a worldwide enterprise, his mind, if not his body, is freer than ever. He's made our dining table an office; every horizontal surface, even the ironing board, is piled with journals. He'll wake up in the middle of the night asking, *What is information?* Does it have a guiding intelligence, or is it a plasma of random collisions? What is the link between human memory and mathematical certainty? What is the role of coincidence? While I'm trying to write a book about my ancestor, he's working on something he calls *"The Natural History of Coincidence."* Twenty-first century technology (speed) makes coincidence, or the appearance of coincidence, inevitable. Speed enhances contact, speed shrinks space and time.

Bish was working on his voice-activated laptop when I got back to the sublet. It's on the ground floor, so we've not had to install temporary ramps.

"Well, I'm healthy, and the baby's healthy. Are you happy about it?"

He logged off. "Certainly. I'm happy, but I worry."

I closed the lid of his laptop. "*Certainly* is not an option. What do you *feel* about it?"

"I feel I can't be a proper father. A baby will make your life much harder. You won't be able to write. I can't get up in the night to feed him . . ."

"Bish, darling, when did you ever get up in the night? And trust me, it's not a he."

"I swore that if I ever had a child again, I'd get up in the night, I'd be the father I haven't been to Rabi. I swore the next time I'd do it right."

I was still trying to remember when I had stopped my nightly wine. I know I hadn't stopped in the first month, when Bish was in the hospital all day and night, and Rabi and I didn't know if he would survive. The second month? Had I drunk through my daughter's brain development and already condemned her to a Haight Street existence?

When we were married, Bish stood six feet tall and walked with a manly stiffness my sisters called Calcutta Cowboy and I called Clint Eastward. An imaginary saddle creaked whenever he walked. Now I stand behind him and look down on his thinning hair, at the gray roots he can't dye out. My oldest sister, Padma, the one I call Didi, didn't marry until her late thirties, and that was in New Jersey to a divorced Punjabi. My middle sister, Parvati, found her own husband in Boston and returned with him to Bombay. Purely by coincidence, he happened to be a Bengali brahmin from a decent Calcutta family, so no one complained. I, as youngest, upheld family honor and married Bish, the perfect groom, in the old-fashioned, arranged way.

He had been a good off-spin bowler on his college cricket team and he played—used to play, that is—killer tennis with anyone who'd learned his game on private courts in tropical clubs. When America started looking for unthreatening, non-European success stories, there was always the "Atherton Communications Guru," "the Swami of Stanford," Bish Chatterjee. Unthreatening, because he was perceived as courtly and approachable. He always gave informative interviews. He had no rough edges. He hadn't started out in rags and gouged his way to the top. He hadn't stepped on anyone, hadn't tricked or absorbed competitors, and didn't keep their shrunken heads in a trophy case. There were no skeletons to haunt his dreams, no off-limit closets. He had no skeletons, no closets. Business writers called him "The Rajah" back then. (That used to give us a big laugh. Rajahs are Kshatriyas and wc are brahmins; my parents would never have sanctioned marriage to a lower-caste maharajah.) Or he was the "Broadband Mogul," and we'd cringe again, since Mughals are Muslim, our historic enemies. They even morphed him once into "The Rajah Mogul, Bish Chatterjee."

Guru, Rajah, Mogul, Swami, and Yogi: They exhausted their exoticizing vocabulary on him. They couldn't call him wise or brilliant without the tag of guru, couldn't explain his success without rope tricks, or his wealth without the opulence of an Oriental potentate. For ten years I was his "jewel in the crown," his "rani" on magazine covers. Smooth, sophisticated Bish Chatterjee inside a walled mansion with tennis courts and a swimming pool. Just your normal, middle-class Calcutta boy with a temperature-controlled wine cellar and on-call wine steward, tending a few

hundred vines of his own up in Napa with a private label, distributed to special friends. Château CHATTY Chardonnay. Bour-
gogne de Broadband. Calcutta and Chardonnay—they thought
they had stumbled on a vast and inexplicable contradiction.

Perhaps they had. The contradictions are vast, but subtle. He
rarely drank wine and now that everything's been lost, he doesn't
miss it. Outrageousness was expected in those boom years, stock
values might have plunged if he hadn't lived up to the hype. He
was talked into buying shares in a racehorse. He hosted splashy
receptions for Bollywood stars when they visited the Bay Area,
though his heart was in recitals of classical Indian music. The
only reality that counts now is that for the past three months I've
been standing behind the Rajah Mughal and looking down on his
head and shoulders and his once-dyed black hair, watching white
hairs spread from his hair-part and the part itself begin to widen.

By twenty-two I had satisfied all my ancestral duties. I was
married; I had a son, material comfort, an admired husband—
what else is there? Eight years later, feeling myself a privileged
prisoner inside the gated community, I listened to all the voices
yammering around me and all the stories on television and in the
magazines and did the right California thing and struck out on
my own.

According to the tabloids, at least, I went on to have a life.
There were men, yes. Bish stayed focused. He stayed inside the
gated community and built CHATTY into the position it
enjoyed until the bombing. Our bombing, not the country's. He
was twice voted "Bay Area Bachelor to Die For," although the
only death recorded was nearly his own. He could not forgive
himself for the only thing in his life (before the bombing) that he
had not seen coming and taken protective measures against, and
that was my defection from paradise.

At the time of the bombing, CHATTY had assembly plants in twenty countries, research facilities on three continents, and a worldwide workforce of well over a hundred and fifty thousand. CHATTY was in broadband and routers; it coordinated operating systems. The CHATTY time signal permitted integrated communication between the world's computers and universal access to the Web. It powered cell phones. Bish was convinced that its full power had never been touched.

He dreamed of a CHATTY that would unlock the mysteries of existence. He used to complain that "communications" was an unworthy word if it referred only to telephones, computers, and television. To him, "communication" extended down to the quantum level. He saw every corner of the universe as a hologram. On the quantum level, time and space break down. He's a mystic in the guise of scientist. And I'd ask, Well, how do you get from here to the edge of the universe? And he'd say, Just find the area code.

In the divorce, I refused the split of assets in favor of child support and Bish's continued benign involvement in my life. In gratitude, or maybe guilt, he'd bought me the house we nearly died in, and paid for its renovation, even after the contractor moved in with me. I knew I'd been headstrong. We got back together on the day of the bombing. I'd been trying to send a message to the man who had invented the modern standard for sending messages, but I didn't know the area code.

In Bish's order of priorities, building networks and endowing the world with handheld miracles was dharma, a duty. Creating wealth for millions entailed the further dharma of redistributing it productively. Marriage had not been part of the same hierarchy of obligation. Marriage was something done once and for all time to satisfy everyone's expectations, then put aside. Marriage was self-sustaining, the way our grandparents' had been. But those are Indian assumptions, not American.

After the bombing, CHATTY's stock value melted, particularly after Bish had been exposed as the target of hidden assassins. He withdrew from active participation. After the big bombs of 9/11, even the potential for broadband had narrowed. His old partner, Chet Yee, came back from semiretirement to run the day-to-day.

For Bish, the divorce, the bombing, the handicap, had all been signs. We come from a long line of amateur yogis and sadhus. He who had walked with statesmen, movie stars, and corporate gods, and soared above the world, now shuffled along its surface, pushed by his wife. Instant communication, possessions, wealth, were maya, he said, illusions. He who had paid no attention to borders and time zones, who had stepped from limousine to corporate jet, now sits by a window overlooking Haight Street, staring out on the homeless sleeping in doorways, the drug-hustle in Golden Gate Park, and the old men and women rooting through garbage cans for redeemable bottles. We still have money, but our life has shrunk to thrice-a-week therapy sessions and the contents of a sublet with institutional crockery and furniture. It's hard to think that the gods or the ruling deities of the wired universe or hippie California wisdom had not decided to deliver a painful lesson.

With this pregnancy, Bish and I are not even married. He'd graduated from the oxygen tent to a wheelchair, and soon, from the chair to parallel bars, then to a walker, with the prospect of sturdy, wrist-gripping canes to follow. In our daughter's earliest memories of him, she might see him walking, carefully planting his numbed feet directly under his weight. In the long future, perhaps by the time she needs a father to walk her to school, he'll regain the flair and enthusiasm that made him the Raja of Silicon Valley.

Of course, Silicon Valley will never be what it was. By the time Bish walks again, it will be a memory, ripe for a twenty-first-century Fitzgerald to make it come alive. *The Great Gupta,* perhaps.

,　,　,

During the twenty years I've been in California, an immigrant fog of south Asians has crept into America. Quiet, prosperous, hardworking, professional—in India they would have been blocked by social convention and family duties. There are Indians in every town, every hospital, every high school and college, in banks, motels, 7-Elevens and taxis, and a startling number have begun appearing in everyday American families. Like Victoria Treadwell's second husband, as girlfriends and boyfriends. I see Indian faces at family picnics in Golden Gate Park.

I noticed the swell of Indian faces for the first time when I was still in Palo Alto. Rabi was three years old. I was cashing a check and one of the bank managers came walking behind the counter. She said to my blond teller, "Missy, you can take your break when Shobana gets back." Shobana? Where had *she* come from? I hadn't even noticed an Indian face behind the grille. I was still an Indian-graduate-student-wife. Wife-of-Bish-Chatterjee was my full identity. If I had plans for the future, they would be to follow my husband wherever he went, probably back to India. Shobana, wherever she was (and in my mind, she's been on that coffee break for the past dozen years), was constructing a different immigrant life. I suffered a twinge of envy for her. I wondered if "wife" was the only role permitted to me, if there was a way of being in this country with my own identity.

The first time I went back to India on my own, it wasn't just to see relatives. I took Rabi with me on my own American-style roots search, into the East Bengal—now Bangladesh—of my grandparents and a hundred generations of Gangoolys and Bhattacharjees. My friends and even my sisters thought I'd gone crazy, or very American. In particular, I wanted to see this place called Mishtigunj that everyone in the family had talked about, but no one had visited in sixty years. "Why go that side?" my mother had asked. It was much better to talk nostalgically and bitterly of that place, "that side," than actually to expose oneself to it. I've gone back two more times.

Until I'd seen Mishtigunj, I thought I was a total Calcuttan. But when I walked through the alleys of the old town, I felt I knew the streets—nothing surprised me. It conformed to a mental image I'd been carrying since childhood, from the stories I'd been raised on. Yes, I thought, this is where my grandmother as a young girl had brought sweets to the Tree Bride, this is the old Hindu primary school she'd attended. I felt for the first time how recent my family's Calcutta identity was, just two generations, how shallow those urban roots were, not much deeper than Rabi's in California. I saw my life on a broad spectrum, with Calcutta not at the center, but just another station on the dial.

3

On my third visit, after the medical formalities, Dr. Khanna led me from her examining room back to her office and asked, "Is my last name of any interest to you?"

"Khanna? It's Indian, of course, but from where? Delhi, perhaps?"

It's a familiar game Indians play, since our names give away everything about us. Unless, of course, you're Victoria Khanna.

"My husband's from Delhi. Do you know many Khannas?"

"None come to mind."

"Your husband studied under my husband at Stanford. Yash Khanna, you might remember."

"Of course!" I said. "Bish spoke very highly of Professor Khanna. Please relay our greetings." Thus, I thought, are destiny and formality served. Her interest in me, and Bish, was easily explained. I said, "How stupid of me, it sometimes seems so long ago."

"Your husband was something special to Yash. He's followed Dr. Chatterjee's career with great interest. I believe they still communicate." The man who practically invented wireless communication now requires my help to punch in a phone number. Irony is not the same as destiny.

"And does my maiden name, Treadwell, mean anything at all?"

"Vaguely," I said. I wished it did. Treadwell is not a name I associate with my destiny, but she seemed so intent on asking, that I felt I owed her something.

And so, just as I had started coming to terms with an accelerated middle age—a mere thirty-six, but in one night nearly widowed and now nursing a crippled husband—no longer the tabloid-interest cutie-pie with the "pixie hair and latte complexion"—I began to suspect that this pregnancy was going to be tangled up with history.

I had no need for amniocentesis; I had been awash in estrogen for over a year. I had been writing a book about my sisters, Padma and Parvati, and our growing up in Kolkata, and then I'd started on something new and strange. This was about a distant relative we called the Tree Bride, my great-great-aunt, a point of light from the remotest, darkest galaxy of my life.

′ ′ ′

Behind Dr. Khanna's desk the windows opened on one of those Bay Area panoramas to die for—the Golden Gate Bridge, the Marin Headlands, and the deep purple of the bay, spotted that winter afternoon by dozens of sails. The bridge seemed just inches away, Berkeley a brief swim, the gray scab of city streets an easy stroll.

She kept her back to the windows and folded those broad, baby-delivering hands over my manila dossier. "I know I shouldn't pry into your life, but I think I shall. You have no reason to answer anything I might ask you."

I told her, "I have nothing to hide, Dr. Khanna," which sounded naïve, even to my own ears. I half-expected an arched eyebrow.

"Victoria, please—just never Vickie. How big a coincidence does it seem to you that my Indian husband taught computer engineering to your Indian husband at Stanford?"

I caught her irony. Even I would say, as Bish might, that's probability, not coincidence.

"He was so taken with your husband that he even put some money into the start-up. We owe you our weekend place in Sausalito. We named it Easy Come."

Only a weekend place? The pixie dust scattered by the start-up, after CHATTY caught on, is a Wall Street legend. Every dollar invested in the start-up returned a thousand, every ten thousand, a million.

"But now the coincidences start to get interesting." She leaned forward. "I'll ask again, Mrs. Chatterjee. Does the name Treadwell ring any bells?"

"Tara," I said.

Treadwell—such an English name! Treadwell was a name like a winter-trapped fly sticking to my face or a swarm of mosquitoes I couldn't swat away. I didn't remember any Treadwells from my childhood, but a name like that was strangely comforting in an old-fashioned Calcutta way. I could have written a dozen stories from the name alone. *Violet Treadwell and her three maiden daughters let rooms in the family's ancestral quarters . . . Treadwell's, a low Eurasian dive off the Kidderpore docks . . . Treadwell & Greavy, the tea-*

*shippers, maintained a godown behind a tawny wall scrawled with movie
posters and political graffiti . . .*

I wanted to be helpful. Her innocent question did not start me
on this quest, but it might help me to end it.

"I seem to remember a Treadwell Gardens when I was a little
girl." I didn't, but it sounded plausible. "My father might have
known a Treadwell, one of those Englishmen who came back for
December parties after Independence."

My father owned tea estates. Even as I write this, Rabi is stay-
ing with my parents in their retirement cottage in Rishikesh.
After Independence, the British planters sold out to Indian entre-
preneurs like my father, but they still returned to Calcutta for the
winter "season," health and politics permitting. Calcutta was the
only place in the world that treated them the way they saw themselves, like beloved royalty returning from exile. Their good old
days became our good old days. Their nostalgia became ours,
their irony and cynicism a mark of our own worldliness. The
urban decline they noted was a fall from standards we'd never
known, but learned to lament. I was a child during the last years
of their returns, when servants had to wheel them past the greet-
ing line.

One of them—a Treadwell, possibly?—even asked to be
buried in the old Calcutta Anglican cemetery. My parents and sisters and I went to the service to "pay our respects," which seemed
like a comic phrase. We were three little girls dressed in starched
white dresses wondering how much we had to pay. The priest was
an Indian Christian from the south. Two old women, English
widows in white gloves with no home to return to and no children to receive them, sat in the pew in their broad hats with thick
veils, while the rest of us, all Indians, passed by the bier looking
inside. Someone had dabbed color on the old man's cheeks and

trimmed his mustache. He wore an expensive woolen suit with a waistcoat and a broad silk tie. The coffin was made of an expensive, lacquered wood with brass handles. The body snuggled against its silk and velvet lining.

It seemed nonsensical. We wondered who would light the funeral pyre, since no sons had bothered to make the trip. Corpse-bearers carried the coffin into the overgrown jungle behind the church. It was a dark, moldering, unswept place, scattered with leaning, mossy, unreadable stones. To our horror, they lowered the coffin into a pit. It was a disgusting thought to us, putting a dead body underground. If the earth contained bodies, then the air held ghosts. It could have been a Treadwell. I was ready to concede it, if she insisted.

"I don't think so," she said. "My grandfather Treadwell left India in 1947 and never returned."

"There might have been a Treadwell girl in my school."

"I doubt it," she said.

What I wanted to say was "Treadwell" is so perfectly English it might not be English at all, but what we used to call Anglo-Indian and the British called Eurasian, the mixed-blood community with Domesday names and a long-vanished link to the fondly recalled mother country. Think of the actress Merle Oberon, so ashamed of her mother she introduced her as a servant. We were trained to despise Anglo-Indians. Now I can say, almost literally, I feel their pain.

I asked, "May I ask why *you* are so interested?"

"My grandfather's name was Virgil Treadwell. They called him Vertie—an acronym, really, Virgil Ernest Reginald Treadwell. He was in the Indian Civil Service. Eventually they posted him to Bengal. He was a district commissioner in Bengal from 1930 up through Independence."

"Bengal was a huge area," I said, about to launch into a familiar lecture. There would be today's Bangladesh, West Bengal, Orissa, Bihar, bits of Assam, and some remote mountain areas we try not to think about. Vertie Treadwell! It really is a Wodehouse world.

"I can narrow it down for you. It was in East Bengal," she said.

I had to ask, "Would you know where in East Bengal, exactly?"

She replied, "I believe I do, my dear."

She went to her corner coat closet and pulled out a white banker's box and lifted it to the edge of her desk. The contents were covered by an old sari. All the identifiable odors of India rose from that box, a century of monsoons, sweet and rancid bug spray, dust, hot mustard oil, fried fish and vegetables, basmati rice, trapped sun, mold, and decades of uncirculated air. Even today I can remember the smells of drying saris, the slippery, never-dry bathroom, the heavy air and fatigue of tropical Sundays, odors that the memory never releases. Under the sari, the box brimmed with old ledgers, silk-tied letters, and loose papers. Dr. Khanna set those gray-green eyes on me.

"So," she said. Oh, yes, she knew exactly where in Bengal her grandfather had been posted, and she knew that I knew, too.

"These papers from my grandfather have been traveling for nearly a century, across half the world, and they've settled on me like a forty-year pregnancy. If you don't take them away today, I swear I'll burn them. I have a feeling that you might be the perfect person for them, Mrs. Chatterjee."

"Tara, please."

"They are a history of a place you know very well, I think. They'll be like a RAM upgrade."

"Ram?"

"Random access memory."

If Bollywood were writing this script, the Golden Gate Bridge would sway and collapse and San Francisco Bay erupt in a wall of water. A cog of history that had been spinning freely for a century suddenly groaned and snapped into place.

"I wonder if you have ever heard of a place called . . . I hope I'm saying it correctly—"

"Mishtigunj," I said. It had to be.

"Yes, Mishtigunj." She smiled. "A strange name, wouldn't you say?"

I could have enlightened her. It was named for a foundling from London via Calcutta, an escaped murderer by the name of John Mist. Or a Lord Jim of the Sunderbans, a Pimpernel, a White Mughal, a visionary. At least, those were the stories I had read. It's not simply a Wodehouse world.

"*Mishti* means sweet, I understand," she said. "They must have grown sugar cane."

"Very likely," I said.

I'm enough of a mystic, like Bish, to believe there are no coincidences, only convergences. Yash Khanna had met and married an Anglo-Canadian, Victoria Treadwell-Percy, in India. They'd left India for Stanford and he'd taught my Indian husband. No Yash Khanna, no Bish and Chet Yee, no CHATTY. Victoria Khanna knew my blood, had typed me and could trace me, if she wished, to the dawn of time. Victoria Treadwell's grandfather must have known the Tree Bride. All stories of Mishtigunj touch, eventually, on Tara Lata Gangooly. She is like the Ganges, draining all tributaries. Hearing the word "Mishtigunj" from unexpected lips closed the circle.

I have visited Mishtigunj three times in the past six years and have been writing about it, and the Tree Bride, ever since. I lay out the old books, the ledgers, and my sheets of paper, knowing that somehow there's a novel behind them that only I can tell. I know a little bit about the Tree Bride—she'd been proxy-married to a tree at the age of five—but nothing about her latter years, except her death at British hands in 1943. In our family, she'd always been there, a living presence. Mishtigunj has always been there. Everything and everyone had always been there, without origin or ending. I'd been blocked from learning about the origins of Mishtigunj, and more about the living Tree Bride, until I made my second visit and an old hajji had taken me aside. That's how it goes; you put the word out, and magic things happen.

Until that moment, I'd been working only with family tales and memories. The Tree Bride was my mother's collateral great-aunt, meaning that she was one of many dozen children from at least ten wives kept by my great-great-grandfather, Jai Krishna Gangooly. Not until the ninth wife did he get the only son he acknowledged, his line's (and my mother's) continuance. But Tara Lata, the Tree Bride, was his third-born daughter from his first wife, born during his early years as a nationalist attorney.

The child Tara Lata had a quick mind and a serious aspect. The dozens of other daughters must have married, they must have found appropriate brahmin grooms in the forest villages of East Bengal. Dowries must have been paid. They are no less members of my family; given world enough and time, hundreds of aunties and uncles could be traced. My cousins probably populate the tract houses across the bay in Fremont. As Victoria Khanna had noted, the deck has been shuffled too often; our genes are old.

Last century's green-gold village of Hindus and Muslims set between the forest called in British days the Sunderbans, and the clean, fish-rich river called the George is now a sprawling city renamed Razakpur, spilling over a scruffy plain, edging a brackish basin in a Muslim country called Bangladesh. Its original name, Mist's intended name, had been George's Bight. There was a time when the extensive forests of the Shoondar Bon, the Beautiful Forest, protected all of southeastern Bengal from destructive storms. Wetlands filtered the salt and silt and sorted out the fisheries between shrimp and carp. Now, the forest has yielded to stagnant paddy fields. Every few years cyclones send walls of salt water through the marshes, carrying off thatched-roof cottages and herds of cattle, wiping out a decade's progress in a single day or night.

The River George is now part of a tidal estuary, its gradient lost, its water unfit for drinking and freshwater fish. I knew Mishtigunj. We've been trained to think of Mishtigunj as home in ways that our adopted homes, Calcutta and California, must never be. Ancestors come and go, but one's native village, one's desh, is immutable.

And so, I answered Victoria, yes indeed, I knew Mishtigunj. In fact, Victoria Khanna and I might be the only persons in the Bay Area, with the exception of a taxi driver I'd once encountered in San Jose, who'd ever heard of the now-vanished Mishtigunj. What a coincidence that your grandfather was posted there! I must have exclaimed. I believe it was Faulkner who said the past isn't past. The past isn't even dead.

"Hold on, Tara. It gets better," said Victoria Khanna.

When she'd been a twenty-year-old English major at the University of Alberta, Victoria had been presented by her father with a duffel bag of moldering papers. Vertie Treadwell, her father's "birth-father," with whom he had never exchanged a word, had died in England. Vertie's widow, Thelma, lived another ten years, but before she died she used World War I military records to trace Vertie's son, Victoria's father, to northern Canada. She'd mailed the old canvas bag to him without a warning or a salutation, and then she died.

It's like a slow-acting chain letter. Since Victoria was the only one in the family with historical curiosity, her father had decided to dump the papers on her, rather than burn them. He was a man of small compass who distrusted anything old or written or coming from England. So, the records survive through a series of miracles, mostly because no one has been interested enough to paw through them.

According to Victoria, Vertie Treadwell must have had a bit of Richard Nixon in him. He thought he would be seen as one of the towering figures of his age, a man of Churchillian depth and complexity. He'd hung on to minute scraps, letters, and articles in the hope they would someday cement his reputation. In the larger scheme of things, Victoria joked, the records had been kept for me.

"My father was born near Bombay in 1897 under what they called 'irregular circumstances.'" She paused, and smiled. "Illegitimate. Supposedly, his mother was the landlady's daughter. He was trundled off to England and placed in an orphanage. Vertie stayed in India, of course, but he had blotted his ledger, so they banished him to an administrative Devil's Island in the United Provinces. Instead of water, he was surrounded by jungles and wild little men with blowguns. And if Britain hadn't lost so many young men in the Great War, they would have left him there to rot. He never forgave them."

"And how old was he?"

"When my father was born? Vertie was all of twenty-three."

I was doing my own calculation. The cone of coincidence continued to narrow, and now it was touching ground. If Vertie Treadwell was born in 1874, he was the same age as the Tree Bride. In 1879, when Vertie was a sailor-suited preschooler, Tara Lata was waiting to get married. Her husband-to-be was a twelve-year-old from a nearby village. On his way to the ceremony, he was bitten by a cobra and died. This was an impediment to marriage, perhaps, but it didn't affect her auspicious horoscope. The marriage rites still had to be performed; marriage is bigger than the participants. And so, rather than die a spinster—second only to widowhood as a personal tragedy—on a cold, foggy December night in 1879, deep in the forest, she had been married to a proxy-husband, a straight, tall, sundari tree. Other girls facing similar fates were married to rocks or crocodiles.

Freed of any family obligations, she spent the next sixty years inside her father's compound, learning to read and write Bengali and English, then teaching and finally organizing and protesting. Every manner of protester and activist came to visit: Mahatma Gandhi the pacifist and Netaji Subhas Bose the militant, American friends of India, Sikh separatists from California, vegetarians and theosophists, Sufis and freethinkers, authors and photographers. One of those visitors could have been Vertie Treadwell.

"My poor father was a Diamond Jubilee baby," Victoria said. "If you were born in 1897, it meant you were eighteen in 1915, and that was the worst year in history to have been uneducated, able-bodied . . . and, well, a bastard. He was gassed in the trenches and in hospital they advised him to leave England for free land and the fresh air in northern Alberta. Old Vertie eventually married a proper colonial lady and had a daughter. When the girl was five, mother and daughter did some trundling of their own. They disappeared into New Zealand. Neither of his children ever returned to India, nor saw their father again. He married Thelma late in his life and died a miserable old man. I tell you, studying his life up close is like looking at hemorrhoids."

I peeked under the covering sari at the neatly tied bundles of letters. Vertie Treadwell kept a neat, flowing, Victorian hand. The ink was sturdy black India, turning slightly olive with age. I couldn't wait to unwrap the years and get started.

"I want to thank you for taking this on. You may find Vertie's accounts of Indians somewhat biased, to be sure. I was about to say that history is written by the victors, but in the case of India it's not always clear who won, is it?"

As I was leaving with the box, she said, "Don't think of me as one of those batty old dames who talks endlessly, Tara. I'm actually a very reserved person. It's amazing, isn't it, the way India opens one up?"

We settled on the next appointment, in two months. Medical appointment, that is. But personally, she said, Yash would like to get together with Bish. And she'd like to know me better. Could they call?

,   ,   ,

Back in the apartment, I set the banker's box on the kitchen table. "Well, Dr. Khanna listened in. Everything's normal," I said. Probably I should have said, Everything's extraordinary.

I prepared Bish's bowl of cornflakes, heating the milk in the microwave, just the way we'd been raised. I still have to feed him. He peered over the edge of the banker's box. "Life . . ." he began. *What?* I wondered. Life *what*—goes on? Life is frightening, unpredictable, a miracle? Tell me, Bish. Too complicated, too wonderful? This time it was just an utterance, with a suck of his teeth. "What's in here?" he asked. "A doctor gives you old documents?" I could see he wanted to unload the box.

Standing over Bish, looking down at his bowl of soggy cornflakes, I was reminded again of Calcutta. Yes, in my childhood it was Calcutta; "Kolkata" is a different time and space. Some days, everything radiates from Calcutta, then I can go for weeks, dreaming myself a native-born Californian. I remembered visiting my grandparents in the outer suburbs. Early every morning in their neighborhood, bells would announce the arrival of the goala, the cowherd and his cow. Servants would empty from the shuttered houses with brass pots to collect the fresh milk, then boil it three times. Before it cooled, my sisters and I would come down for our breakfast. What the humidity hadn't done to the canisters of cornflakes, the hot, pungent milk would finish off.

Soggy cornflakes on the Haight. My mother's mother and her husband had both been born in what is now Bangladesh, and she remembered visits in her childhood to her oldest relatives in Mishtigunj. This would be before the war, in the 1920s or '30s. Her parents would dress her up in her best white dress and take her to the biggest house in town to deliver a gift of sweets for Tara-mashi. *Shondesh* for the Tree Bride. From my grandmother, through my mother, I learned the purer strains of Bengali, the Mishtigunj dialect, the voice of East Bengal. And from my grandmother I learned the happier parts of the Tree Bride's story.

Sog beats crunch. Mush means love. Cold milk and crunchiness make our teeth hurt. In America, we took revenge on Grape-Nuts by heating them with milk in the microwave. Drying cornflakes were stuck to the sides of the bowl like bits of an exploded paper sack; it seemed to me, as I scrubbed it clean, a promise of continuity. Dried, stuck cornflakes seemed a sign of something inexplicably tender. If I were to speak, I would cry, and I don't know if it's nostalgia or new hormones kicking in.

Like a child with a toy, Bish took an interest in Dr. Khanna's box. Not the contents, exactly, or even trying to untie the silk ribbons that sealed the ledgers and stacks of letters. Twenty years ago, when I'd asked him to explain what he and Chet Yee were doing in the basement, he'd say, "assigning tags" or "sorting information." Since the bombing, he could devote the same concentration to a crossword puzzle or a game of solitaire that he once had to cutting-edge technology. His eyes sparkled over the prospect of sorting so much chaos.

I asked, "Do you remember a Stanford engineering professor named Yash Khanna?"

"Yash Khanna changed my life."

So, Bish had not sprung miraculously from his own forehead. I could see he was anxious to begin his work. "Would you mind stacking the ledgers here, and the loose papers there, and the clippings—"

"Well," I said, "his wife is my Dr. Victoria Khanna. Quite a coincidence, no?"

"Yash Khanna invented Information Design. And there are no coincidences."

Twenty years ago, Yash Khanna had taken his students, including Bish, to San Francisco's main post office to watch letters zipping through the system. Think of each letter as an electron, Yash had said. Look at normal pieces of mail as the flow of electrons. Scanners started by looking at zip codes; a first-generation replacement of place-names by numbers, a kind of primitive digitizing that overrode inherited notions of time and space.

"What is this?" Bish asked, pointing out a sheet of old newsprint from Victoria's box. " '*Mishtigunj Mourns Death of Tarama. Famed saint and recluse dies of heart attack in police custody. DC Virgil Treadwell denies police involvement.*' "

It was at that moment, with a scrap of brittle, yellowed paper from an English-language newspaper (provenance undisclosed) pulled from a box that had traveled around the world to land on my dining table in San Francisco, that I can date a kind of cosmic mystery. Voices began to speak; ghosts took flesh. Bish always says, "Nothing in the universe is ever lost," and I hadn't fully believed him, or understood. It's physical and chemical and historical and finally psychological. Every discovery has a motivated seeker.

The Tree Bride had been little more than my grandmother's and mother's bedtime fable. When I realized that Tara Lata had been an actual little girl who grew up surrounded by other little girl servants and had taught herself to read Bengali, English, and Persian, it seemed to me a miracle on the order of Helen Keller. The fact that she then taught the languages to the girls and boys of the village made her an Annie Sullivan, and that she had fought against the colonial authorities on the side of the Indian nationalists, a Joan of Arc. It became my dharma, my duty, to set her story down.

My mother gave my sisters and me an odd bit of advice when we were children. She'd walked into the bedroom that Parvati and I shared and found us absorbed in the latest issue of *Time* magazine. She said, "Trust to dreams to tell you the truth."

I must have been around seven, Parvati ten. We'd recently discovered how easy it was to dazzle the nuns in General Knowledge quizzes if we studied *Time* and *Reader's Digest,* which my father always brought home from his office. The teachers believed that General Knowledge, by which they meant knowing what was going on in Europe and America and being able to name U.N. officials, American movie stars, and Davis Cup players, would turn us into the kind of wives ambitious bridegrooms working for multinationals would desire. The nuns did not approve of dreaming.

When we were kids in the high-ceilinged house in Ballygunge Park, my mother was a mesmerizing storyteller. In the long, dark hours before dinner while my father bathed, then chanted long, loud prayers in Sanskrit, and after the prayers settled into a divan on the wide veranda for his nightly two pegs of Scotch (with

Padma perched on an ottoman, keeping him company with the half glass of shandy that she was allowed), she kept Parvati and me spellbound with stories about the kind of people she must have come across in novels or looked up in her prized encyclopedia.

We sat on wicker stools at her feet on the veranda. A filigreed brass lamp in a far corner was the only light, so as not to attract mosquitoes, and we let her voice carry us to exotic places in bygone centuries. Her favorite novelists were Marie Corelli, Erich Maria Remarque, and Mary Renault. She probably embroidered the adventures of historical figures that she'd read about, as storytellers often do. She made us weep over poor Marie Antoinette, waiting to be guillotined, in torn, dirty clothes. The Kolkata nights of storytelling smelled of mosquito repellent, incense, deep-fried cocktail snacks, and sandalwood soap. My mother morphed into a defeated Napoléon, despairing, longing for home; or Julius Caesar, betrayed and staggering from stab wounds; or Pritilata Wadedar, fearless freedom fighter who was cornered by colonial troops and who swallowed potassium cyanide after making sure that her fellow revolutionaries had made their getaway. It's almost funny, thinking of little Bengali girls crying about Marie Antoinette, Napoléon, or Caesar, yet I always thought of them as Bengalis like us. Their defeat, often as a result of intimate betrayal, was our history.

Of all her stories, the one that moved me most was about my namesake, Tara Lata, the Tree Bride of Mishtigunj, the five-year-old almost-widow who was forced to marry a tree as surrogate husband and then expected by villagers to lead a life of resigned self-abasement. Caste tradition forbade remarriage. But destiny works in mysterious ways, my mother said. Who better than an abandoned child, free of wifely duties and fear of consequences, to lead a village into dignity and freedom?

Last December, on my last night with my parents in Rishikesh, my mother, now rigid with Parkinson's, began a story about the Tree Bride that I hadn't heard before. My parents hadn't known I was writing a book. When I mentioned my interest in any stories of the Tree Bride she might still know, my mother tried to lift her hand as though to stop all other conversation. Only one admonishing finger rose from her fist. Her tongue was slow and heavy, her face a mask of stone. Only her eyes were still alert and impatient with what her lips and tongue could not do.

If I deciphered her correctly she said, "Tara Lata, and the English writer."

The idea that any member of our family had ever "taken up the pen," as the nuns taught us to euphemize literary ambition (lest any of us be foolish enough to take our assignments too seriously), was so striking to me that I nearly violated family decorum and asked her to explain herself. Bish would say the answer was always present, circling around our heads, lost in time and space, until it found the proper question. The area code. I'd announced that I wanted to write, and suddenly a previously unknown writer entered our family history.

"What was his name?"

She didn't get too far into the story. "Name . . . Je . . . je . . . je . . ." and I could see she'd forgotten it. At least, if first syllables are to be trusted, it wasn't the usual colonial chroniclers like Forster or Kipling, which was a partial relief. Her eyes seemed to beseech me. To do what? Find out as much as I could? Then she gave up, exhausted. "Go . . . Mishtigunj," I heard her murmur. But I couldn't, I needed to get back to San Francisco to find a place for us to live. Bish was about to be released from his germ-free hospital room.

"I could ask Rabi to go. He'd love that."

Her head jerked. No. "You," she said.

I had never heard of any Gangooly or Bhattacharjee having contact with the literary world, prior to my own attempts. I knew that the Tree Bride had had visitors and contacts from the outer world, mainly political with a few spiritualists thrown in, but an English writer? I couldn't imagine who, or why.

In their Rishikesh retirement cottage, my father has set up another ritual. The live-in servant, who has worked for them nearly fifty years and who came with them to Rishikesh, heats up milk in a stainless steel cauldron, pours it into glasses for them and a brass tumbler for himself, adds a heaping spoonful of isab-gul, a fibrous laxative, to the two glasses and tumbler, then carries the glasses on a silver tray into the living room. Rabi is partial to ritual, even this one. He doesn't complain that the milk isn't fat-free and that isab-gul is gritty. After the milk has been drunk, which my father does in one draft ("I used to drink a pint of bitters that way in Reading," he jokes), he takes out the small sandalwood icon of Vishnu he carries in the pocket of his wool vest and walks from person to person among whoever happens to be home, touching foreheads with Vishnu and chanting a blessing to ward off evil.

That last night in Rishikesh, as she watched my father press Vishnu to my skin, my mother whispered, "The magic of Mishti-gunj . . ."

I didn't tell her that my trips to ancient Mishtigunj or modern Razakpur are now relics of my life. I have been there three times and only once was the experience fully magical. The first time, in that innocent time before the bombing, I went with Rabi, just to show him the ancestral homes. The second time, I met the hajji, and gained possession of the documents that have taken me this far, at least, in the Tree Bride's story. The third time, I felt myself a vulture, like someone picking through the trash. Everything is gone; nothing remains for me there. Modern-day reality is catching up with myth; the abuses of history have desecrated the corpse.

5

ere is my confession.

I come from a highly religious, orthodox Hindu Brahmin family, but to know me in California, you'd never guess. My sisters and I received a typical upper-middle-class Calcutta convent-school English-language education, but we were not of that cultural persuasion. We left school and returned to a world of tales, prayers, and a shadow universe of myth and legend. Our family, whatever its outward signs of Westernization (and they were plentiful), had never joined forces with the truly Westernized, progressive traditions of nineteenth-century Bengal. Those progressives, Hindu reformers, scientists, writers, and artists are called Brahmo-Samaj. The communal reaction against the secularizers is called Arya-Samaj. Our family, beginning with Jai Krishna Gangooly, father of the Tree Bride, became antisecular, and the traditions of piety remain. For this, I am unapologetic.

I am ashamed to say, however, that I grew up inside a group mythology that blamed our expulsion from that eastern paradise—modern-day Bangladesh—on the beastliness of Muslim fanatics. And I grew up with a more generalized second myth, reinforced by the schools I attended and the class I belonged to: The British were, with many famous exceptions, generally decent. It has taken me twenty years to realize that Muslims had nothing to do with our "relocation." It was the British, always the British. And it wasn't the 1947 Partition. It started in 1833.

Here is my rant.

It is easy for an English-educated, middle-class Indian (or Pakistani or Bangladeshi) to fall in line with colonial prejudice. Thirty thousand British bureaucrats and "factors" were able to rule ten thousand times more Indians by dividing Muslims from Hindus, Persian Zoroastrians from Muslims, Sikhs from Hindus, and nearly everyone, including Hindus, from castes like lazy brahmins and money-grubbing banias. Sikhs and Muslims were declared "martial races" and rewarded appropriately with army and police positions. Muslims and Jews and Anglo-Indians were traditional, Western-style monotheists in the way that Hindus were not seen to be, and were rewarded appropriately. Parsis were fairer-skinned, leaving dark-skinned Hindus to be treated with contempt and labeled potbellied vegetarians and sensualists, deceitful and cowardly. But behind gymkhana doors, all of us, martial races or not, fair-skinned or dark, were referred to as niggers.

Since Calcutta was the headquarters of the East India Company and seat of Empire, Bengal had the longest exposure, among Indians, to the British and to the English language. Bengali brahmins in particular were targets of British ridicule, since their priestly functions demanded a certain degree of literacy. Brahmins were naturally drawn to education. It was our caste dharma to test ourselves spiritually and intellectually, which put us in direct competition with the British. In any discussion about the future of India, Bengali brahmins were seen as the potential winners. Keep the Bengalis in their place, especially their disputatious brahmins, ridicule their pretensions, defame their character, mock their religion, and the Empire will rule forever.

It was the wealth of India that underwrote the industrial and commercial prosperity of England. Britain started its India trade by purchasing Indian textiles. A hundred years later, to keep English mills operating, Indian textiles were banned, Indian weavers were killed, and India was forced to buy inferior British cottons. In the nineteenth century, twenty-five million Indians were allowed to starve because India's "excess" harvests were shipped to England. Commodity brokers were encouraged to hoard and speculate. The "invisible hand" of the market became the supreme adjunct of imperial authority. Intervention by government, in the form of emergency relief, would merely sap the self-respect of the Indian peasant and make him even less capable of feeding himself in the future. Undue generosity would send all the wrong messages. Recurrent starvation was blamed on Indian laziness, on their beastly, fatalistic religion, their money-lending banias and corrupt brahmins, and it served as the ultimate colonial sanction.

It all began in 1833: the seeds of the Brahmo-Arya split, the active encouragement of English, and the creation of a native, English-speaking intellectual aristocracy. It's the year that created my hybrid family of orthodox Hindu, Bengali-speaking, cricket-loving, Shakespeare-acting, Gilbert and Sullivan–singing, adaptable-anywhere brahmins. That was the year the brilliant young parliamentary orator, Thomas Babington Macaulay, only thirty-three at the time, delivered his famous "Minute on Education." I say "famous" but of course it is known only to scholars of

India, even if it is part of the cultural baggage of every "Westernized" Indian with an English-language education. Bengalis are its target, and potential beneficiaries. Macaulay set out to define a range of British attitudes toward India that began with liberal, enlightened self-interest, and ended in sheer contempt.

When I first encountered the "Minute" in my old Calcutta convent school, I'm sure it was presented as India's central moment of cultural deliverance. Some of Macaulay's language is thrilling, even today:

> It is scarcely possible to calculate the benefits which we might derive from the diffusion of European civilisation among the vast population of the East. It would be, on the most selfish view of the case, far better for us that the people of India were well governed and independent of us, than ill governed and subject to us; that they were ruled by their own kings, but wearing our broadcloth, and working with our cutlery, than that they were performing their salams to English collectors and English magistrates, but were too ignorant to value, or too poor to buy, English manufactures. To trade with civilised men is infinitely more profitable than to govern savages.

There you have it, the nineteenth-century utilitarian's rationale for twenty-first-century globalization.

I would say now that Macaulay was responding to a collision of values that the existing structures of British power, and the East India Company, could no longer contain. Earlier generations of European visitors had been seduced by India. They were enthusiastically adaptive to Indian ways. By Macaulay's time, however, management problems had arisen. Better, Macaulay thought, to turn natives into surrogate Englishmen, easily controlled, making the English language and Western values desirable to them, than to rely on British adventurers whose embrace of Hindu and Muslim practices made their basic loyalty suspect. For them, Macaulay had nothing but scorn:

> *I have no knowledge of either Sanscrit or Arabic—but I have done what I could to form a correct estimate of their value. I have read translations of the most celebrated Arabic and Sanscrit works. I have conversed both here and at home with men distinguished by their proficiency in the Eastern tongues. I am quite ready to take the Oriental learning at the valuation of the Orientalists themselves. I have never found one among them who could deny that a single shelf of a good European library was worth the whole native literature of India and Arabia. The intrinsic superiority of the Western literature is, indeed, fully admitted by those members of the Committee who support the Oriental plan of education.*

Sooner or later, the mood of 1833 will figure in Tara Lata's story, just as it figures in mine. Perhaps a well-trained colonial administrator like Vertie Treadwell had vague knowledge of Thomas Babington Macaulay, but certainly no one else involved in this story had reason to. Yet the bookends of Macaulay's argument— uplift the natives to make them better subjects, uplift India to make it more profitable, ridicule India for its superstitious ways—will apply to nearly all of them. Except, of course, John Mist and the Tree Bride.

In my mind, the history of the British in India is a story of adventure gone bad, where the thrill of new encounters, the lure of transformation, and the frontier of second chances slowly, inevitably, started drying up. There was passion in the early days, vision, and—dare I say it?—a strong sense of gamesmanship, even of fun. Maybe there's a limit to the human capacity for wonder or the ability to absorb the truly alien without trying to reduce its dimensions and tame its excesses. Maybe the Spanish felt it in Mexico and all the other empire-builders felt it as they hacked their way through jungles or trekked over deserts.

Then came the time when a serious-minded bureaucrat said, "All right, enough with the silks and spices—where do you keep the gold? And while I'm at it, the gods you worship are frankly offensive; here's a better one." All the could-have-beens and should-have-beens of history, the best of the East meeting the best of the West, etc., etc., shrink from grandeur to petty profit-taking.

In my school days, I'd been made to feel ashamed of my ortho-dox Hindu background. My friends in school were effortlessly Westernized. Some were Armenians or Jews or Indian Christians, but many had come from Brahmo families, inheritors of the most enlightened and progressive elements of nineteenth-century Ben-gali society. Tagore was Brahmo. Satyajit Ray was Brahmo. My distant relative Jai Krishna Gangooly, confronted with the choice between the English language and British law, and a return to Sanskrit and the *shastras,* made a choice that still affects our fam-ily. He hung up his lawyer's wig and robes, and abandoned En-glish altogether, leaving Dhaka and drifting down to Mishtigunj on a river boat.

My father drank scotch and read English mysteries and posi-tively idolized Doris Day, but at heart he had always been plan-ning his retreat from this world. The life of prayer he now leads in Rishikesh is perfectly in keeping with all his precepts.

Everything about my convent-school education, our Shakespeare Society and British Council debates and our Gilbert and Sullivan evenings, had trained me for one certainty: We could trust English models. Those models might be cranky and blustery, but they embodied a notion of fair play and scholarship we would do well to emulate. The British were the most reliable source of knowledge about ourselves, because they had lifted us from the deep slumber of decadence, they had injected us with the spirit of inquiry and reverence for art and culture, and of course manly competition and fair play, and we'd do well to emulate them. I had never doubted their ancient, bewhiskered authority, like elderly relatives who rarely visited. I am a late defector from their ranks.

6

When Victorians dreamed, they dreamed of the future. I dream of the past.

The men who prospered a century and a half ago in the swamps and jungles we now call Bangladesh live on as legends, supreme in their hearts of darkness. Maps immortalize their one-time passage. Wonderstruck Englishmen: Who was the Cox of Cox's Bazaar, the Abbot of Abbottabad in the Punjab, or the McCrory of Macrorigunj? I can answer only one name with confidence: I know the John Mist of Mishtigunj.

The great horde of strutters and fretters never made it on the maps—they disappeared into docket numbers, charge sheets, and prison records. One or two in a hundred, or a thousand, persist through two centuries of riots and disasters, tropical rot, and the casual indifference of bored officials—Mughal, East India Company, British, Indian, Pakistani, Bangladeshi—dumping out their administrative drawers. A few usable accounts linger, often by accident. From one old book pulled from the shelves of the Berkeley South Asia Library, I came across an 1822 receipt made out to a *"Redd Sahib"* who purchased from one Naseer Ahmed Khan of Mymensingh *"150 maund Rice . . . 2 chest Tea . . . 40 maund Salt . . ."* and rented a two-masted *bajra* along with a *"porter, cook, helmsman, translator, guide and pilots."* But there, "Redd's" official history ends. A ginger-haired would-be-empire-builder put out from the docks of Jessore, Tangail, Sirajgang, Dacca, or Mymensingh in 1822, and disappeared from history.

They headed south toward the Bay of Bengal. It wasn't the bay that attracted them, but the Shoonder Bon, "the Beautiful Forest," a dense, tiger-and-timber-rich jungle that separates the sea from the fragile interior. The treasure and the terror of East Bengal is its limitless fresh water for rice and fish and the "blue devil" indigo and the forests of sundari trees, straight and tall with a purplish density more resistant than iron. In a spar- and mast-hungry age when rounding the cape nearly always involved the loss of booms and topmasts, he who provided reliable wood to the world, especially to the British navy and the East India Company, and the means to supply shipyards along the way, owned riches more convertible than gold.

Swollen rivers rush from the Himalayas through the low, flat plains to the ever-thirsty bay, pouring waters so broad one wonders how even an ocean can absorb the engorgement. They twist and tangle, as the poet says, like women's hair spread out and drying in the sun. Tagore even dedicated one of his books to the rivers of Bengal. The Meghna, the Ganga, the Padma, the Brahmaputra, the Jumna, and their meandering tributaries flow to their own twists and curls, flooding fields and villages, ending in the mangrove tendrils of the Shoonder Bon. All is peace. In the

Beautiful Forest, the jungle canopy obscures the sun. The gradient falls, the rivers merge, and waters pool. And that's where Bengal is at its most dangerous.

The Bay of Bengal is never at peace. It is a thousand-mile-long, three-hundred-mile-wide, ever-narrowing, ever-shallowing blind canyon of water, lapping against the flimsy wall of the Shoonder Bon. Disturbances a thousand miles south have nowhere to go but north, in an ever-rising bore.

The empire-builder who'd one minute been admiring the green and gold incontinence of East Bengal hears a distant rumble, dry thunder on a cloudless day. Helmsmen drop their oars and swim madly for shore. Redd Sahib calls after them, "I'll report you!" and picks the floating pole out of the glassy water. And before he can find the river bottom and lean his full weight into the pole, the rumble has become a roar and great clouds of birds are rising from the trees and there in front of him racing up the river channel faster than an avalanche down an Alpine slope comes a wall of muddy water, twenty, thirty feet high and growing, and the last thing he will see are huts and trees and cattle caught in the water like currants in a pudding. A week or so later when the waters subside and people dare make their way back to what had been their village—though now the river has changed course and the forest has been shaved to splintered stumps—their remains are discovered half a mile inland and, depending on the religious allegiance of the unfortunates who stumble upon them, are respectfully burned or buried. Jackal meat, food for dogs and packs of hyenas and the basking garials. What a way, and in what a place, for an Englishman to die.

Or perhaps Redd and the others succeed. The bore doesn't rise; the crew does not desert. They trade along the way, plucking mangoes from the trees, shooting meat, hauling lazy carp from the teeming waters. The natives aren't hostile. They find work in the indigo plantations and stay, or they reach the forest and blend in, like tigers. They work harder than native labor, they ingratiate themselves to the Muslim nawabs or Hindu zamindars. There is no lack of resources in that warm and fertile Eden. No one starves in that original paradise.

For two hundred and fifty years travelers from China to Portugal have remarked upon Bengal's tormented beauty, its murderous seduction of the senses. Plentitude is its feeble precaution against starvation. In all that water, there are droughts. In all that wild profusion, starvation looms in shades of green. Muslims can take four wives and brahmins from my subcaste any number, all in the hope that a single son might survive.

One unassailable attraction stands out above all others. The forests lie outside the jurisdiction of the Honourable East India Company and of the British administration, both of them housed in Calcutta, less than a hundred miles to the west. The Empire stretches around the world but doesn't quite penetrate the Shoonder Bon. When a European arrives in the Beautiful Forest his records are wiped out, he becomes free of all debts and oppression. He is the freest man alive, freer than even we can possibly imagine, free to invent past and future, free to discard every scrap of inheritance. He seeks, or surrenders to, alien codes.

His ancestral faith being lightly rooted, he becomes Muslim or Hindu, or a less constricting combination known only to himself. He takes wives and fathers dozens of children. His British name slithers into versions of Persian or Bengali. Even today, after a flood has carved away the centuries, one comes across mossy headstones topped by alien crosses, or scattered clusters of worn grave markers (*John Thomas, husb. Gauri,* or *Benj. Wylie, husb. Fatima*) propped against the fragments of a clay-brick wall. They were fragile predators, like the big cats they resembled; enormously strong, able to survive unspeakable hardships, yet still capable of dying in a single day. Not every pioneer pushes westward in a covered wagon or breaks the prairie sod with a wooden plow; some head south into bewildering abundance. Such a man was John Mist, and the village he created is that magical word in my native language, my desh, my unseen home.

' , .

I can imagine the sort of men they were, outcasts of the British Isles. Second and third sons cut off from inheritance. Cornish seafarers, Manxmen, Scotch, Welsh, and Irish, theirs were the names on charge sheets; the escapees from debtors' prison, the common criminals and mutineers. Others had absconded from contracts of indenturement or other binding agreements. The literate among them might have forged documents or libeled authorities. If they finally reached the Beautiful Forest and secured timber or indigo concessions, they would operate through native middlemen or the omnipresent Portuguese, lest their presence be detected.

After many years, they would emerge from the shadows, confident of their immunity, resplendent as the new nawabs of indigo or timber, and later, of jute and tea. By the first quarter of the nineteenth century, the "blue devil" indigo had created its own British planter society, insular and profitable, hostile to outsiders and newcomers. Indigo turned native farmers into poorly paid laborers and transformed paddy fields into plantations, driving up the price—or, as they preferred to put it, the value—of rice. The cycle of starvation had begun. In a Benthamite age, indigo planters pitied themselves as maligned heroes, industriously creating the nation's wealth by raising land values and selling everything that grew on it at the highest prices the market would bear.

They were not all criminals. Some were victims of circumstance, the orphaned, the abandoned, and the foundlings. Blessed were the foundlings, who'd been granted lives without memory or patrimony. No regrets, no laments. No legends of lost inheritance to cloud their thinking. They knew what they were, and they were unbeholden to any man or king or god or state. The excluded became the unlimitable. Having known constraints, they guarded their freedom like hyenas at the kill. Having come from nowhere, they had everywhere to go. Having been given nothing, they were free to fashion anything they pleased. Such a man was John Mist.

7

e could scrawl his name, but he never learned to write. He must have been able to calculate, but he lived too far from civilization to be photographed. I imagine him in full Victorian bewhiskered glory, under a turban, in full kurta-pajama. For more than a century and a half his name has clung to the houses he built and to Mishtigunj, the village he created. The sprawling river-port city that has grown up around the original settlement is called Razakpur, after a local politician with the proper credentials, from the majority community.

Six years ago, before Abbas Sattar Hai, before the bombings, when Rabi and I and my ex-hippie contractor were living quietly on Rivoli Street, I made my second visit to Mishtigunj, this time, alone. When I stepped down from the rickshaw just outside the Tree Bride's house, an old man was standing by the gate as though he had been waiting for me many hours, maybe years. He was tall

and gaunt, with a tuft of white beard and a lacy, intricately cro-
cheted skullcap. I'd deliberately dressed down in one of my
mother's old Calcutta cotton saris. To anyone's eyes I was just a
simple Calcutta Hindu woman on an old-fashioned roots search. I
spoke the local dialect. I wore no jewelry, but for a single gold
bangle. Since I was divorced, I had not put vermilion powder in
the parting of my hair. I wasn't trying to disguise my religion—
we're too good at mutual detection for that—if anything, I'd been
trying to hide my Americanness and ward off the fear, or resentment, that it might engender.

He identified himself as Hajji Gul Mohammed Chowdhury.

I shocked him by extending my hand. "Tara Bhattacharjee," I
called myself, my maiden name, a little too perkily. He wasn't
fooled. His face said: Ah, brahmin. Calcutta. No wedding ring,
no *shindur,* but something isn't right. She gives off innocent trust
and confidence with none of that Calcutta brahmin arrogance.
She's like an American. Six years ago, unlike today, I was (frankly)
too pretty not to be married, and well married at that. Divorce is
not part of the calculation. So, he probably thought, a mysteri-
ously unmarried lady from Calcutta, brahmin from her name,
speaking the local dialect, traveling alone to an isolated place like
Mishtigunj? What kind of woman does a thing like that? Only
someone with a Mishtigunj desh. A Mishtigunj brahmin like, say,
a distant descendant of Tara Lata Gangooly? Come back to claim
ancestral lands, perhaps? And in my gait, I was far too American.
I didn't walk confidently wrapped in a sari. I hadn't worn a sari in
years.

I could even see him putting it all together: *Click, click, click!*
For years my picture had been in the Indian press as the wife of
Bish Chatterjee. All juicy Calcutta gossip eventually seeps over
the border to Bangladesh. He'd recognized me. I had been—and

in the hajji's mind would always be—the wife of the world's richest Bengali. He probably remembered the interviews and my proud claim of a Mishtigunj desh, with a great-great-aunt, Tara Lata Gangooly, the Tree Bride, as a namesake. I'd claimed it all without ever visiting or knowing much about the Tree Bride except the circumstances of her marriage and the rumors surrounding her death.

I, too, was making my calculation. His name announced that he'd made the pilgrimage to Mecca, and from the beard I guessed he was a scholar, perhaps an imam. He was a Muslim of the old school, gracious, gentlemanly, and protective. We touched antennae and exchanged information, like ants at the tip of a branch. "Cholo," he said, "kajey hat lagao." I hadn't heard that phrase since my grandmother would herd us girls into bed. A very forceful "let's get on with it."

He opened the gate. "Mist Mansion Number One. They called it the Mist Mahal. Here is where the Tree Bride stayed." The government of Bangladesh had erected a small hand-lettered plaque in English and Bengali on the wall outside the gate: *Home of Tara Lata Gangooly (1874–1943), Freedom Fighter and Martyr. Known to the world as Tara-Ma.*

"Do many people here still know her as the Tree Bride?" I asked. Tara-Ma, freedom fighter and martyr, seemed so cold and official.

"You of course know the legend." It was not a question.

"It's not a legend," I said.

"I know," he said.

At the time of my first visit, Tara Lata had been dead for fifty-five years. Hajji said, "In Mishtigunj many old people still remember her." He himself was eighty-two, making him twenty-seven when she died.

"I first came through these gates when I was a boy of fifteen," he said. I did the mental calculation: 1930. If my grasp of Indian history serves, 1930 was the year of Gandhi's Salt March, part of what we now call the Second War of Indian Independence. The Irish nuns in my former convent school called it the rebellion, the mutiny, part of the long decline from noble origins.

Children who'd been playing in the scruffy yard ran back inside. " 'Merica memsahib!" they were shouting to their parents. "America" is a bad word. It means that a rich, America-settled Indian, probably a motel-owning bania, has found an ancestral deed to a Bangladeshi property tucked inside a trunk, probably folded inside a great-grandmother's wedding sari, and for sheer vengeance has decided to lay claim to pre-Partition family property. Poor, god-fearing Muslims would be evicted from the only floor and roof they'd ever known. In Mist Mansion Number One a dozen families had claimed their squatting rights. Hajji raised his hand, palm up, and bent back at an obtuse angle in a kind of benediction, and the shouting stopped. "Inside, many families," he said. "Nothing of your auntie remains."

And so I asked, "Hajji, what was the Tree Bride like?"

"She was our mother," he said.

The concept is alien to both our religions, but I almost asked, "Our virgin mother?" "You said you were fifteen—"

"When she called me. My father was her physician, so she knew me for an honest boy. She said Gandhiji was organizing a march against the British and all women could help by selling their gold and giving it to Congress. Everyone knew she had been married to a tree and that her dowry was buried somewhere in the forest."

"At the feet of her husband," I said.

The stuff of legend, but in that magical place, true.

Where generations of Mishtigunj men had gone out at night with picks and shovels, digging around the stumps of every felled tree in hopes of finding the Tree Bride's buried dowry gold, young Gul Mohammed had set out one night in 1930 armed with a map drawn by the Tree Bride herself. She who had never left her marriage-house asked only that he place a flower-garland around the tree and say a Sanskrit prayer. "We know the Hindu rituals," the hajji said. "She was an inspiration to all of us. I was honored to serve and protect her. I was in the British prison with her."

She had told him, "Your name will be praised." Echoing Gandhi, she said: "No boy is too young, no sudra too poor, no woman too weak, to fight for the freedom of India." And there in the roots of a dying sundari, his pick found the rotting saris that had been buried on her wedding night fifty-one years before. They fell into pieces as he tugged them from the ground. For half the night he piled gold into the jute sack she'd given him.

Her gold put Mishtigunj on the map. Congress officials singled it out: A village in the remotest corner of our country has contributed more to our freedom than some of our richest cities. The Bengal Congress chief himself, Netaji Subhas Bose, came all the way from Calcutta and orated before hundreds outside the school. *Mishtigunj jai hind!*

In the new imperial capital of New Delhi, the lavish contribution was also noted. East Bengal? the British viceroy demanded. Bloody Hell! Call our man in Dacca. Call Calcutta. Send a detachment. There's a hotbed of sedition down in the Sunderbans (as their maps spelled it); see to it that it doesn't spread.

⸝　⸝　⸝

Hajji proposed a walking tour of Mishtigunj, using the old name. "That way, we can avoid Razakpur," he said with a solemn smile.

So we walked along the river where the old buildings seem to cluster. Other Mist Mansions, numbers two through eight, had been schools, counting houses, a Hindu temple, a mosque, and a pukka market that wouldn't melt under monsoon rains or blow away when cyclones struck. All of it seemed vaguely familiar; either it made sense because of the planning, or because of stories implanted in my childhood, the architecture of dreams. The ruling nawab had maintained his own tax-collector's bungalow—they were dutiful in the collection of money, devious in paying it out—and there was a small courtroom attached to a police *thana* and a detention cell, all courtesy of John Mist.

Just outside that police *thana* is the public square where John Mist and Rafeek Hai were hanged in the fall of 1880. In that same police station, the Tree Bride died.

When the British finally marched into Mishtigunj in 1880, they built their own collector's bungalow next to the whites-only gymkhana. Only now, after reading through the box of Victoria's papers, can I see the full picture; it served as Treadwell's last retreat, the place where he read his reports, meted out justice, and wrote his diaries. For the last sixty years of the Raj, the grim years of hanging on, all sense of adventure abandoned, inside that gymkhana the dozen or so whites, the police contingent and the teachers and secretaries and petty magistrates, fought over copies of the latest papers, backstabbed, complained of the ingratitude of the natives, and drank themselves to nightly stupefaction. Now its front room serves as a small Hindu temple in a town of ardent Muslims.

How many Hindus had stayed behind? I asked.

"Many good families," he said, "poor people only. Like us." Which meant that the rich banias, the land-owning zamindars, and the brahmins with their caste-consciousness had all fled with their sacks of gold to Calcutta. Like my grandfather's family, but without any gold.

My ancestors had been lured to that emerging village by the persuasiveness of John Mist. He offered them a chance to exercise their professions free of British influence. A doctor and his lawyer son, both British-trained, both, in their way, weary of Western ways. When Mist began his recruitment drive, there had been nothing there but a bend in the river, George's Bight, with forests lapping the water's edge. Mist decided that a well-run society needed a professional class: teachers; doctors; a newspaper and journalists to write in English, Bengali, and Persian; and, of course, lawyers. Jai Krishna Gangooly (as the British spelled it) had been a Dacca (as they spelled it) barrister. His father was a doctor. Jai Krishna gave up the wig and black robes of the second city's High Court to become little more than a backwoods vakil, arguing native cases from native precedent, before local judges. His father reveled in the title of chief surgeon, though in reality he was little more than a dispensing, homeopathic chemist.

In the case of East Bengal, with its Muslim preponderance and Hindu wealth, Mist's governing philosophy was "two of everything," like Noah and the ark. High-caste Hindus were generally the better educated, the more proficient English-speakers. Without external restraints, the minority upper-caste Hindus would dominate, an unstable situation for any society. And so Mist recruited a Muslim doctor, and a Hindu, a Hindu lawyer and a Muslim, two kinds of teachers, two kinds of journalists, and built two kinds of schools. In his time, when the buildings were whitewashed and landscaped and clustered against the river and a backdrop of forest, it must have been a beautiful village. Locals still call it Mishtigunj. "Razakpur," after forty years, has not caught on.

When I say "the village he created," I mean something more than the ghats—still in use, by the way—where the various forms of native boats loaded and unloaded, and where, one day in 1879, the wedding *bajra* of the Tree Bride's husband-to-be was anchored, and her groom exhibited, dead in his father's arms. I'm referring to more than his still-standing mansions, numbers one through eight, or the English school where Jai Krishna's son taught and my grandfather attended, and even the town infirmary where my great-great-grandfather became chief surgeon. In an age of vast extractions, when indigo wealth was squeezed from labor and the East India Company bought Indian goods cheap and sold British goods dear and remitted the guaranteed annual six percent back to London, John Mist simply counted his fortune in a different way. He spoke of a legacy, not of profits.

The hajji invited me to his home for tea. "I have something of interest for you," he said, and when I pointed out that he didn't know me or what might be of interest to me he merely crooked his finger and waved me forward.

It was a small, dome-shaped structure, a kind of miniature mosque situated slightly off a narrow alley. The hand-painted signs above the door were in Bengali and an Arabic-scripted language, Urdu or Persian. It appeared to be a school, named for a local pir, or saint.

"My youngest wife is expecting us," he said.

"Hajji—" I started, but he held up his hand in that same stop-all gesture. The door opened without a key. He turned on the overhead tube of bluish neon, lighting up a single room with desks and chairs. I followed him through a doorway of beaded curtains into a kitchen area. Indeed, a woman not much older than I am now, but gaunt and with badly misaligned teeth and hollowed-out eyes stood smiling by the two-burner gas ring on which water in a tea kettle was already boiling. Her arms looked too frail even to lift the kettle. She could have been pretty with straightened teeth; now she looked skeletal.

"This is all very strange, Hajji. No one knew I was coming, yet you were waiting for me. You know about me and you know about the Tree Bride."

"You have come to Mishtigunj on a mission, isn't it? You said as much in Dhaka when you booked the car and hotel room."

Ah, the network, I thought. Of course someone would have called the hajji. Nothing would proceed without his blessing.

"Purpose of visit, research into history of Tara Lata Gangooly," he said, as though quoting from my visa application. "Since I am a little familiar with Tara-Ma, I thought we might profit from a meeting."

"I am profiting. You know far more than I."

"Not for long." The shy young wife handed us our tea, and again he crooked a finger and said, "Come." Now we were in their sleeping space. A high platform with a thin mattress nearly filled it. The bedspread was kantha-work shawls sewn together.

"Mishtigunj is the story of John Mist," he said. "Tara-Ma comes much later. Mist-sahib died long before my time, but my grandfather was his closest friend."

"So, you know the story of John Mist?"

"Mrs. Chatterjee"—he paused for effect—"I know many things. I know how Mist-sahib lived, and why he died." He opened an old wooden trunk and lifted silk-tied packets of letters off the top of two thick, leather-bound volumes. "Life is more important than death, isn't it?"

He laid two thick books on the bed. The title of one was hand-written in Arabic script. He translated, running his finger from right to left. *"Mist-nama."* The second had no title.

All the great Mughal emperors—Babur, Akbar, Shāh Jāham, Aurangzeb—wrote and had illustrated their own *"namas,"* their dynastic histories. They are among the glories of Indian civilization, detailing court life, battles, hunts, love, education, and faith, with sidelong glances at family, politics, and the economy of the imperial court. The *Mist-nama* was no less flamboyant; the mini-epic of a poor English boy's life.

"It was my father's and my grandfather's project," Hajji explained. "Mist-sahib dictated it in spoken Persian to my grandfather, but it was my father who assembled the notes and put them all together into literary Persian. Mist-sahib and my grandfather perished on the same day in 1880. It says here, 'Dictation taken by Rafeek Mohammed Hai, English calendar, 1878–79.' That was my grandfather. 'Edited and assembled, Dr. Hajji Shafiq Mohd. Chowdhury, 1932.' He is my father."

The ominous name of Hai had not yet entered my consciousness. "Chowdhury" is an honorific, bestowed in olden times by British authorities for services rendered to the Crown. Nothing in the universe is ever lost, or dead; it just circles overhead, waiting for the proper question.

He flipped through the pages. Beautiful, like all Muslim calligraphy, but for me only art, no meaning. I paused over dozens of vividly colored illustrations in the style of Mughal court painting: a disfigured face missing an eye, a beautiful woman in Regency dress walking a deck, renderings done in the style of early British lithographs of a river and forest and the first encampment that must have become Mishtigunj. Tents are pitched, two elephants bathe in the river, a camel nips fruit off a low branch. Eden, I thought. Fertility, peace.

"Here," he said. I was greatly relieved when he opened the unillustrated second volume and I could read the Bengali script.

"The life work of an old man," he said. "I have tried to render the *Mist-nama* into Bangla." The Persian text had looked like a medieval illustrated Bible. The Bangla was more hastily composed, with cross-outs and marginalia, and no illustrations; it welcomed the eye.

"From what did they perish, Hajji?" I asked.

He replied with a smile, then a sharp jerk of his hand. "Jute."

I asked if I might carry it off for a few days to read it. He said he no longer needed it. His life's work was done. He had made his pilgrimage, raised fourteen children—four now in America—buried three wives, and had participated in the liberation of India and then of Bangladesh. All he wanted now was to preserve his final legacy, the school. He proposed a trade; the Bangla version of the *Mist-nama* for some money. "You must see that the book is translated into English. You can translate it," he said. "Sell it to the Americans, sell it to the world. All I ask is a five-thousand-dollar contribution to the school, Mrs. Chatterjee."

When I first encountered the Tree Bride as an adult, it was through her own writing in a little pamphlet stored deep in my parents' Calcutta memorabilia. I thought they'd rid themselves of all books, except for holy tracts and the ubiquitous volumes of Tagore's stories, novels, and poetry. Rabi and I were making our first visit to their cottage in Rishikesh. Rabi was starting to take an interest in his Indian heritage, at long last, and his grandfather was embracing his every question.

We were having twilight tea on the flat rooftop. I went downstairs with the servant to help with the preparation, and that's when I spotted an unfamiliar wooden crate in the hallway outside the spare bedroom. I'm sure there's a practical explanation; perhaps the servant had been cleaning under the bed and forgotten to restore it. Obviously, my mother was in no condition to have moved it.

I refuse to believe any logical explanation.

For some reason, my mother had accumulated her own little trove of Gangooly-family memorabilia, and it had been mixed with my father's holy books, and they'd not been willing to relinquish them. And when I needed them, they appeared.

Tara Lata had written of her childhood, but infuriatingly, not from a modern autobiographical perspective. I wanted facts, word-pictures; she gave parables, moral lessons. But she did provide three or four memories of her early childhood. She remembered the day of her near-widowhood and the night of her marriage. A year later, at the age of six, she remembered the night that British troops and their Indian conscripts arrested the chowkidar, then broke through the gates. A feast was in progress; John Mist had been visiting that night, the Gangoolys had just sat down, or reclined, on the floor. The feast was to honor Rafeek Hai and his family. It was during Ramadan that the British came, not that native religious practices registered on their consciousness.

Here is my second shameful confession: I cannot do justice to my own surprise that in 1880 an orthodox Hindu family, brahmins to boot, would not be practicing strict religious as well as caste segregation. A Ramadan feast, served in a Hindu house! I cannot imagine a similar tableau anywhere in India at that time, unless it were in the house of a progressive Brahmo, out to make a point. The magic of Mishtigunj, indeed. Certainly it would have been unthinkable in my grandparents' time, or in my Calcutta childhood. And the idea of such a scene being vandalized by troops, Mist and Hai pulled away in chains, and Jai Krishna running after them, promising legal help. A week later, she remembered her last time outside the walls of her family mansion. She sat on her father's shoulders in the town square, and witnessed her two favorite "uncles," John Mist and Rafeek Hai, being hanged, and, in the words of "Sweeney Todd," she never forgot and she never forgave.

Tara Lata wrote that as a small child she and another girl, Sameena, the daughter of the cook, would play in the dark glade of uvaria trees and be allowed to select the fattest pullet for special feasts. Not the cocks, but the slower hens, which they would chase with a special net so they couldn't get off the ground. Sameena would dive for the legs and bring it squawking to her father. Sameena is a Muslim name; the cook's name was Abdulhaq. Tara Lata and Sameena were five years old, both recent brides. Tara Lata called Abdulhaq "the cook" not "a cook." For an orthodox brahmin like Jai Krishna Gangooly to take food from a Muslim's hand would bar his path to salvation. We know he became super-orthodox, that in later life he turned his back on any kind of ecumenical accommodation with Christians or Muslims. Yet, in a certain place and time, before the hardening of his ways, it must have happened.

Abdulhaq would stretch the chicken on the chopping block, one swift blow, and the hen would flutter and dance, fanning the yard in headless flight. "Won't it hurt?" Tara would ask, and he answered, "The All-Merciful does not allow animals to suffer."

And now you know. It was a time and place of magic. I have tried, in a way, to translate all that Hajji and my parents and Bish and Victoria have given me. It is part of a larger story, *The Natural History of Coincidence*. So far as I know, all the things I'm about to reveal are true.

Part Two

1

etween the watchman's rounds, sometime after two o'clock on a cold, London night in the year 1820, a propped-open seaman's chest was deposited outside the doors of the Orphans and Foundlings Betterment Trust. A trail of prints, those left by a woman in rag-bound feet, and by a man in boots, led through new snow up the stairs from the footpath below. The baby's parents at least intended that he be saved. Most Trust babies were plucked from the docks or the stinking backrooms of public houses where they'd been birthed.

"Bast'd. Snow," he was called, to distinguish him from the half dozen other bastards—Straw, Turnfoot, Mole-Face—collected in the same manner during the same week. He was cleaned, swaddled, and set on a wet nurse's teat.

Not quite a dungeon but far from a home, the Trust stood as a beacon of rectitude above the squalor of the east London docks.

The Betterment trustees, Benthamites every one, saw no conflict celebrating moral uplift while honoring the book-balancing values of their trades. It was understood that the poxy sailors and the women who served them inhabited worlds beyond the reach of moral accounting. Just as God-fearing parents take responsibility for their children's misdeeds, so should well-trained children be held accountable for their parents' failings. With repayment in mind, the foundlings were fed, inspired by sermons, and set simple tasks in preparation for lifetimes of service and sobriety. For more than a century, the Trust had placed its best boys in what were termed the sanitary trades, or farmed them out as footmen, hostlers, and grooms, often in the trustees' homes and businesses. Some even rose to positions requiring skill and grace as drapers and tailors, bakers and butchers.

What had worked in previous centuries, however, was now under assault. No sooner had Bonapartism been routed than new challenges arose. Hell had climbed from the bowels of the earth and taken up residence in every port and city. This brutal new thing would soon go by the name of Industrialism. Devils of industry were running free where trout and salmon had once filled creels, in tidal basins where the poor had raked for shellfish, and on village greens where flocks had fed for centuries.

Urban immigrants streamed from the abandoned villages. Worker-ants poured out of taverns and brothels. No longer could it be said to Betterment Boys that honesty, loyalty, and a cheerful attitude were certain to be rewarded. No one cared for piety, ancestry, or letters of introduction. Industry cared only that its hirelings show up vaguely on time and sober enough for work.

See what you've wrought, Adam Smith and Jeremy Bentham? the trustees cried. Wealth of nations, indeed! The Betterment Trust and everything it stood for would disappear within the decade. Into this gluttony, this noisy revolution, Jack Snow, at six, was sent to work.

, , ,

Jack Snow was not known to speak. Cursory examination revealed no deafness or gross deformity. Silence being held more a virtue than a failing in a child, "Jack Snow, Mute" found easy placement sweeping animal waste and gutter slime. Brothers of the Spade, the supervisor, Henry Wiggins, called his boys, a diminutive army of scavenging rats, although he preferred the model of the immaculately clean, white-bibbed gull. "Mark the seagull," he told his boys, "or I'll send you up a chimney with a scouring broom."

In the nightly exhortations delivered by officers of the Trust, the boys were admonished to extract positive lessons from their daily tasks. Averting pestilence was a holy calling. Morals could be gleaned from clearing the gutters of horse manure and carcasses—mainly canine—that had failed to clear the flashing hooves of a team or trap. After cleaning up dead rats left by teams of terriers, it was morally instructive, albeit contrarian, to cheer on live rats feasting on the body of a dead Alsatian.

The postdawn sight of whores picking over the sleeping mounds of comatose gentlemen, their purses and pockets slashed open, their shoes and belts and watches redistributed, could also serve a higher purpose. Moral weakness carries a heavy price. Less obviously, gentlemen in a hurry to cover their tracks often drop coins and stickpins, foulards and cigar cases, and are too tipsy to find them in the dark. A moral that proved the wisest of all had come from Wiggins himself: *You never know what the next thrust of the shovel might turn up*. A patient, sharp-eyed boy built close to the ground, a regular seagull of a lad, was free to generate his own amusements and occasional income on the East London streets.

The well-timed thrust of the proper shovel could indeed unlock a door.

At night, back in their cells and away from the wardens' lamps, Wiggins's little army examined their day's haul and calculated its possible value. Master Thorne, oldest of the lot, took half of everyone's swag even before Wiggins and the wardens extracted theirs. Master Thorne was ten years old, built large, and handy with a knife. Without him, the wardens would have taken everything. With Thorne, the boys got a bit of it back. But even Thorne never suspected the existence of the mute boy's cache.

And so Jack Snow passed through his sixth and seventh years as unaware of the need for speech as he was of reading and writing. To him, words were necessary only for people who gave orders. He knew what he had to know: the parts of the body as targets of the nightly caning. He knew the streets radiating from the Betterment home. He knew the docks and some of the men and women who gave him food or drink and a penny for special service. Jack Snow, Mute, was an innocent, capable of cleaning himself and his quarters, enduring punishment, and moving through a fallen society without taking special notice of it.

He was already a ladies' favorite. *"Oh, I fancy the silent types, I do,"* the tarts would coo, and fetch him indoors and warm him before the coal-grate till his cheeks flared, then feed him fried eggs, coffee, and larded toast. They'd loosen their bodices and pass him from lap to lap like a monkey and give him hanks of cloth to wrap about his ears and throat. Their bodies were hot and powdered. Sweat accumulated between their breasts. The women were forever coughing, dabbing their scarlet-stained kerchiefs in camphored water. Their ringlets lay plastered to the sides of their heads, their faces and bosoms glowed red from gin and the blast of flames. Once seated on pillows around the hearth they wouldn't venture from the grate except to sprinkle more clots of coal.

Because he was mute, they believed him to be deaf. The unfettered exchange of gossip and special intimacies between women with grievances was another hoardable commodity for a growing boy. Any of them might have been his mother, especially the darker ones with a hint of the Spanish. Any of the passed-out men in the room's cold corners could have served as a likely father, but this never crossed his mind.

Through his exposure to dockside women, Jack Snow had formed the opinion that generally women were of a kinder and more forgiving nature than men, though the eruption of their fury was unpredictable. Men could inflict greater pain over a longer period, but usually at regular times for a stated purpose. A woman would not devote two hours a day to flogging a row of bare-arsed boys, or demand a show of overturned hands for corrective caning with the same cold efficiency as a man. But the wardens would not draw a knife and slice a boy's eye out with not so much as a scream or oath, as women would.

All in all, predictability and impersonality, the handshake when the swollen hand could not close for its battering, was preferable to the ebullitions of womankind. He could well imagine the comfort men took in untying those frills and bows—he'd been urged by the women to try it himself—but there was treachery in it, the fear that he might demand too much or produce too little. He knew men who'd paid for those demands or failures with a razor slash across their faces, or worse.

And then, a chance encounter outside a grog shop forced out an utterance, a scream, a command. Shortly after daybreak on a handsome autumn morning in 1827, Jack Snow's shovel, feeling tentatively under leaves, branches, bottles, torn clothing, and the usual residue of dockside carousing, struck a battered body with holes in the face where you least expected them, some of them freshly bleeding, others devoid of flesh. For the first time in his life he plucked words that had buzzed about him like flies in the summer. *Help!* he cried. *Blood,* he screamed. *Bring help!*

╭   ╭   ╭

Tom Crabbe a-walking was not far different from Tom-in-the-gutter, a living reproof to the pain-addicted ways of plunder-and-payback. Jack Snow, Mute, was but a child, with a boy's innate credulity and want of belonging. There was much he had seen in his first eight years, but precious little he'd actually done. He'd not spent a day outside the narrow compass of the Trust home. He could not read or write and his formal learning was confined to the Scripture he'd been read. Compared to the roistering ways of Tom Crabbe, who'd been twice around the world by Jack Snow's age, he might as well have spent his first eight years inside a Dorset vicarage.

Old sailors bore their amputations with swagger, indulging in ivory pegs and Sheffield-forged claws, fine silk patches and silvered teeth. Every tick-tock of the mortal clock roamed the London streets in full display. Crabbe's face resembled a carved mask fixed in rage. One blue eye turned outward, the other was but a cavern, a leeched glene. His nose had been split, an ear yielded to the Moors, the other shriveled for want of circulation. He could close his mouth, inflate his cheeks, and expel air through the glene, flapping the eyepatch like a shade caught in the breeze.

On the high seas, a man's "subtractions," as Crabbe liked to put it, bought a kind of professional exemption. Even papists might find their blood lust quelled, knowing no more earthly pain could extract conversion from one so inured. Any hostile boarding party would go first for a slice of cherub, a fatty slab of virgin piss-pant. He sucked smoke from a long clay pipe and expelled it in tiny jets from half a dozen unstopped vents.

His stories became Jack Snow's education. He offered deliverance from the wardens and the likes of Master Thorne, for example. Why not gut the little bastard? Crabbe asked. What's a mate for but looking out, eh? Lure him on the street, point him out, and I'll whittle him down to kindling. He took out his knife and stropped it twice on the gray callus of his three-fingered hand.

Avast! the strictured grays of the Betterment Trust, the sermons and nightly canings. No more Bible readings from the pulpit above the rectory table. Welcome to the grog shops and harlots, the blood, the blubber, the torn limbs, the intimate scavenging over bones and bounty. Crabbe had worked slavers, he'd survived the cannibalizing of his mates and delivered prisoners and orphan girls to Van Diemen's Land. He'd seen the Indies and traveled up the Amazon, he'd made four sailings on thousand-ton Indiamen around the cape to Calcutta and China. He'd tapped sperm whales for casks of oil, and salted cod till all the juices in his body lay caked upon his shriveled fingertips. He'd seen wild half-men, kangaroos, and thylacines.

And, he reckoned, Jack Snow had the makings of a mate.

"Ah, life at sea," he'd extol. "You foller me and you'll see the best and the worst of life. That's the meaning of it all, ain't it?" The talk turned to sex. In selected waterfronts off the shipping lanes, where old enemies met as mates, half-mended faces like his earned respect and the attention of the finest women. "There's many a fine piece to be had in the world, but none in London. You probably wonder why."

The boy had been thinking only what "the best" might be. He assumed he saw the worst every time he looked on Tom Crabbe's face. Jack's fantasies ran to food, soft beds, and warm clothes, but Crabbe and his cronies talked only of the grog and women and money to be made in private dealing off the ship. They were always arguing over where to find the best liquor, who had the best women and the easiest life. If they'd been drinking, these arguments were something they could kill over.

"London's too rich. Poor men like us only get the dunwithums. But take George Town or Hong Kong. Everybody's poor, so a face like mine gets a choice." Devastation counted for more than an admiral's silks. "This old face of mine," he swore, "fetches up girls King Willie can't get." Bearing the scars of blue water service, speaking the tongue of every flag, Tom Crabbe could always find a ship to bear him onward, no matter where in the world he washed up.

What boy could resist the call of the sea?

⸙　⸙　⸙

The tales Tom Crabbe told left a lifetime's impression on the boy who would become John Mist. At the time of writing the *Mist-nama,* John Mist was fifty years and half a world removed from his London origins, but still quoting Tom Crabbe and trying to please him, or at least not disappoint him. I read and I grieve, because Tom and John had nothing in common except the turn of a shovel on a particular morning in a London gutter. He was John's mentor, in the best and worst of ways, just as he'd promised.

"What about those black balls around your neck?" Jack asked one day.

"Balls? These?" Tom tilted them upward for a better view. The black leather balls he was always talking to and sometimes brushing with his lips were four tiny heads, lips and eyes sewn shut, but their noses and ears perfect.

He drew Jack's finger to the row of heads. "Say hello, boy. They're sorry they can't shake your hand. This'un here's my man Doom, this is Li'l Ike, say hello to Nigger Sam, and this boy here is Isaiah. Isaiah could sing like an angel."

Third time out he'd caught on with a whaler out of Sag Harbor. They called him surgeon's assistant. Fetching Captain Carter his tea and grog was more like it. They had a near full load of sperm, but chased a pod way south off the Guineas all the way around the bulge of Brazil.

"Dangerous Portugee waters and the captain was a right fool. Nothing new there, eh? We seen dolphin, so we chased them, too. Who ever heard of sweet water dolphin? No one thought to taste the water. We was in the river mouth even before we knew it for a river, and not just any river, but the Amazonas."

The boy thrilled to that word: "Amazonas."

That's when they'd been captured by Indians. "Damn fool captain and officers got gold fever, couldn't be stopped or turned around. Up the Amazonas with monkeys firing shit balls down from the trees and little fish with razor teeth could rip a jaguar down to a tuft of his tail, even before he drowned. Saw a tree all black and slithery like it was bleeding pitch, but it was a million black leeches up from the water, whelping new ones."

He'd spent two years on land with monkey-eating savages, forgetting English, thinking every minute might be his last. He never knew why he'd been spared and the others were eaten. He'd passed into manhood under their watch, twice the height of any man. He reckoned half the tribe would grow up tall and light-eyed. And one day, when he'd practically forgotten the life he'd known, he heard a first mate's cry, "Ahoy!" from deep on the river, and never mind the devilfish, he plunged in and swam to the channel and was taken aboard.

What red-blooded boy could resist it?

"What about your missing eye?" he asked.

"Ah, noticed it, did ye? Observant little scamp."

A Barbary skirmish, he said, with the fool captain lying drunk in his quarters, the first mate setting no watch and the other officers playing cards on the deck under a lantern light. Too hot and smelly belowdecks for their fine English noses. Why not invite a few Spanish cutthroats aboard, eh? Why not send out a little skiff? The good lads that didn't fall by the sword were shackled together and brought belowdecks to the captain's cabin.

Crabbe wasn't shackled. He thought he'd been spared, like on the Amazonas. "There's a lesson for you, boy. Don't ever think there's a fat goose waiting for you at the captain's table."

"I don't," he said.

Crabbe thought the priest would try to convert him, which was a damned sight less painful than what the Mohammetans do. If he'd been younger, it might have turned out that way. Papists want you young or just before you die, but he was now a man of sixteen. The billowy prelate was preparing an altar to celebrate the victory, sipping anise and holding his egg spoon over a candle.

"Fat beast was wrapped in silks and satins like a lady-in-waiting. He'd been hiding inside a closet till the fighting died down. Last thing this poor right eye of mine ever seen was his big fat cross dangling in my face. He gets his egg spoon hotter'n a forge and plunges it in and lets it sizzle before decerpting. Our shackled boys was watching and they started crying, and it weren't for my pain."

Then Tom Crabbe took out his gem-studded dagger, sharp

enough to shave with and stropped to keenness on that flat, gray callus. "Can't say I haven't helped myself to a few priestly parts myself."

Egg spoons! thought Jack Snow, the best and the worst coming together. Is there nothing in the world not used for misery and mayhem?

Leeches cleaned it up a few days later, reducing the glene to polished bone, and that's how it stayed. Of course, losing an eye saved his life, a rough equation not lost on Jack Snow. The other lads, pleading squabs that they were, had not been mutilated at all, in the beginning. They screamed for a week, till their tongues were taken and then their lips and eyes and noses. The priest guided the crew slowly down their Protestant bodies, cutting as they went, and the cries were piteous.

What Betterment Boy could resist?

A life at sea hinted at access to something larger than the moral codes of the Betterment Trust. It was the lure of special knowledge, an opening to the world that could be tied to words as simple as "Amazonas" or as fearful as "egg spoon."

And the other thing Crabbe had hinted at, with his tales of mates dying for one another, the loyalty they felt for those who'd fallen, and the contempt he held for all authority, was the presence at sea of a loyal community. In the Betterment Trust, for all the talk of Christian fellowship, there was little he'd seen but lies and thievery. From Crabbe with all his talk of knifings and torture, vengeance and retribution, his apparent indifference to pain and suffering, there was uncommon gallantry. It was Jack's instinctive call for help the morning he'd spotted helpless Tom in the gutter that had alerted the sailor to the boy's special quality, and led him to believe that he belonged with him at sea. He had the makings of a mate.

On the strength of Crabbe's recommendation, given the testimony of his face, there'd always be a place for Jack as cook's cabin boy, a beer-drawer, a foremast boy, or, better yet, a surgeon's apprentice. They fancied small fingers, the surgeons.

2

Crabbe had warned him, and now he saw it for himself: The great days of sailing were coming to an end. Sealanes were as crowded now as Piccadilly Circus. The better ships paying the higher wages had grown so vast, so laden with iron fittings and teak furnishings with mahogany panels that sailing itself had lost its soul.

The newer ships could sail themselves. Just aim them, said Tom, and if any tight maneuvering is required, best begin it a day in advance. The newer Indiamen had staterooms for women and children going out to Calcutta to join their husbands. There'd be no more exemplary lashings or hand-nailings to the mast. The captain's table, where the ladies dined, served bottles of wine stored middecks, where they also kept pens for goats and fowl and beds of vegetables. What was next—a fishpond? Chickens and cabbages got more light and air than two hundred sailors stacked in the dark, sleeping in a shit-smelling oven.

The basic design of an East Indiaman, British, Dutch, or Danish, had not changed in two hundred years. They'd been sleek and beautiful at three masts and five hundred tons, then at six and seven hundred, but the companies' trade kept expanding and their ships grew heavier and more luxurious. Masts towered higher than the tallest tree, topped with a second mast subject to easy snapping. In a gale, they could be overmasted. Their appointments were like a floating inn's. They didn't need rigging-monkeys or fo'c'sle boys anymore. It would take a pair of leather lungs for a warning to be heard from such a height. And with the continental wars over, retired artillerymen with no naval skills had taken over the cannon.

Crabbe was right, of course. The days of the sail were nearly over. He had reached his conclusion by Crabbe-like logic, however. Because *his* days were numbered, so were sailing's. Because *his* experiences were no longer valued, neither were anyone else's. And if there was no honor in the "subtractions" he proffered, neither was there value in bravery and forbearance and a lifetime's practical experience. Tom Crabbe had become an anomaly, and it's the nature of the anomalous to condemn the world as out of step.

′ ′ ′

Diligence Partridge of Penzance, captain of the Indiaman *Malabar Queen,* was a new sort of East India Company officer. Most captains were seasoned blue water salts, marked by the crowsfeet around the eyes, spyglass squint, and sallow, weathered skin. They could take a scurvy crew and pare away the malcontents with a single exemplary lashing. They returned their ships to port seaworthy, and their crews got something more than base pay in their purses.

Partridge, however, was younger and educated in something he called the Nautical Science, which he'd mastered in a class-room of a naval academy. He was small and trim, his uniform tight, his face unscarred. Sideburns stretched across his cheeks, starting sharp but fading out, unable to link with a silky mus-tache. He settled young Jack and old Tom on the deck and pro-ceeded to lecture them on the fine art of modern sailing. It's a wonder Crabbe didn't take out his knife.

In silent, serious Jack Snow, a boy who watched him steadily, Captain Partridge sensed a hostage to the future. And the disrep-utable old guardian, or whatever he was, his face pitted with more holes than a smoldering coalfield, was an amusing enough sort if he stayed out of the path of gentle passengers. And so, Crabbe and Snow signed on with an Indiaman at last, fifteen hundred tons, on just its second voyage out to India and China. The promised pay was enough for Crabbe to consider retirement to a tavern in the Straits or the Burma coast.

There was a price to pay, and that was having to listen to the nonstop lectures of Captain Partridge. According to him, ships were guided by currents as well as winds. Oceans were braided with strands of water, sweeter and saltier, warmer and cooler. Warmer water lifts the air, setting up convection currents, bring-ing wind. Temperatures and salinity would be tested hourly—your job, Master Snow. The saltier the water, the greater the buoyancy, hence less drag. Colder water is denser, offering greater resistance. From the point of view of a modern ship's captain, air and water share the same properties. Waves pass through them in the same way.

"Contrastive hydrology—sorry, the science of waters—will be as important as reading the ship's glass and wind direction in determining costs and timing."

The boy nodded. He had been lost from the first mention of "braided water." Crabbe's expression could not be interpreted.

"In short, less time on the water, more gold in the purse."

And then Captain Partridge said something that he had heard only once before, and that was from Tom Crabbe, an unreliable source. "We are not long for the world of wind and sails, I fear. Mark my words, the time is coming when wind is irrelevant. Man himself will generate the wind."

About generating wind, I'll grant him that, Tom Crabbe said later.

It was summer, 1831. He would turn twelve early in the new year, somewhere off the coast of Africa if they held to schedule. The next year would change his life.

"Round the cape in the dead of summer, it's the only way," said the captain. "December-January, I mean." The boy took in that little absurdity without objection. Sailing with a captain who took hourly temperatures of water but didn't know his seasons would make a good story, later.

Captain Partridge had seen the future, and the future was steam, human-generated wind, directed under pressure. He'd seen the steam locomotive outrun and outpull the finest span of horses in the land. A network of rails was spreading from London to every city, and from every city to every village. The stagecoach was finished. The horse-drawn hayrick plodding along a country road—what earthly use was it now? Horses might as well be sold for slaughter. That's what a three-masted Indiaman was—horse-drawn! The world would not tolerate the vast speed differential between land and sea. The nautical future was in steam and iron-hulled ships ten or twenty times the tonnage of the *Malabar*

Queen. Fifteen hundred tons? It would take that much coal just to reach Gibraltar.

"Are you with me, Master Snow? Much will depend on your measurements."

"Yes, sir," he lied. He was with the spirit, if not the meaning, of the captain's disquisition. As imperfectly as he understood it, he realized that Tom Crabbe and men like him would know even less. The boy could at least grasp the logic. Tom would reject it as raving lunacy. Jack Snow had become the master.

A modern captain provisions fruit and keeps a milch-goat, this one, named Pippa, to provide at least a drop or two of milk for tea every day. The crew should remain healthy at least till the Horn, when more fresh provisions could be boarded.

"*Doom, my man,*" said Tom Crabbe, brushing his lips on his necklace of bumpy scalps as he and the boy claimed their hammocks, "*in my life I've seen many a strange thing. But a partridge flying out a goat's arse   that I have never seen.*"

*   ,   ,   .*

Twice a day Captain Partridge would stroll the deck with his first mate, Mr. Listowel; the ship's surgeon, Dr. Vanstone, and the captain's young assistant, Master Snow (never without an empty bottle tied to a very long cord); and whatever passenger might feel himself—or, given the lady-passenger on board, herself—in need of a preprandial stretching of the limbs. Forty-two circuits of the deck constituted a mile, a numbing ordeal in solitude, but pleasant enough in gentle company. The captain's stroll also braced the crew. It is a captain unworthy of his rank who could not detect a shortcoming and assign a reprimand in any brief encounter with any common seaman.

Captain Partridge was not above a touch of vanity. In his stateroom he'd installed brass bars upon which he lifted himself fifty times on waking and fifty more before retiring. While suspended, he performed fifty gut-tightening leg lifts. For the final half dozen, Jack was usually called in to help.

The evening stroll and the dinner that followed gave him a chance for formal dressing in a snug-fitting uniform. Jack administered the final, button-closing squeeze. The captain thus incapacitated from bending, the boy affixed the polished boots. Because there was an attractive and witty young lady aboard, he shaved more carefully and defined his sideburns ever more sharply. Jack stropped his razor twice a day. On deck, he struck poses fitting of Nelson on the bridge. The crew might see him as he saw himself; the captain, majestic in dress whites with his assembled family: two brothers—Listowel and Vanstone—a wife— the lady-passenger—and a son—Jack Snow Mute—his brass spyglass furled, slapping it impatiently across his open palm.

Thanks to his years of tutelage from Tom Crabbe, Jack Snow had absorbed the mutinous sentiments of the lower ranks. Mates, passengers, and, above all, captains, were by their very nature ignorant of the basic rules of survival at sea and indifferent to the suffering of the crew. Without the quiet subversion of captain's orders and sullen collusion among the ranks, he'd been taught, no ship would ever sail or return intact. Of course he was wise enough to suppress the least sign of disrespect.

Now, Jack found himself the captain's pet, the surgeon's assistant, the first mate's attendant, and the lady-passenger's "bright, bright lad." She'd even invited him to stay on with her new family in Calcutta as a cook's assistant and apprentice butler. He'd been brought up to midships, sleeping on a pallet at the foot of Pippa's stall, the easier to milk the beast and sweep away the pellets. Tom Crabbe acknowledged his defection with a snarl whenever they passed. If errands sent him below, or placed him alone in a darkened corner, he feared he might find himself gutted like a cod and tossed overboard, so bitter was Crabbe's sense of betrayal.

The captain encouraged and participated in the widest range of civilized discourse. Jack was privy to every discussion. With the lady, the captain discussed music and theater; with the surgeon, diseases and their therapies; and with his officers, sailing risks and advantages. With everyone, however indifferent, he expounded his ideas of future travel and where navigation was heading. Jack was silent throughout, but attentive. He was receiving the best education available for one schooled in silence and credulity.

The future Mrs. Humphrey Todd-Nugent, for now Miss Olivia Todd, was to meet her husband-to-be in Calcutta. She was a twenty-seven-year-old governess from County Armagh, tall and forthright—"horsey" was the applicable word on first impression—a sober and sensible woman, Protestant of course. At the captain's table one evening early in the voyage, she confessed to never having entertained the notion of going out to India, or of becoming the wife of an East India Company official. The prospects of marriage and of managing the house and domestic affairs of a high-ranking, socially demanding East India Company director turned her giddy. Thereafter, the captain was smitten.

"Don't you find our guest a handsome sort?" he'd ask young Jack, who of course replied, "Which guest do you mean, sir?" and he would pursue, "The lady, I forget her name . . ." and he would stutter while Jack supplied, "Could it be Miss Todd, sir?" and the captain would release a long "Ahhhh, yes, of course," as Jack helped lift his legs for the final six pulls. She played Irish airs on her harpsichord. She had a delightful singing voice.

For the first time in his life, Jack Snow found himself in the company of a woman who paid him respect and attention, and placed one affectionate hand on his shoulder as they strolled, and the other hand on the captain's arm. "And what does my bright, bright lad think of that?" she'd ask after nearly any adult conversation between the captain, herself, or the senior officers.

She questioned the captain about the hierarchy, the social etiquette, of East India officials in Calcutta. How should she prepare herself? What could she expect?

"A woman such as yourself should find no lack of women friends," the captain replied. East India Company officers were all of them married men, but for the occasional widower. She would find Calcutta a full and vibrant society, at least from his limited experience of it. She seemed reassured, but the boy knew the captain to be lying. Among themselves on the afternoon stroll, without the lady, the captain and officers joked of Calcutta's carryings-on, men with native concubines called bibis, of certain semisecret "visitations" timed for the months when husbands, or wives, were back in England. The boy knew that some women went out to India and found disaster.

"For example, Captain Partridge," she asked one night, "would you think it disrespectful of me if we invited you to dinner? Would that be overreaching?"

"Miss Olivia, nothing would give me greater pleasure, but your husband far outranks a mere ship's captain. I cannot dine at the table of a man to whom I report."

Egg spoons, the boy thought. *It's all about egg spoons.* Aboard ship, she dined at his table every night. What's so special about Calcutta?

And she confessed to knowing nothing about furnishing a home that comes with a set of ready-made children, her widowed husband's boy and girl. "I was a governess, never a mother," she said, and the boy heard her to say, *I never intended to be a mother*. She seemed to grow prettier each day.

"You will find Calcutta supplied with very competent help," he said. "Entrust the children to the ayah they doubtless know better than their parents."

And so, the give-and-take went on around him. He was picking up words, codes, the insecurities of people in positions of power.

After three months at sea, sharing dinners and evening perambulations, the captain found his susceptibilities to Miss Todd growing, suppressed with the utmost difficulty. He upped his exercises. The boy lifted him ten times, a dozen. He added a second morning stroll with the boy alone. He saw himself successfully fighting this "erosion of resistance." The crew was snickering behind his back. One morning he mentioned, "I think I shall marry on my next shore leave. Yes. One finds oneself . . . susceptible, no?" Dr. Vanstone prescribed a tonic. Certainly Olivia had taken to the boy, whose wild tales of life at sea and of cannibals in the Amazon, or his cruel abandonment and institutional upbringing, had initially left her close to tears. Now his grisly tales engendered her own light, Irish rejoinders. "Lost an eye, did he? Only one? Oh, Master Snow, surely he just slapped a poultice on it and proceeded along his merry way."

Her marriage had been arranged through cousins. Mr. Todd-Nugent was a man in his mid-forties in need of a wife, having lost the mother of his two children in the previous year. If Jack were to be employed in her household, he knew he'd have trouble with her husband. He had no right to one so fine, merely by snapping his fingers and saying "bring me a pretty young woman who sings and plays and draws and makes men happy just to be around her."

Mr. Todd-Nugent and Miss Olivia were not only betrothed,

they were related in some complicated, north-of-Ireland fashion. She was a Todd. When she thought of the life in Calcutta that she would be leading, she pictured her harpsichord in a parlor, and her children—that is, Mr. Todd-Nugent's and her children should she be so blessed, as well as Mr. Todd-Nugent's older son and daughter—standing around the instrument as she played a chaste selection of country airs. She would teach them to draw—she had a good hand—and to paint. She'd been a governess on a large estate. In her field she came highly recommended.

She'd not yet accustomed herself to thinking of Mr. Todd-Nugent as possessing an actual Christian name, which she remembered but did not articulate as Humphrey. At some later date, her cousins predicted, his full name might be Sir Humphrey Todd-Nugent, given the extraordinary profits his sharp trading returned to the Honourable Company. Mr. Todd-Nugent himself had suggested in a letter, God willing, they'd put in ten more years in India consolidating his fortune, then retire to a country estate and round it off with a Tory seat from the Home Counties. She counted herself a fortunate woman, indeed.

Olivia spoke of her betrothed's architectural pride. He'd adopted native building practices. Marble exteriors to cool the air even before it passed inside, windows placed in shaded alcoves to circulate the air that had been previously cooled. He would hang strips of wet muslin, not merely to exploit the benefits of evaporation, but also to trap the particles of dust that were, unfortunately, everywhere in the nonmonsoonal months. Broad overhangs, marble floors, a lawn and fountain, and of course the cunning use of angles to catch the river breeze: the genius of tropical design.

She had kept all of her betrothed's drawings. She'd even shared them at dinner, or sometimes taken them out in her quarters and spread them on her bed to study the architecture of her coming life. The boy would study them with her. "This will be your room, Master Jack, what do you say to that?"

What do you say to that? She pinned extra ringlets to her gathered hair. She took out a long braid that she sometimes wore on top of her head and chased him about her cabin, more like another kid or a sister, threatening to turn him into a pigtailed Chinaman, and he finally let her. "I think you have a future in China," she laughed, when she let him see himself in her glass. "Mr. Snow-Snow. I think I'll call you Mr. Snow-Snow and say I found you in Hong Kong."

And at dinner she'd ask the captain in that same teasing voice, "My betrothed is a genius, wouldn't you say, Captain Partridge?" and the captain would brace his shoulders and respond, "Employing European reason and native materials is indeed a wise course." It hurt him to admit another to the select company of the world's finest thinkers, but for her sake he was willing on occasion to do so.

"Indeed, madam, one can live through the hottest months of India in utter comfort," he'd say. Then add, in case Mr. Todd-Nugent might follow the normal custom, "I personally find it an unforgivable extravagance to escape to the hills for summer."

⁓ ⁓ ⁓

Miss Olivia had been confined to quarters since Christmas with a touch of summer cold and fever. The heavy, humid air had been anything but salubrious. It was December in the last week of 1831, and in those southern latitudes to the east of Madagascar, the very midpoint of summer. All agreed that it was a short-term relief to feel beads of moisture, condensing fog, settle on one's brow.

"Such a gray, glassy sea, Captain Partridge," she exclaimed. "It's like punting on a pond."

"Yet . . . ," he started. But why rouse sleeping ghosts? "Many years ago, this was considered the most lawless sea between London and Calcutta. Captains' wisdom would say, 'You don't want to find yourself off the bulge of Africa in the summer when the big cyclones are brewing, or rounding the cape in the winter, when those southern gales can snap your masts—but the Mascarenes at any time are far more perilous.' Or *were,* I should say. Piracy, slavery, mutiny, unspeakable beastliness—the rest of the world progresses, but the Mascarenes remain a test." Jack knew the stories; the captain had filled him in just that morning. His imagination had been fired with tales of pirate treasure in Madagascar, whole cities of plunder protected by sword-wielding cutthroats mounted on elephants.

From a captain's perspective, this voyage had been perfection itself. They had arrived off west Africa after the season and rounded the cape under ideal conditions. And the boy had worked out well, labeling everything promptly and consistently. A scientific and commercial marvel; perhaps even a social coup, should this friendship with Mrs. Todd-Nugent be preserved.

"And how long ago was that, Captain Partridge?" she asked.

"Things have quieted considerably. The French are no longer a menace in these waters."

He unfurled his spyglass and performed a full ocular sweep. Endless gray on foggy gray, but the gesture at least appeared commanding. The French were not the problem. But Mascarene fogs were a problem, in the way that high grass is a problem. It favors the predator.

Fog accumulated on these banks. But why, she wanted to know. Fog she associated with Irish winters, not the stifling tropics. Wasn't it dangerous, under full sail with even the bow obscured? The captain was indeed worried, but tried to keep his explanations scientific. Just like the fogs in Ireland, it's the temperature differential, colder water clashing with the heated, humid atmosphere, wringing vapor from the air itself and no breeze to push it off. *Colder water up-pouring from the valleys below. Did you know, Master Jack, we are presently sailing over mountaintops? There are deep trenches down there, trust me.* Shallower waters, he might have lectured on another occasion, are far more dangerous. Shallow waters—case in point, the Bay of Bengal—engender exaggerated wave formation.

Best not to speak of professional matters. Best to keep the conversation light, keep it moving, and keep it on her.

Wind and waves were not the problem tonight, when they were unable to make satisfactory headway through a becalmed sea. With any kind of normal wind, they could make Mauritius in three days, maybe four. Port Louis meant boarding fresh produce, perhaps a goose or two, some pork, and decent wines, which were nearly depleted. Give the crew a break, the reprobates, make them better sailors for blowing off some steam. Maybe even a waiting stack of journals and some news from home, or from Calcutta. A fresh wind would clear the fog and help pick up the pace toward the trades. After Mauritius, they were nearly home, just threading the Straits, a peek at George Town, perhaps load some cargo, sell some English goods, and then north, into the bay. Home, at least for her. He still had China, then back to India, the endless rounds.

"The glass, Mr. Snow?" the captain asked.

"Rising, sir," he answered.

"Fair tomorrow, Miss Olivia," said the captain. "I predict a stiff breeze—"

"All the way to Calcutta!" she sighed.

They carried on at dinner over slices of Christmas goose, creamed corn, and pudding. Now that they had rounded the cape and were heading northward again, she felt they had crested a mountaintop and the voyage had somehow turned downhill.

"The most demanding part is certainly over," the captain agreed. "Another month, depending on trades, might put us in hailing distance, all things being equal."

"I shall miss our little strolls and conversations," she said.

"Oh, you'll be too busy to remember me," he replied.

"And these dinners. Your cook's assistant is a gem. I intend to keep him for myself in Calcutta."

Milking the goat, Jack Snow beamed. Unlike Tom Crabbe or the captain, he figured to be happier on land.

She allowed herself a second glass of the captain's Lisbon-loaded Madeira. The talk had been of Calcutta, of what she'd heard and read, and of what the Captain knew from earlier visits.

"The richest city in the British orbit," he said, "some day, I trust, to be enfolded within the British Empire."

This was not, he realized, a politic statement. He was a Company captain. In the long run, the British Empire and the East India Company were competitors for wealth and power. His dinner companion did not seem to notice.

"A city of grace and sophistication," he added, "the cleanest city I've ever known, but for squalor in the native quarters. Spacious housing, with gardens, and the open sky visible from every balcony."

But she seemed distracted. Jack cleared the table.

"Captain Partridge—the most extraordinary thing!" The captain's back was to the porthole. The boy turned, plates in hand. Pippa bleated. Olivia's face was white, her hands embracing her cheeks.

"What did you see, my dear?" The captain smiled, explanations of odd events being his special calling.

"Fire! I just saw a ball of fire falling—"

"My dear, that's quite impossible," the captain began.

"Captain!" came a pounding on the door and before Partridge could rise or inquire as to the nature of such an intrusion, Jack Snow had dropped the plates and opened the door. Through it burst First Mate Listowel. His arms were thrown wide, his eyes unseeing, his throat slashed. He staggered two steps and fell at the captain's feet.

3

*T*he weekly *Oriental Patriot* of Calcutta reported three months after the fact that on a foggy December night in the southern summer of 1831, two Danish-flagged marauders, little more than frigates half the mast-height of the Indiaman, had risen from the Mascarene mists, and—guided by the scent of tobacco smoke and the nostalgic piping of a Mauritian cook above decks—closed on the *Malabar Queen,* drawing along each side without detection. Some three dozen brave Company officers including Captain Diligence Partridge and First Mate Alistair Listowel were cut down in the early minutes of the engagement. The lone passenger, Miss Olivia Todd, betrothed of Company director Humphrey Todd-Nugent, was presumed lost at sea. The paper called upon the British government to offer armed escorts to East Indiamen passing through Mascarene waters, including the entire transit between Durban and Port

Louis, and to be particularly solicitous toward the female passengers now that civil society in Calcutta, Bombay, and Madras had so rapidly developed. We are, after all, no longer a company of bachelors wresting profit from the jungle factories. We have evolved into a civilization with a network of schools and churches, based in large part on the comforting solace of the fairer sex.

The newspaper account would have closed the matter had not one agitated Company officer, the above-mentioned Humphrey Todd-Nugent, brought charges of mutiny against the surviving crew. "A scurvy lot," he called them, begging any witness to scan their faces and draw his own conclusion.

According to his claim, the tale of piracy was an obvious fabrication. The piracy fable was concocted to cover up the attempted molestation of the lone female passenger, and the theft of her property. When she detected the theft, they had threatened her. When she disclosed the plot to the captain, he'd threatened them with the brig and death in the nearest port, which could have happened as early as Mauritius. That's the only version that comported with reality. Naturally, the first people killed would be the captain and officers, and then the brave cannoneers.

The proof?

Very simple. Mascarene pirates, if they still exist, are known to scuttle boats and to leave no witnesses. Why would *this* crew and ship survive?

The penalty for mutiny was automatic death, and a painful one at that.

Jack Snow had seen most of it and heard it all, but Jack Snow, the boy, had died that night, and John Mist, the young man who rose in his place, did not speak. During the two months adrift before arriving at the Kidderpore Docks, he had fallen back into his earlier silence. He had witnessed the beheading of the captain, the surgeon, and other mates. He'd watched the pirates swill the brandy, slaughter the guinea fowl, and carry off Pippa, the prized milch goat. The captain had died on his knees, bawling for the nanny. The boy heard his last piteous cry, *"You fools, I could—"* and through the slats of Miss Todd's trunk he'd seen the broadsword coming down and the expression on the face of the cutthroat wielding it, a black man whose face was already smeared in gore.

Jack Snow, a prized little oyster if he'd been detected and pried apart, remained silent and undetected in the chest at the foot of Olivia's bed, where she'd stashed him.

The homesick Mauritian was trussed and tossed. Cannon and ordnance were transferred and the artillerymen dispatched to a watery grave. Being Danes, by flag if not by crew, they were less intent on carving up the common sailors than on making an orderly transfer of serviceable goods. "Captain Moans," as he was called (later identified as the notorious privateer Mogens Jespersen), had gathered as rapacious a gang of savages—Malays, Turks, Zanzibaris, and Moroccans—as could be safely confined on a single ship without turning upon one other. To lengthen the odds of hot pursuit, the charts of the *Malabar Queen* were burned and her food stores scattered for trailing sharks. But John Mist would not speak.

The captain's safe had been blown open and the crew's collective payroll, which by company policy had been held hostage till their arrival in port, was taken. Captain Moans forced Miss Olivia to play two airs on her harpsichord before it was chopped into kindling and she was carried off, screaming.

From the hold, pirates helped themselves to transportable valuables from seven relocating London mansions. Books and paintings were slashed and tossed, but the pewter and silver, the damasks, the gentlemen's and ladies' silks and velvets, were all off-loaded. One could imagine cutthroat popinjays and smartly dressed Comoro tarts strolling the dockside in La Réunion, drinking from Irish goblets and eating off pewter with silver spoons.

Egg spoons, the boy thought.

On that warm summer evening, a gale of piteous prayers, a teleological cacophony, had arisen from the Indiaman's deck. Mohammedans appealed to the all-Merciful, papists fell to their knees, kissing a cross. Protestants raised their voices in a feeble chorus of "A Mighty Fortress," praying the Danish flag was more than a bloody banner. For anyone who pleaded convincingly enough for entry to paradise, the invaders were accommodating. A few old salts, experienced in the nimble art of expedient survival, proffered their services to the newer flag.

Before the boarding, the crew had started dreaming of George Town whores and Calcutta tarts, of iced drinks and soft, warm food. The captain would reach into his safe and advance them a guinea or two, man to man, even this pathetic little insult to the fleet. They'd passed the cape, La Réunion was near, and then Mauritius. Crabbe was planning his Rangoon Taverna. They'd let their guard down. The Mauritians were piping and blowing smoke. They deserved the slaughter, but they still needed someone to blame.

It was the passionate intervention of Tom Crabbe that saved the ship and the remaining crew. The integrity of his face spoke to them all. He spoke in Danish to Captain Moans, in Spanish, in Turk, in Portuguese. "I'm calling on you as men of the sea," he cried in English. "You took us fair and square, you have a privateer's right to all you can carry. We understand the killings. You know how we feel about lifting our wages, that's a foul deed and God willing, you'll answer for it. The woman does not belong with you. You must not harm her. You must set her free. The smooth-cheeked cabin boy you're looking for is . . . (and here Jack Snow had bitten into Olivia's silks and cottons) . . . dead. He fell from the topmast. Leave us the ship so's we can make port. Leave us a crew, who've done no harm to you or anyone."

These were the visions John Mist held inside him. (*You fools, I could—, I could—* and the crunch of an executioner's sword. *What* could the captain do?) And the eloquence of Tom Crabbe, who'd saved a hundred lives that day. But it was Tom Crabbe who'd warned him in the weeks at sea against speaking out ever again.

With the murder of the officers and captain and the loss of their pay, it was the officers' pet lackey, Jack Snow, who was held to blame for the theft of wages. Every member of the crew had been in line for fifty pounds, maybe more. The boy alone had access to the cabin, what had he taken for himself? Where had the captain kept *his* pay? Behind a panel, perhaps? They ripped the panels out. Only by acting dumb and performing acts of self-debasement did he allay their suspicions. Crabbe became his personal tormentor, lest favoritism be suspected. Little Jack Snow, who'd walked with the captain, who knew the captain's thinking, who laced his boots and pulled his cinch-belt tight, who'd made himself the captain's little monkey . . . well, then, little monkey, they'd say—let's see you dance. Climb the riggings. Climb higher, Jack o' the Mists! Eat this. Drink this, fresh and foamy. Jump. And Tom Crabbe took the lead.

After the theft of wages, Crabbe got them dreaming again. Bring the damaged vessel home, he told them, tell the heroic tales, and fall on the mercy of the Company. Perhaps they'll reimburse us for saving their ship and some of the cargo at least. Or we can claim high sea salvage and maybe sell the *Queen* and turn a bigger profit. We will always be the crew who rose from the dead. We'll have stories to tell for the rest of our lives and we'll drink on those stories and go down in history as the survivors of the last Mascarene piracy. Women will throw themselves on heroes like us.

And so, early in March 1832, they arrived in the bustle and tangle of the Kidderpore Docks, across the Hooghly from the white mansions of Garden Reach, expecting their heroes' welcome. They told their stories to the *Oriental Patriot*. They enjoyed two memorable nights of women and rum, and on the third morning Company guards—brutal, turbaned, sword-wielding brutes from the northwest frontier—pried them loose from adoring women, sobered them up with buckets of water, and tossed them inside a long train of camel-drawn conveyances.

The acting captain, Tom Crabbe, the cabin boy Jack Snow, and other so-called officers—the ringleaders of the mutiny—were taken to the brig of Fort William, pending trial. It was familiarly called the Black Hole, a dank oubliette worthy of a Turkish castle. They suffered the further indignity of being guarded by Indian troops, sepoys, who had orders to kill if they dared raise a ruckus.

The charges against the men were rooted in twisted logic, and driven by fear. There had not been piracy and loss of life on an East Indiaman in at least a dozen years. Every officer in the Honourable East India Company, or his family, made a passage to London at least every two years, and no man in Calcutta ever considered his wife or family in danger from anything more serious than mal de mer and boorish companions aboard a company ship. More men were lost to polo, and women to confinement, and both to tropical diseases, than to criminal activity at sea. If piracy was even suspected it could prove disastrous to profits and the sense of composure long associated with the Honourable Company. The Company traded on its image of omnipotence.

Had the day arrived, the *Oriental Patriot* editorialized, when the Honourable East India Company could no longer guarantee the safety of passengers or the sanctity of property on ships carrying its flag? If so, had the time come for the British navy, the undisputed master of the seas, to take over these duties from a failing company? And would this be the beginning of a larger takeover, the absorption of the largest commercial enterprise in the world into the world's greatest empire?

In the long run, Captain Diligence Partridge would have been proven a prophet. Indeed, *he could, he could* . . . Wooden boats and sailing ships were doomed and iron-hulled steamliners would take their place. Mascarene pirates would melt back into the ports and jungles bordering the Indian Ocean. All the navigational challenges and advances that Captain Partridge foresaw were real. Science and progress would be served and heroes would emerge, but the proud and vain Diligence Partridge would not be a pillar of the new establishment. In the next twenty-five years, the political ambitions of the British Empire and the commercial interests of the Honourable East India Company would be found incompatible. After the mutiny and the humiliation of British soldiers and civilians at the hands of sepoys in the Black Hole in the distant year of 1857, Viceroy Canning would dissolve the Company and absorb it into the Raj.

For the next few years, the foggy latitudes of the Southern Hemisphere off the coast of Madagascar would harbor privateers. They were known as the monsters of the deep, their wanton destruction almost self-defeating in an era that had begun to discover the profit in renewable plunder. The politics of the region still seethed with unsettled scores. The slave trade flourished.

Monsters were still out there, the forces of an older, pre-Industrial feudalism. Crews of the dispossessed from north Africa to the East Indies, those whom the Dutch and the French and the Portuguese had burned from their villages and shackled into slavery, could be counted on for plunder and vengeance. Those who had broken free became pitiless men wielding swords, manning the galleons of retribution.

Diligence Partridge had seen it coming but kept it to himself, lest it upset Miss Olivia, or his own faith in progress. He could have alerted the gunnery mate, but hadn't. He should have enforced total silence above decks and curtained his porthole while entertaining her. And a boy like Jack Snow, who had been meticulous in all his duties and had even begun to plot his own ocean charts according to the principles of contrastive hydrology, might well have settled in Calcutta under the expert tutelage of Olivia Todd-Nugent, learned gentle manners and to read and write. He might have gone to a school and then to a college and even an academy and become an adjunct in some branch of the new nautical science.

But not this Jack Snow, for whom life held a different fate. When the *Malabar Queen* arrived in Calcutta in March 1832, Jack Snow no longer existed. In his place stood John Mist, Johnny o' the Mists, they called him when Crabbe sent him up the riggings to the fo'c'sle looking out for food, any food. Globefish, that's what they were looking for, and thanks to John Mist they found them, immense flat lazy disks soaking up the sun. They sent him to the end of a boom to chop it off and fashion a crude harpoon.

After the privateers disappeared with their loot and the woman, captaincy of the crippled ship had devolved upon Tom Crabbe. It was as he'd said: in the company of common sailors, his face compelled respect. Their charts were gone—not that he would have used them—but he knew east from west and north from south and which way the wind was blowing. Having seen tall ships swamp in stiff ocean breezes, he sensed the *Queen* was overmasted for the trades, now that they rode higher in the water. He ordered his little monkey to chop off the three topmasts. Sooner or later, the crew held with their accidental captain that blind luck and sea-faring experience would take them through the Straits, up the bay and into the estuary of the Hooghly.

And that's the tragic story of the *Malabar Queen,* and the clash of nations and temperaments, and the immaculate conception and virgin birth of John Mist, and eventually, the founding of Mishtigunj.

, , ,

One's first view of Calcutta in the early 1830s, particularly of the whitewashed, double-storied mansions of Garden Reach as seen at a comfortable distance from the far bank of the Hooghly, was likely to invoke visual echoes of Athens and Rome at their pinnacles. Gentlemen on horseback are often included in the picture, with the horse seen nibbling a fringe of grass, the gentleman in riding coat and breeches and a high, Regency-style hat, staring out over the river or perhaps back to the mansion and the Edenic profusion of flowers issuing from a well-tended garden.

The view of the river from Kidderpore itself, however, is a-blur with movement. Paintings should be accompanied by a sound track. The hushed serenity of Garden Reach is blocked from view by three-masted Indiamen moving cautiously in the channel, flanked by the skiffs of riverine traders, long-bearded men in decorated skullcaps. Their little punts are brightly painted and flower-bedecked, piled high with baskets displaying Oriental commodities in garish abundance (and promising more, yet unseen): crabs and chickens, companionable songbirds for the long voyage back, dried fish, monster carp with their gills still heaving, kid goats, lambs—some still tethered, others already skinned and skewered waiting for a pit of coals—and (buyer beware!) gold and gemstones and a bearded old man with brass scales for weighing them out. Wives and daughters display ornate silks, draping them suggestively over their shoulders—think what *your* cheap women will do to *you,* for *this,* they seem to say— and the traders' little boys in skullcaps are sent up the side of the Indiaman, scaling rope riggings like inspired monkeys, faster than any pirate, hauling up the silks and bottles of grog, the dried fish and savories, the stuffed garials, the sacks of fruit—the first sweet thing these men have eaten in half a year—while the crew passes down hoarded items from Europe and Africa, the prices agreed to by shouts and insults, the little boys holding purses of gold in their teeth.

For the ex–cabin boy who had sailed past the Houses of Parliament on his way out to India some eight months earlier, who'd had it beaten into him at the Betterment Trust that London was the center of the world and the glory of civilization, the dazzling white buildings of Temple Square were finer by far. London streets were horse-clogged and squalid, festering with vermin. There was not an alleyway in London not infested with crime and disease, no footpath not cluttered with whores and drunks, beggars, madmen, and thieves. Children ran everywhere, shrill and unattended. Public buildings were gray and soot-streaked, the winter air foul and bilious.

Calcutta streets, on the other hand, were wide and the pace was slow, set by ox carts and camels. A small army of bent-over women and children swept the roadways. Even the cow and camel dung was quickly picked up and piled into baskets. Children no older than he had been when he started out on the London streets balanced baskets on their heads. The baskets carried the foulest garbage in the world, yet the children looked happy, smiling, waving to him as he passed. He thought briefly and fondly of Master Thorne and Henry Wiggins's Brothers of the Spade. *You never know what the next shovel load will bring you,* and that little homily had proved true. Every push of the broom can lead you . . . here, around the world. Trees lined every road and were not confined to a few locked parks and private gardens. He had never seen so many parks, as though it were a divine mission to preserve greenery in such heat and dust. Monkeys chattered on the branches and begged for food, then snatched it. As in London, dogs ran free; unlike London, so did cows. One could see open sky between each blinding white structure, and every house was blessed with garden spaces, river access, and a small forest of well-tended flowers and fruit trees.

He closed his eyes and remembered Captain Partridge's descriptions of Calcutta. Destined, he'd said, to join the British orbit. Calcutta was the seat of British governance, but also the base of the Honourable Company. As a commercial and political entity it sat next only to London in the Empire, and might even surpass it. He remembered Olivia Todd's dream-life, the harpsichord evenings in the mansion at Garden Reach and her promise of a home for him with his own room, her "little butler" and companion to her husband's son. He'd probably passed Humphrey Todd-Nugent's mansion, set off behind a wall beyond an extensive lawn, angled to catch the setting sun off the water and to avoid the late-morning, early-afternoon extremes of heat and glare.

Jack Snow had hated Humphrey Todd-Nugent before ever meeting him, just for his presumption of ownership over Olivia, the way even the mention of his name suppressed her gaiety whenever she spoke of him and his great accomplishments. He sensed the captain felt the same way, for his own complicated reasons. And now, John Mist hated him for the deceiving coward he was. He would have his life, and that of a brave crew, to satisfy his broken pride.

Unfortunately, Mist's first impressions of Calcutta were formed via glimpses behind the bars of an ox-drawn conveyance leaving the Kidderpore Docks under armed guards, fording the Hooghly just south of Garden Reach and following a leisurely course along the main road to Temple Square, thence to the Black Hole. Five of them were shackled, including the chief mutineer and instigator. The Crabbe Gang, they were called, then the Crabbe Cabal. A fine target they made for the citizens lined up outside their walled mansions throwing rocks and rotten fruit and hurling their choicest curses. It was assumed that he and the other villains would linger in the Hole pending the simple formalities of their trial and conveyance to the jungle fortress of Hazaribagh, where their expeditious execution would take place. Mutineers were the cattle-rustlers of that time and place; no greater crime could be imagined, or committed.

4

umphrey Todd-Nugent was not an evil man, unless his accumulated character flaws were considered in aggregate, but he was a man being driven mad by the public perception not of his tragedy, but of cuckoldry. His fiancée had been killed at sea, perhaps dishonored on a company ship, and the only witnesses to his humiliation had sailed blithely into the harbor of his city, expecting rewards from his company. His public tragedy earned him less sympathy than he felt his due, and roused his sharp trader's need to settle scores.

On March 12, 1832, the arrival of the *Malabar Queen* had been hailed in the *Oriental Patriot*. "Three weeks en retard, victimized by piracy off the coast of Madagascar . . ." "Crew regroups under a common seaman, Tom Crabbe, who brings the crippled Indiaman to port . . ." "Damage considered minimal, the loss of a boom and topmast, torn canvas, and the armaments . . ." "A feat to rank in the heroic annals of Company sailing . . ." "In sheer heinousness the worst piracy in modern butchery . . ." "Over forty deaths confirmed, including those of the Captain, First and Second Mates, Gunnery Mate and Chief Surgeon, and three dozen brave crew. And the tragic loss of the lone passenger, Miss Olivia Todd of County Armagh, Ireland, en route to marry her betrothed, Humphrey Todd-Nugent, of this city, a director of the Honourable Company."

As details revealed themselves in the following days, Miss Todd's death was ascribed to a gunshot wound, then to drowning, and finally to suicide. The implication of the latter could only be the attempt by pirates to dishonor her. Either she had resisted, then realized the futility and chosen to drown herself, or she had been molested, and drowned herself in shame. Whatever had occurred, said her husband-to-be in the March 19 issue of the *Patriot,* not one of the craven crew we saluted so patriotically last week did anything to prevent it.

"Stop it?" Mr. Todd-Nugent was quoted. "I would not be surprised if they did not instigate it. What evidence do they present that the Indiaman was ever boarded? I charge, and challenge any to disprove it, that the crew of the *Malabar Queen* rose up against the East India Company captain, Diligence Partridge, that they had collusion from discredited forces in that cauldron of French adventurism, the Mascarenes; that the heroic officers and captain had got wind of the conspiracy and in attempting to suppress it, were murdered by the mutineers. Either that, or they rose up for even more despicable reasons that I dare not enumerate outside closed court. Men at sea are caged animals, one must remember. It adds grief to the burden of my loss to ascribe their motives as not being, shall I say, entirely mercenary. There is clear evidence that my beloved wife-to-be was disgraced unspeakably at their hands."

The Company director exercised his influence and got his official inquiry.

,   ,   ,

A three-decked Indiaman is a floating allegory of heaven and hell. Below the middecks staterooms, where Company officers and families enjoyed safety and a measure of luxury, seethed a devil's spoor of rampant degeneracy. True gentlemen like Diligence Partridge and Alistair Listowel and Dr. Morley Vanstone supplied only a veneer of respectability. In the lightless hell belowdecks, two hundred swillhounds of dubious morality lay stacked like cordwood on fetid hammocks.

"Yeah, but cordwood don't shit and piss," said Tom Crabbe, on hearing the description.

A reporter (fancifully named "Virgil") sent belowdecks described (March 26, 1832) the stench of sweat, rotten food, body waste, and stale, spilled grog to be overpowering. Vermin of every description, crawling and flying, swarmed the galley and sleeping space. Air never circulated, the hammocks were never cleaned, and floors never swabbed. "And this," Virgil wrote, "is the condition with the boat in harbour, and the quarters empty."

"The noxious fumes of incontinence," he continued, "seek to find a destructive release."

The following week, a "humble Bengalee reader" signing himself "Dante" wrote that Virgil had perhaps been so overwhelmed in his senses by the raw stench of base humanity that he had not drawn the necessary link between squalor and lawless behavior. "In the *Divine Comedy,*" he wrote, "my cognomen swooned on two occasions at the sight of so much suffering. If we expect human beings to act as befits the children of God, perhaps we should afford every human a certain God-like respect. Could it be that our friend 'Virgil' had not walked the crowded native quarters of our own fair city?"

That is the implacable, self-taught, self-righteous, utterly prophetic voice of Bengali Brahminism, probably in its Brahmo phase.

"Dante" did not blame the crew for any crime they might have committed if their living conditions were even half as distressing as Virgil described. Nor would he blame our dusky fellow Calcuttans for future uprisings, even worse than the alleged mutiny on the *Malabar Queen*. It is not inconceivable for a whole people to rise up, and for someone in authority to call it mutiny.

No counsel stepped forward to protect the interests of Tom Crabbe and the suspect crew, and so a retired barrister by the name of David Llewellyn Owens, a noted defender of lost causes, was entreated to appear on their behalf. His opening statement gave fair notice: "I realize, milord, I am here not to defend, but to add a touch of legitimacy to a process already decided." Sitting at his side busily taking notes was a young assistant, native by the look of him, despite a certain European fashionableness. Owens introduced him as "Mr. Rafeek Hai, the fastest and most accurate transcriber, English, Persian, or Bengalee, in all Calcutta."

✦ ✦ ✦

(Rafeek Hai! I caught my breath and let it out slowly. Bish asked if I was crying. I cried, all right; I shouted out "Eureka!" It had been six years since that innocent day in Mishtigunj when I purchased the *Mist-nama* from Hajji, six years of desultory reading and attempts at rendering it into novel form, six eventful years in my life with just an M.A. to show for it, and only a year since I decided I wanted to write the history of the Tree Bride, and just half a year since everything I owned was wiped out. The name

"Hai" now sends shivers up my spine. The hajji was a Hai, under the honorific title of "Chowdhury," for his father's unspecified services to the Crown, and probably the title had been granted by Vertie Treadwell himself. It hadn't registered on me at the time; it had no reason to. Six months ago, my San Francisco house was bombed by a Bangla-speaking Hai. My husband is crippled on account of Mr. Hai, my son is under permanent threat by Mr. Hai, a nephew was murdered by Mr. Hai, and he is still out here in San Francisco. There have to be millions of Hais in Bangladesh, just as there are millions of Gangoolys and Chatterjees in West Bengal. Even if the names are coincidental, I knew that the best transcriber in all Bengal, Rafeek Hai, sitting that day in a Calcutta courtroom, would make his way to Mishtigunj and die on the same day as John Mist, after taking down the Persian dictation of his *nama*. My Eureka! was a scholarly thrill. Because of my research and writing, I suddenly knew the future and the past. Some of those Mughal paintings in the *Mist-nama* had come alive. And I knew again, in case I ever forgot it, there are no coincidences.)

＇ ＇ ＇

"So long as he confines himself to transcribing, I have no objection," said the judge, although technically natives were not permitted in British courts. Natives would not be admitted to law school and allowed to practice for another twenty-five years. By that time, young Mr. Hai would be a middle-aged vakil in a new village known as Mishtigunj.

David Llewellyn Owens was then a man of sixty-plus years, shiny bald on top and portly, "a perfect Welsh egg," even to the porcelain pallor of his skin. A lifetime spent under the Indian sun had not darkened a pore, at least to outer appearance. He'd been born and educated in Calcutta and was known as one of the last of the old "British Hindoos."

He dressed in Indian clothes outside of court and kept four Hindu wives in a block of houses in the native quarter of Sealdah. He was an embarrassment to the British establishment of Chowringhee and Garden Reach. He had resigned from the Calcutta Club and published his notice and the reasons for it on the front page of every paper. "It is a continual embarrassment to associate myself with the attitudes and actions of the so-called 'Club-worthy' members of the white Calcutta establishment," he had written. With that little gesture, he had passed beyond token eccentricity into the realm of disloyalty. His ancestry, however, fixed him at the center of Company nabobbery. Publicly, he favored a British takeover of Company assets, but secretly, the community charged, he favored an India returned to its native princes to rule as they pleased. His private religion appeared to be a personal amalgam of the least restrictive aspects of Muslim and Hindu. His children numbered over thirty, all acknowledged with his name.

For its part, the Honourable East India Company admitted that in previous decades its factors and officers had not always lived up to the Company's full title. Three or four generations of Mr. Owens' own relations bore convincing evidence of that. An editorial on the subject appeared shortly after his public resignation letter: "It is an honourable course that Mr. Owens has set by acknowledging his many dozen dusky children. Perhaps in the same spirit, he will enlighten us with the names of his more numerous dusky cousins, uncles, and aunties."

The historical fact is that 1832 marks the end of evolution in British/Indian accommodation. Macaulay's "minute" on education would appear a year later, and Macaulay himself take up residence as an East India Company official a year after that. In the earlier century, a man like Owens would not have seemed misplaced. Many Britishers came to India and became more Indian than the natives, learning the languages, practicing the religions, eating the food, and fathering half-Indian children from a virtual harem of bibis. They did so while still holding important offices within the East India Company. But with the turn of the nineteenth century, Christian missionaries were admitted to India, mainly Protestant, and they brought with them the doctrine of sexual abstinence and strict separation of the races. There had been a time when British and Indian values were in a kind of balance, when British felt themselves capable of gaining instruction from India as they spread their own enlightenment to receptive Indian youth, but by 1832 that time had passed. The sight of Owens in his kurta-pajama and turban, trailed by his wives, was as anachronistic as the vision of the hideous mutineer, Tom Crabbe.

,   ,   ,

Tom Crabbe was the focus of the inquiry. He was everything the East India Company and the British navy feared, a throwback to the days of blue water anarchy. So long as the fearsome Tom Crabbe stood in the docket, all manner of horrors were imaginable to the good citizens of Calcutta.

He didn't help himself. Was he bitter, was he envious, did he feel superior to his captain in navigational skills? Yes, to all counts. Did he feel all his rather, ah, striking sacrifices render him worthy of a higher rank? Did he feel humiliated that a man of his . . . obvious . . . experience at sea was marking time as a lowly deckhand? Yes to all.

"I returned her to port, din't I?" he pleaded. "Without charts and proper officers and not even an academy-trained captain, I returned her to port without further loss of life and nary damage to the ship. I ain't no privateer."

Mr. Owens asked the judge to consider the fact that all the cannon were missing from the ship. If the crew had truly mutinied, would they have been so stupid as to strip themselves of their lone means of self-defense? And if they had mutinied, why would they return to the lone port where their directors were likely to challenge them? If they were in collusion with anyone, why would they not have delivered the ship to the enemy port?

A fair point, indeed, the judge conceded.

Owens explored a more radical approach. The self-pitying, aggressive-to-pugnacious Crabbe was a disaster to his case. He called upon the mute young man called John Mist, whose name did not even appear on the original crew manifest. He'd boarded in London as Jack Snow, a cabin boy, but anyone could see that he had emerged as a man, fully deserving a name of his choice. John Mist was introduced as a proud product of a strictly Christian, purely naval education. He'd been Captain Partridge's loyal cabin boy and cook's assistant. He'd seen the dreadful events of that night, and his youth removed him from any taint of self-promotion.

Forced to speak, John Mist found his voice. It was as though he were plucking words from the air, in the new refined language of Olivia Todd and Captain Partridge. *We live in the Industrial Age, milord. Sailing is doomed. We are sailing over the highest mountains and deepest valleys in the world. You fools, I could, I could— Is my husband not a genius?* He confessed that it had been the reversal of expectation that had crushed his soul and taken words from his mouth. He had expected welcome from the city and especially from Mr. Todd-Nugent, and a bed, food, and soothing language. For ten weeks adrift in the seas, he had dreamed only of arriving in Calcutta, living for the sight of Calcutta and the welcome, and then dying happy. When they'd reached Kidderpore, they ran from the boat, scattering to the grog houses, begging a drink of any and all, and receiving a proper warm welcome from the Portuguese and half-bloods who ran the docks. They knew what the crew had been through. They sympathized. *Ah, Captain Moans the Dane,* they'd say, shaking their heads. *Out again, is he? He's a wily one. He's a cruel jack.* They thought he'd been trapped in the Danish enclave of Serampore.

Mist answered prosecution questions about the lethal fog—temperature differential, milord—the boarding, the rapid takeover of a complaisant crew, and the captain's mild distraction with theories of contrastive hydrology, which by then he was able to demonstrate. He spoke of his own special work, the braided water and stoppered bottles and how his work, too, had been lost, and of the captain's fascination with steam and iron hulls and the twilight of sailing as we knew it. And then he spoke of Miss Todd. "I wish to settle the issue of her demise," he said, then went on to describe how she had stood between the cutthroats and himself, declaring that no one should harm a hair on his head, and when she would not move aside, the vicious beasts had shot her dead.

"That is your sworn statement concerning the mode and manner of death of Miss Olivia Todd?" he was asked.

"She died in the act of saving my life, yes, milord," he cried in open court. "No more noble a woman ever bestrode this earth."

"It is the court's opinion that you are a most extraordinary young man," said the judge.

As for Mr. Crabbe, a man he had known and sailed with since his earliest childhood, a man who was the only father he'd ever known, he could say without contradiction that nothing of his knowledge of the sea, or of the honor of exceptional humans, or of human bravery, would be available to him without the example set by Tom Crabbe.

"He is a fearsome looking man, but no finer specimen of English sea-dog exists on this planet."

Where had it come from, this sounding drum of pieties?

The judge called a recess. Mr. Owens had scored a coup. The Company lawyers were in disarray.

 *, *, *

In the end, before the appeal process, the senior crew was found innocent of mutiny, but liable for damage to the ship and the loss of twenty thousand pounds' worth of the plaintiff's personal possessions. Crabbe and a dozen other ad-hoc ship's officers were sentenced to ten years' hard labor in Hazaribagh for dereliction of duty, including failure to mount a defense, permitted pilferage, and loss of ship's stores and charts. Pending appeal, they would be returned to the brig in Fort William. The *Oriental Patriot,* by now a supporter of the crew and an outspoken critic of the Company and its practices, considered the verdict a cowardly capitulation to the injured vanity of a powerful official, company power, and government incompetence.

Hazaribagh had a reputation as a place of jungle entombment, not imprisonment. If diseases didn't kill you, then the heat and labor would, and if not the work, the punishments. Anyone contemplating escape would face a hundred miles of tiger-rich jungle, bounty-hunting deoghars, and pernicious little tribal men trained in tracking and rewarded for aiding in apprehension. They'd bring in an escapee's ear for grog and a biscuit.

The only person involved in the trial who benefited from the event was young Mr. Mist. The judge deemed him a young man of exceptional talent. Therefore, acknowledging his youth (twelve years) and family status (foundling), he would be placed on three years' probation and assigned to the nearby Hickey Home for Orphans to learn a useful trade. Jute, it was thought, might suit him well. Mr. Todd-Nugent objected, feeling that the boy had shown himself a more accomplished liar, more complicit and less redeemable, than many others.

The prisoners waited outside the court, shackled in their grays, waiting for the cart that would transport them to the brig. Mr. Rafeek Hai, Owen's faithful stenographer, had changed from his English court clothes back into his native garb, and he drew John Mist aside. "Mr. Owens wants you to know he will fight the Company for the release of Mr. Crabbe and the others. No one survives Hazaribagh. And he is telling you one more thing. Even if Mr. Owens wins your case on appeal, Mr. Todd-Nugent is a powerful enemy who considers you the agent of his humiliation. He will not rest until you are dead. When you are free, you must leave British and Company lands. You understand, Mr. Mist? You must go east, into the forests, to the Indian lands. It is my desh. I will give you names."

* * *

Once again, at the age of twelve, John Mist found himself in an orphanage. At least there were no sermons, few beatings, and an actual trade to learn, and to perform.

There was one high window in the weavers' room. Floating threads and dust motes of dried hemp danced in the sharp, focused light. The stench of bodies in the stagnant air reminded him of the ship's hold, mercifully without the waste. Hemp fibers cut like razors. Young girls, many of them half-English or Portuguese, Christian of a sort, stood around the tables, sewing crude

sacks for the transport of tea chests and spices. The Hickey over-
seers fancied small fingers, boys till eight, girls till twelve.
Weavers were forever sick, coughing and sniffling, their eyes running, their fingers sliced raw and bleeding. At the end of every
day, as the girls made their way to the rectory for soup and cha-
pati, their black hair was matted brown from the settled dust.
Whenever he entered the room with his morahs of dried hemp, to
the cacophony of their coughing and the high pitch of their dawn
to dusk Bengali talk-talk, his eyes swelled and he could think
only of pulling a sack to a corner of the room and sleeping. They
lost a high percentage of girls every month to consumption,
before they could place them as servants with some Company
clerk.

Mist was a delivery boy. He carried boatloads of raw hemp to
the retting vats, then helped to peel the outer fibers from the useless inner pulp till his fingers ran red from the slicing. Hemp was
a fast-growing weed, but he reckoned it to be stronger and
sharper than tempered steel. The younger boys had fun with
strands of hemp. Many mornings he'd find rats and lizards, sometimes a mongoose, hanging from tree limbs by just a strand or
two. They were almost impossible to cut down.

After the retting and peeling, he'd lay the wet fibers out in the
hot sun a day or two, then load a bullock cart with great mounds
of sun-dried fiber and take them to the girls in the batching area.
At least his duties left him enough time in the open air to clear
his lungs and dry his eyes. He was said to be a good worker, yet he
had no idea what work he was doing, if he were good at it or not.
And anyway, the years at sea under the tutelage of Tom Crabbe
had ruined him for systematic work of any kind.

In the Hickey Home he was obliged to think of jute twelve
hours a day, but jute could have been another Calcutta joke, like

at the trial when he'd come in expecting praise and a little money, and came out an orphan with three years' probation. Jute was a slave trade. People talked of indigo and tea and timber, but no one ever spoke of jute. Perhaps the judge had thought it a joke, placing him with pathetic, grieving orphans when he was a proud foundling. He'd suffered too much to think of himself as a dupe.

He slept on a narrow charpoy, three boys to their dark little cell. His cellmates had English names, though none of them looked it, not a drop, nor could they speak a word of it. Unlike the foundlings, orphans tended to blubber a lot and dream of reuniting with their mothers. He was, by far, the whitest boy in Hickey Home, even with his vaguely Spanish looks. He was old enough and strong enough now to play the role of Master Thorne to these younger and weaker boys, had he been inclined. He could have snatched extra food or a blanket in winter, but the reality was there was nothing in Hickey Home he wanted. The only thing in Calcutta he still thought about was his enemy out there who would kill him if he could, and the luxuries promised him by Olivia Todd and snatched away by her husband-to-be.

The only thing the younger boys talked about was the weaver-girls, all safely bunked and guarded across an open courtyard. All of the boys would find their wives from among the Hickey pool. The boys lived for that moment, when they would leave with a girl selected by the wardens and a letter attesting to their competence and virtue. The old ways still worked in Calcutta; they were lucky. At thirteen, the orphans would be expelled to the streets and expected to survive, using their Hickey skills. For Mist, this meant being on his own in less than a year, with another two years of probation, without the protection of the home, a terrifying thought given what he knew of Humphrey Todd-Nugent. There would be no wife for him, nor did he want one.

In the year and a half that Mist had spent in the Hickey Home, he was often called upon to accompany a Company warden to Kidderpore to pass on the validity of a woman's claim to be the real, the true, the resurrected Olivia Todd, escaped from the pirates in the Mascarenes. Humphrey Todd-Nugent himself had no portrait of his betrothed, and had never met her. He was forced to rely on the expertise of young Mr. Mist.

On the first few occasions, Humphrey had viewed them from a distance and declared them offal, crude imitations of a British gentlewoman, or deranged, or low-class harlots. He suspected that "Olivia Todd" was more a banner than a proper name. He feared his name was known in British outposts from Africa to Burma as a comic cuckold who'd even lost a legal case to a notorious blackguard in a Company court. The shame of it all would hasten the day when he would leave Calcutta for good. Women kept showing up in Kidderpore; he embargoed the entire procedure.

The young warden was named Doncaster Hapgood, called Donny. He also occupied a part-time position on Mr. Todd-Nugent's private domestic staff somewhere between house manager and personal butler. He was a proper-seeming sort, and spoke to John Mist as gentleman-to-gentleman. Though Donny called for him at the orphanage in a horse-drawn Company conveyance, he showed no reluctance to enter orphanage grounds and no condescension toward Mist's lowly status. The ride to Kidderpore and back, including tea and tiffin and the ferry to and fro, took all day.

"You can imagine, can you not, Mr. Mist, the sort of woman would like to get her claws into a Company official? Especially a Company rajah like Mr. T-N himself."

"I can," said Mist, feeling his personal loss on the same score. Donny Hapgood might be holding the valet's job Olivia had promised him.

"Mr. T-N says not to trust any of them. They can fetch up a tale of woe could soften the hardest heart."

"I pay no attention to any tales," Mist said. "There's only one woman fits the description, isn't it? Either 'tis her, or 'tisn't."

The tale of Olivia Todd, *"Ollytodd in the Mascarene,"* had spread across Indian Ocean ports and up the Straits. There was a popular ballad set to music about *"a right proper Irish lass / left from Armagh on a day so green / in a soft wool dress and a hat of blue / and buckled shoes of velveteen . . ."* and the bawdy verses that followed detailed the successive unlayering of her stays and buttresses and the brutalities inflicted on *"an innocent lass with a bony arse / . . . in the Mascarene."*

The real Olivia Todd, if she still existed, might be in line to claim certain damages. The first pretenders had shown up in Kidderpore even before the *Malabar Queen* had limped to port. Some of the women who'd claimed the title of Ollytodd were half-French or -Portuguese, the others half-Indian or -African. They barely spoke English. Two of them had fancy silverware engraved with the Todd name, which meant the pirates' loot was in general circulation.

No one in Calcutta except John Mist (and the crew waiting on appeal in the Black Hole) could identify the real Olivia. Mr. Todd-Nugent took the position that his affianced had been murdered at sea, as attested by John Mist at trial, which justified his public pose of immutable suffering. Any claimant after the fact of her murder was, prima facie, a lowborn consort of devilish privateers. John Mist wanted to believe that Olivia was still alive, since her spirit and resourcefulness matched his own. He counted it his greatest failing in life that he'd not been able to save her in the moment of her greatest distress.

"Mr. T-N says not to trust any of them." And this time, Donny Hapgood was communicating an order that an institution-raised orphan, cabin boy, and ship's dogsbody could easily understand. "He's a contented man, the way things stand now."

"And how do things stand now with Mr. Todd-Nugent?"

Since Mr. Todd-Nugent had initiated the case of mutiny and had succeeded in sending most of his mates off to certain death, John Mist made no attempt to hide his sarcasm.

"He has companionship, in case it concerns you."

"That was very quick of Mr. Todd-Nugent."

Donny could have stopped there, not picked up the challenge, and the outcome of John Mist's life might have been very different. But, like Mist in his sarcasm, he couldn't help himself in defending the director.

"You misunderstand my meaning, Mr. Mist. It is not 'quick' at all unless you count fifteen years as quick. He has his bibi. That is why there will be no Mrs. T-N on the docks today."

Mist felt his rage building up. I've been duped, he thought, a little monkey dancing on everyone's string. And he knew even as they rode through Garden Reach on the way to the Hooghly ferry, that the woman in Kidderpore that day a year and a half after the fact of her abduction was going to be Olivia. He asked, "What was his first wife like?"

"I have already answered, although I find your question rather impudent, Mr. Mist. He has a bibi. He has always had a bibi. To the best of my knowledge, Mr. T-N has never married. The children are with the bibi, but they stay in the cooking house and never show their brown little faces."

Mist thought again, as he rarely did these days: *egg spoons*, the smug assumption of murderous power. If he'd had a knife, he would have killed this young man who, in a less cruel world, could have been himself. So, there never was a bereaved boy and girl to stand around the harpsichord singing airs, never a lost, beloved wife, never even a marriage. It was worse than Olivia had feared.

Is my husband not a genius, Captain Partridge?

"Mr. T-N is an influential man," said Donny, as they descended from the ferry. "An important man. Your period of probation will soon be over. The right word today could set you up with a proper job in the Company."

"And the wrong?" He looked down at his scabbed and bloody fingers.

A flicker of condescension crossed his lips. "Are you really that keen on the company of Mr. Crabbe?"

       ⸱ ⸱ ⸱

When they arrived at Pereira's taverna in Kidderpore, a crowd had already gathered, blocking the black space that served as a door. Some falling-down-drunk habitués were singing "Ollytodd, Ollytodd, Where's my Humphrey Gone?" The woman had been placed on a stool inside the dark interior, with just her exposed legs showing in the sun.

Donny Hapgood pushed through the crowd and stood at the entrance. "Ladies and gentlemen," he shouted, again with that slight flicker of condescension, "today we have a special treat. You all remember the mutiny trial of the Crabbe cabal!" A chorus of "Ayes!" spiked with "Hang the bastards!" drowned out Donny Hapgood's next sentence. He held his arms out till they quieted. "Today, one of the Crabbe cabal has come all the way from the

Hickey Home to identify our Princess of Pretence." Scattered applause broke out. "Master Mist, come forward."

Inside the black interior, a roughened but familiar voice cried out. "I know no John Mist!"

He took a few steps forward, through the parting crowd. A few men slapped his back. "Don't let us down," they whispered, but he didn't know for what they were pleading. Bets, perhaps. The same voice from inside damned the drunken men— "Git yer filthy hands off me!"—who were lifting her stool, singing the ballad, and ruffling the front of her dress as they carried her into the sun.

The woman squatting before him, violently tossing her head to and fro, her matted hair half-hiding her face, her eyes wild and bloodshot, bore no resemblance to the Olivia of the deck strolls, the Olivia unfurling house plans on her cabin bed, and the memory he still cherished of her hand on his shoulder. In profile, he could see that the woman's mouth had collapsed, her teeth were missing, and her chin and nose were hooking together.

The Olivia he knew had been his fantasy mother. Because of her, all the fear and harshness he'd harbored against women had been erased. She could not have done ill or raised her voice to any man, yet now she screamed like an Amazon monkey, using words even Crabbe might not have heard. She excited the crowd, who shouted their own insults back. Mist was back in his London days, with the tarts who'd passed him from lap to lap, and their deranged threats to the sleeping drunks.

"So, what do you think, Master Mist?" asked Donny Hapgood. "Is this our fair princess? Do we hear the sweet song of a director's wife?" His smile was bright, exuding confidence. Donny moved closer to her and reached out to place a hand on her shoulder, which she swatted away. Then she looked up at John Mist, and for a moment, her face looked exactly as he remembered it, fresh and hopeful with a young girl's freckles, looking out at her future with modest trepidation.

"Mr. Mist, your judgment, please," came Donny's voice.

"My bright, bright lad, how you have grown!" the crone cried out and raised her arms toward him. And he could see, with her face up close, that what he'd taken for freckles were poxy pits, and her remaining teeth were black. Her hands had been tattooed, stars and other signs in the webbing of the bay between her thumb and pointing finger.

"Tell them, Jack," she croaked. Her filthy, tattooed hands fumbled for his arm, and now he caught a whiff from her clothes and the blackened cavity of her mouth. When they touched, his arm flew out, pushing her backward off the stool. The crowd cheered, and Donny clapped him on the shoulder.

"The judge has spoken!" shouted Donny Hapgood. Pereira's men dragged the pretender back inside and even if Mist had wanted to he could not have saved her. God had answered his prayers, and he'd swatted God in the face. He didn't know what he wanted, what he should do, what he could say, since he had been silent throughout—he could not have broken through the ring of congratulatory celebrants.

'　'　'

As Donny led him back to the Company rig, he said, "Next, they'll haul up a dugong and say it's Olivia Todd." Mist was in no mood for joking. All the egg spoons of this earth come from words, he thought. If only he could take back everything he had ever said. "This should be the last one. Mr. T-N wants an honest accounting. Six girls have come forward, and six struck down. He will be properly appreciative."

"Where did she come from?"

"Down in George Town. A common whore by all appearance, goes by the name of Patsy Derozio, but down on the docks she calls herself Ollytodd. Reckons she can make a little more that way, eh? Her pimping Chinaman thought he had a chance of running her in the sweepstakes."

He thought then of hemp, how many strands might it take to hang a man?

"Likely she was what she said—not Olivia Todd, of course—a saucy Irish tart taking a chance on India, maybe got disembarked in the cape and sold to pirates and after they'd used her up they sold her to Arabs and then to the Chinaman. You saw the branding on her hand?"

"You could have told me."

"What? And prejudice the outcome? We run an honest competition here, my boy. Which, I should add, has turned out well for everyone."

Never in the rest of my life, he vowed, which, God willing, will not be long, shall I speak another word. Donny continued his nattering all the way to Hickey Home, promising this and that, the Company job awaiting him, perhaps in jute now that he'd mastered that beastly procedure. Did he realize how lucky he was? The Company didn't hire boys his age in England for service in India, but an English boy like him, already in India, conversant with the languages, fit the norm exactly. "When you're free of your constraints, Mr. T-N would like to become your sponsor," Donny beamed.

5

*T*en strands of braided hemp wrapped around his wrists held without breaking as he lifted himself like Captain Partridge used to, and dangled under a beam in the retting shed. He added a dozen more just to make sure, and fashioned a noose. He'd seen hangings on shipboard. He'd seen hangings that had somehow failed, miscalculations of weight and drop and the under-scaffold moans that came from stretching and not snapping, moans that would send a warden and doctor scurrying while the crowd started cheering. He didn't want that. He wasn't hoping for the gentleman's agreement that sometimes applied. "Not today, gentlemen," the executioner would say, "neither God nor the Devil wants this wretched soul." Try it again, or release the son of a bitch.

All the Betterment sermons came flooding back. He was

Adam, he was Cain, he was Judas who betrayed the Lord and Peter who denied Him three times. He heard Crabbe's voice after the boarding, *"If ye'd jist crawled out of the lady's trunk when they was askin' was there a boy aboard, they'd wouldn'a taken that ugly old woman and we wouldn'a bin sent into the jungle to die. There's things a boy can do, can't no woman do. It's the most thing a cabin boy's good fer. Why'd I bother savin' yer wretched life when ye ain't got an ounce of a mate's common decency? Ye've cooked us all to save yerself . . ."* Until they'd reached Calcutta, the crew had muttered "yer damned" at him whenever they saw him. *Drink this. Hot and foamy, fresh from the tap and it ain't from a goat. Eat this. It's what ye'll be feasting on in Hell.*

He had not denied Olivia to get a Company job, as piss-pant Donny assumed, or to save himself from the vengeance of Mr. T-N. He had been trying to find the strength to acknowledge her, to throw up his arms and cry, "Olivia Todd is living still!" knowing it would be the death of them both, especially if Mr. T-N had a bibi of his own, but it would have been death with honor, not this thing he was about to commit. Her fingers raked his arm and he could smell the filth and foulness of her clothes and breath and it came over him like it had when he was just a lad on the streets, turning over a moldering corpse, the smell rising, the near-human parts turning black and starting to melt, and for a moment he was overcome.

They were the same fingers that had caressed his shoulder and brushed hair from his eyes and guided his hand in drawing. He remembered her white, unblemished hand with its long fingers and clear, lacquered nails, pointing out his room in her Calcutta mansion. *"Here, my bright, bright lad, will this be suitable? It's on the ground floor, but it's in the main house, not the kitchen house."* How long had it been since he'd cried? He couldn't remember, but memories of Olivia, even in their good times, brought an ache to his throat and when he tried to imagine her life since the boarding his shoulders started shaking and if anyone had walked into the shed at that moment he would have lost all his rank and privileges. Hickey's orphans did not cry—that was the first rule. Even if he was crying for another's life and not his own loss and misery. He truly did not deserve to live another day. And when he thought of her hand again, there had been only filth and torn nails, the scars of branding and other burns. He sat on the chair with the noose around his neck and vomited.

He prayed in silence, feeling that his earlier vow never to speak again was holier than asking forgiveness aloud. He would not plead with the Lord that he had never meant to cause such grief in the world, or that on some fundamental level he just did not understand what was expected of a man. Not that ignorance or the lack of parents or Christian models made him less guilty; he knew that he'd been given chances at repentance and had simply turned away. He'd not been listening when the Bible was read and he'd been too swept up in selfish pleasures and adventure to think of others. Why, oh why, had he turned that shovel in the leaves, why had he called for help and saved Tom's life. *"Let sleeping sea-dogs lie,"* that was Tom's advice. He reckoned maybe he'd already paid a little for his sins—there had been years of Betterment beatings for things he had not done, explained as precautions against future sins, like now—and he prayed that counted for something. Bless Tom Crabbe, he prayed, bless Olivia Todd, and blast to Hell Donny Hapgood and Humphrey Todd-Nugent.

He stood on the chair and leaped.

The cords cut, then scraped. He gasped with the pain, but it was not the mortal agony he'd imagined, or even craved; it was endurable, a thousand small slashes. The rope didn't snap, it sagged and lengthened, depositing him on the floor even before he'd lost his first breath. He was left with a deep cleft and raw patches, something we'd recognize now as an attempted suicide, but not in that time and place. It left a lifelong scar, which in later life he sometimes covered with high collars, a gold chain, and later, with an intricate tattoo. Scars are legacies, and the gift he'd been left with that night was the assurance that his prayers had been heard and his attempted sacrifice had been rejected. Partial payment on his redemption had been received and credited. In recognition of the unexpected blessing of a longer life, he vowed to keep his promise of silence and never speak another word. From everything I've been able to gather, it was a promise he kept, after his fashion.

Not so many days later, he was visited at Hickey House by his old defender, that perfect Welsh egg, David Llewellyn Owens, and his assistant, Mr. Rafeek Hai. True to rumor, Owens was dressed in a white kurta-pajama, his bald head wrapped in a turban, and a colorful shawl draped over his shoulders. Mr. Hai wore a dark English frock coat over his white pajama bottoms.

Their initial news was not good: death had already carried off twenty of the Crabbe Cabal. The better news was that Crabbe himself had been granted an appeal. Mist nodded, and smiled. The best news was that Mist would be released from parole slightly ahead of schedule. In fact, he would be permitted to walk out of Hickey House with his advocate that very day, should he wish, never to return.

"How do you feel about that, Mr. Mist?" Another nod, and smile.

"I understand the Honourable Company will offer you a posi-

tion." He frowned. "They would like to send you to the East."
Mist shook his head.

"Are you having problems speaking, Mr. Mist? I see scrape
marks on your neck—are you injured in some way?" Mist stared
vacantly.

Mr. Hai cleared his throat and asked in Bengali, "After a year
and a half, have you forgotten the English language? Would you
prefer we continue in Bengali?"

And for the second time in his life, John Mist was able to
gather words from the air. He had not spoken the local tongue,
but he had been living in it, listening to it exclusively, moving to
its demands, smiling at its jokes and humming its songs. When
he thought about it, he couldn't say if he'd been talking to his cell
mates in Bengali or not—but he must have been, since they
didn't speak English. None of the girls in the batching room
spoke English, none of the boatmen, and no one at the retting
vats. Only the wardens, who spoke to him exclusively in English,
but asked him to relay their messages to everyone else. It was as
though he'd been struck blind without memory of sight; he had
no memory of speaking English. It seemed that every conversation he'd ever held with Crabbe, with Olivia, with Captain Partridge, had been in Bengali. The God he prayed to, the God who
had granted him extended life, obviously did not speak a heathen
tongue. He would not be offended. It would not be a violation of
his vow.

"I no longer speak English," he said.

"Khub bhalo!" exclaimed David Owens, clapping him on the
arm. "Now we can really talk."

He felt reborn, all his sins washed away, the boy he'd been lay
buried under a mound of language he no longer spoke. The sound
of English, in fact, sickened and enraged him.

"Here is what I suspect, Mr. Mist," Owens went on. "I suspect the Company will offer to send you east, out where indigo planters are starting to experiment with hemp, and they'll say they're making you a purchasing agent—"

"But you don't trust them, isn't it?" Mist said.

"I think they will find you floating on a river some dark night. You have supplied Mr. Todd-Nugent with the perfect excuse. He hires you out of gratitude, making him look exceedingly generous, but he knows as well as you do that the last woman—"

"Patsy Derozio—"

"Patsy Derozio, indeed, was the true Olivia Todd."

Mist touched the thick, ugly scab now formed on his neck, and caught the flicker of recognition from Rafeek Hai. "I betrayed her," he said. "I did not mean to and it was not because I was afraid of Mr. Todd-Nugent or that I wanted a reward from Mr. Todd-Nugent. I wanted to bring him down to the mud and gutter and when the time came to do it, I failed."

"Life is long, and justice prevails, Mr. Mist," said Rafeek Hai.

Owens continued, "At the moment, Mr. T-N has the best of all worlds. All he wants is a show of endless pity. If he is exonerated by one of his enemies—you—he gets part of what he wants, but only half of what he needs. He knows his credibility rests with you. But his permanent security demands you die. So he must publicly reward you, and then, tragically, you must meet with an accident in some remote corner of Bengal far from any inquiry."

And so they worked out an agreement. Mist found himself a clearer thinker and better negotiator in his adopted language. He would forever think of Bengali and Persian as ladders to safety, shaded from the scrutiny of God.

"Mr. Hai has family in the East," said Owens. "Once you arrive, they will look after you."

"But you can get there only under Company protection," said Hai.

"And take some other protection," said Owens, and handed him a long, thin, jewel-handled dagger. "Mughal, Emperor Aurangzeb's court. A family treasure," he winked.

Owens didn't think they would waste much time. Not on the trip, of course, which would arouse suspicion, but some plausible, out of the way place where they could claim an attack by common goondahs. Don't linger anywhere they might deposit you, he was warned. Don't accept offers of Company accommodations. If they know where you are, they will kill you at their pleasure.

"Better yet," Mist suggested, strong now in his newfound authority, "Mr. Hai can take me directly to my new posting. I will have a Company letter. His relatives can meet me along the way, and *they* can say they were attacked by goondahs. They buried me in the forest."

"A very, very sad story," said David Owens. "Such a promising life, cut tragically short."

"My sympathies to your family," laughed Rafeek Hai.

′   ′   ′

Olivia's dream, a white mansion along the river, a broad carriageway, chowkidars lining the drive, had come to life. A well-appointed carriage dropped John Mist outside the gate. The chowkidar stood, saluted, and swung it open. Mist exchanged a few pleasantries with the old man, waved off the carriage, and walked up the long, crushed stone drive. He was fully grown now, but for the absence of facial hair, almost manly, almost a commanding figure.

The mansion had a name: Armagh Bhavan, in honor of the owner's late fiancée. The rest was as he'd imagined. Pools of water connected by narrow tracks, wide protective eaves, barred windows angled for maximum river breeze, and Mr. Todd-Nugent standing at the door with a drink in hand, welcoming him indoors. *Is my husband not a genius?*

In the year and a half since they had met in court, Mist had grown several inches taller than his erstwhile tormentor, who now appeared old and nervous. The top of his head was hairless and shiny as a mirror, a comic effect that he attempted to disguise with billowing, upswept swirls of graying temple-hair. Flaring gray sideburns fendered his ears.

Under a bay window looking out upon the Hooghly stretched a long, white marble table set upon a mahogany pedestal composed of four carved lions' heads. Fresh flowers had been arranged in a massive China vase, around which were scattered recent issues of the *Oriental Patriot,* and the latest edition of the London papers, now several months old. "Do you read, Mr. Mist?" asked Mr. T-N, then he apologized for the embarrassment even before Mist could shake his head. "I'm sorry, of course you've not had the advantages of a proper education. No matter. I merely wished to point out your name, here"— his finger came down on the first line of print under a line of something darker and larger—"in connection with that unfortunate woman."

He cleared his voice, picked up the paper, and read in a preacher's voice, " *'Ollytodd Claim Refuted.'* And here you are: 'John Mist, *Malabar Queen* cook's assistant and close attendant to Miss Olivia Todd during their months at sea, today forcefully spurned a Penang woman's fanciful pretence of identity with the late Olivia Todd, betrothed of . . .' etc. etc."

Mist shrugged modestly.

Mr. T-N took a seat on a damask-covered sofa whose legs continued the carved lion motif. "Please sit, Mist." He did as he was told. His host called sharply into the dark interior rooms and a bearer appeared with a silver tray of drinks. The coconut oil lamps were lit, and a familiar fragrance spread through the room.

"Please try the drink," he said. "A Company officer must have practice holding his gin and quinine." Mist sipped the foul liquid and let his gaze wander about the room. The contents of this single room, the carved bookcases and piano, each with the same, if smaller, lion's head legs, the chairs and ottomans, the sofa and several tables, the carpets, vases and paintings, could have filled half the hold of the *Malabar Queen*. If every room of the mansion were so decorated, a mahogany forest and an entire Company fleet must have been involved in carving and transportation.

"You're very silent tonight, my boy." He smiled and raised his hands, palms out. "I understand, it can be a mite overwhelming. Imagine the loneliness of not being able to share it with a wife." The boy nodded his sympathy. "Well, enough dwelling on the past. We're here to talk of your future. You've been in jute, I understand?"

He nodded agreement. "You speak the Bengalee talkee-talkee?"

"Indeed I do, sir," he promptly responded, to which Mr. T-N raised his hand. "Sorry, I don't speak it myself." He shouted "Donn-eee" into the dark interior. "We've had a long and sorry tradition of Company officers coming out from England and getting too enamored of local customs. In my estimation, it starts with learning the language. Keep a clear and defined distance, that's been my advice and I'm glad to say it's been adopted. We'll have no more of these wretched White Hindoos or whatever. Good English drinks, English food, English dress. Agreed?"

He nodded.

Donny joined them with a drink in hand. "I've been attending to matters in the kitchen, sir. Mist, don't rise."

"Tell him, Donny."

"The Company has arranged a junior position for you in the Mymensingh district, considerably east of here. It's in jute, with which you have gained familiarity. Formerly, the property to which you'll be attached had been an indigo plantation, so your responsibility will be to oversee its conversion and by showing a profit, the conversion of other indigo plantations in the eastern districts. You of course share in all the profits at a mutually bene- ficial rate to be negotiated with the Honourable Company. It could not be more straightforward. If you agree, a simple mark will suffice."

Mist smiled, and nodded his head enthusiastically. Donny produced the letter, and handed it over with a solemn bow.

Mist thrust out his hand. Donny took it. The Mughal dagger dropped down the sleeve of his borrowed English jacket, into his left hand. He held on to Donny's hand longer than normally required and pulled him half a step closer, tight enough for one quick thrust into his gut, then up and across, and withdrawal.

Donny's glass clattered on the marble floor. Humphrey turned suddenly. "Don't worry about a little spill, Donny. We'll have it cleaned up in a—" Then he watched in bemusement as Donny teetered, opened his mouth, sighed, and slowly, almost comically, sagged to his knees. Humphrey started laughing. "I say, Hap- good, you're sinking to your knees like an elephant, or is it a camel?"

Then he stopped laughing. "Donny? Something the matter?"

Donny tried to raise his head, and then to rise—Mist had a sudden, sharp memory of Listowel stumbling into the captain's cabin—he tried again to speak but then stared down at his cupped hands, like a Mohammedan at prayer, he thought, and at the blood pouring into them. He fell forward dead, slapping the cold marble face-first with a hollow thud.

Humphrey looked at Mist, perhaps to launch a series of orders, but then he caught a glimpse of something in his eyes or the set of the mouth, something that caused him to take a step in retreat. In his panic, he had not remembered the placement of the sofa, which sent him reeling backward amid the pillows on the yellow damask. Now Mist stood directly in front of, and above, him.

The perfect shiny scalp had sprouted tiny blisters of perspiration, and for just an instant Mist felt pity for the poor man's vanity, the sideburns swept up like a hedge to hide his shiny dome. The glass of gin had somehow remained in his fist, unspilled and unrelinquished. The last thing he will see is me, thought Mist, holding and turning the dagger high in his face. Perhaps he was trying to raise an alarm, but all that came out were desperate appeals to mercy.

"I am an old man, Mr. Mist, a father, have mercy. . . . I have sinned, but as God is my witness, I—" and Mist thought well enough of him in his final moments not to desecrate the face for services that would surely follow, and plunged the dagger home between the top buttons of his English coat, leaving the host with his mouth half open, lips pursed in a ring of astonishment.

He wiped the gory knife on his black coat sleeve, then lifted Donny to the facing chair. He had never seen so white a face; all the blood in his body had drained away. He lowered the coconut oil lamps till they sputtered on their faintest flame. By low lamp-light and the last rays of the setting sun, the gentlemen appeared somewhat relaxed, engaged in friendly negotiation. He seeded the dagger in Donny's hand. Somewhere in the interior rooms there was a servant who would guess it might be time for refills, but he would not enter the room until he was called. Mist drew the parlor doors together and turned the privacy key.

He walked up the crushed stone drive, waking the chowkidar to open the gate. They chatted a bit. "Sahib said he would not be going out tonight. He said you should lock the gate now and take your leave. He even said he won't be needing you tomorrow."

The well-appointed carriage pulled up, over-teamed for Garden Reach or any urban lane by a double span of black Arabians. Mist climbed aboard. Mr. Rafeek Hai lowered his paper. A seaman's trunk lay at his feet.

"Mr. Mist—may I drop you somewhere?"

"The Shoonder Bon, Mr. Dante," he replied, using the name Rafeek Hai preferred for carrying out unofficial duties. Within the hour they were well south of Calcutta, into the encroaching forests and the dark Bengali night. Along with not speaking the English language, Mist added another vow—never to wear English clothes again. He tossed the borrowed jacket out the window. The seaman's trunk held the entire native wardrobe, kurtas, pajamas, shawls, and turban, which he would need or own for years to come.

6

ow I know where it comes from, that painting of the Eden-like encampment with camels and elephants and gentlemen's tents pitched on a lush riverbank that I remember from Hajji's illustrated *Mist-nama*. The river was the George. The bank must have been the spot where the ghats were dug and the stonework laid and John Mist built his first house, which Jai Krishna Gangooly would take over, add to, and where his daughter would spend her entire sixty-five years. The bearded man in a turban must have been John Mist, at fifty. Mist is creating his village.

Six years ago when I'd made that first trip to Mishtigunj and Hajji had let me leaf through the Persian book, I hadn't known enough about Mist even to ask a simple question. If only I'd put in a bid for that illustrated, Persian *nama*! Ten thousand, twenty thousand, for his school. Now it is too late. When I went back two years ago, I was told Hajji Chowdhury had died and his school was closed. His last widow had melted back into the countryside. One of his America-settled sons, a cook on Sixth Street in Manhattan, was occupying the house. He knows nothing of any *Mist-nama* and I believe him. He looks desperate enough to sell anything remaining of his father's life.

He had dropped his father's honorific of Chowdhury, and returned his family name to Hai. The bombing of our house still had not happened, I had no reason to stiffen at the name of Hai, or to ask if, perhaps, he had left a son named Abbas Sattar behind in New York. I keep telling myself (as Bish continually repeats) that what writers call "coincidence" is merely a function of mathematical probability, nothing else. If the man who bombed our house is the grandson of the man who sold me the Bangla *Mist-nama,* it is perfectly explicable in mathematical terms, without recourse to fate and the magic of Mishtigunj. For Bish, the only real communication is between numbers. Everything else is chaos.

Maybe the illustrated Persian version of the *Mist-nama* will show up as an antiquarian curiosity in an Orientalist catalog, but I can imagine a different fate. Someone, perhaps this son, or another, or a sweeper or a student in the closed-down school, tore out pages and sold them separately. A few pennies a page would look like a fortune to an enterprising son. Even a framed page of nineteenth-century Persian calligraphy is beautiful enough to return a few dollars in Hong Kong or Singapore (*Biographical material, Bangladesh, c. 1870, Transcriber anonymous,* it will say). The paintings are very different. Together, they tell a story worthy of a medieval tapestry, but were they bought as a single lot and kept together for a museum-style sale? Or were they scattered to Berlin and London and others to Sotheby's, and more, perhaps many more, eventually coming to rest in specialty houses on

Madison Avenue? I once had it in my hands; now it will be my life's avocation to reassemble it. Until then, there is only this novel.

The scene on the riverbank must date from 1870. The other men could be Rafeek Hai, and my great-great-grandfather, Jai Krishna Gangooly. In four years, the Tree Bride will be born. She will carry the name Gangooly, but he'll return to the pre-British spelling of Gangopadhaya. I've seen a photo of Jai Krishna when he was a young graduate of the first law class in Calcutta; he was remarkable for the gravity of his face, the thick single bar of eyebrow, the lack of a beard and mustache. His daughter will inherit his eyebrows and his solemnity. If I ever find that painting, I'll be able to identify him.

He had been persuaded to leave the high court in Dhaka and launch a new career in a village without a name. He is at the crossroads in his life, when Calcutta was calling, even London, and his fellow Dhaka jurists like Keshub Mitter and Harilal Das Gupta went on to Calcutta, wealth, fame, and eventual knighthood. By then, Jai Krishna had become a circuit-riding vakil, with a different wife and family of daughters in every village. The Tree Bride grew up in Mist Mansion Number One, and never left it.

John Mist, perhaps, enjoyed the give and take of High Court argument. I can imagine him seated in the spectators' gallery and approaching Jai Krishna, perhaps introduced by his old friend Rafeek Hai. "Mr. Gangooly," he might have said, "I am told that you find British law and British customs oppressive to your fine sense of Hindu justice."

In fact, I don't have to imagine the scene; I know it—or something very close to it—to be the case. I'm only speculating that Mist had something to do with it. Jai Krishna veered from the path of so-called enlightened thinking at just that time in the history of Bengal. Most of his Hindu colleagues on the High Court were Brahmo, strongly attracted to British models of justice and modernity. They were using their mastery of English as a springboard into French and German. Jai Krishna's contrarian impulses were taking him, even then, back into Sanskrit. While his colleagues grew increasingly rationalistic and openly contemptuous of Hindu tradition, Jai Krishna declared his reservations, and then, his deviation. Though he still wore the robes and wig of the colonizer, he returned at night to native clothes and hours of prayer.

The invitation to Mishtigunj came at a moment of spiritual crisis, the crossroads between his soul and his career. As a family, we never talked of crises. People misbehaved but they weren't able to control it, and there never seemed to be a motive or explanation beyond the familiar: greed, vengeance, or jealousy. I don't remember anyone in my family suspecting that Jai Krishna might have been undergoing an actual spiritual crisis, or that the crossroads in Bengali history had bifurcated the path of his own career. Family tales simply don't go there. Had he chosen differently, we might have become Brahmos. *Baas,* as we'd say, end of inquiry. Together, Hai and Gangooly/Gangopadhaya would serve their two communities as vakils.

In 1870, Mist was emerging from his self-imposed anonymity. He had been underground for thirty-eight years. In the Mist-*nama* he says only that he traveled. There is no mention of wives or children; I do not take this to signify their absence. He trekked to Ambarnath, the sacred ice-cave in the Himalayas where the Ganges comes to life; he visited Benares and slept in alleyways with the beggars; he prayed in mosques and honored the burial sites of every pir; he tramped the length and breadth of India, surviving on the generosity of strangers. He was taken for Indian wherever he went. His origins were never suspected, even when passing the occasional Britisher. We are the same people, he wrote. A hundred miles east into Burma, a hundred miles north into Assam, and my foreignness could not have been disguised. We are perched here at the edge of Europe. He had forgotten the English language. In a century when such total transformation was becoming increasingly rare, John Mist stands out as the perfect, and maybe the last, "British Hindoo."

Quietly, he had amassed a fortune in timber concessions. Rafeek Hai's relatives had opened the door. But just as Diligence Partridge had predicted, the age of sailing ships had ended, and with it the need for masts and spars, even for ship's timber, except teak and mahogany for interior trim. Sundari trees had a secondary use, he discovered, and that was for the framing of indestructible furniture.

He turned his major investments to hemp, now that its weaving into jute had been industrialized in Scotland. The world had turned to jute for all its sacking. Monster ships could swallow a year's output of tea and rice and retted hemp in a single gulp. Mishtigunj became a leading port on the Bay of Bengal, midway between Port Canning and Cox's Bazaar, open to the sea but connected by river to the interior. A native fleet stood at hand, awaiting the transfer of finished goods to the interior, or raw materials from the plantations to Europe and America. Mist was always the silent partner, buying up the abandoned indigo plantations and converting them to jute, or back to rice.

Hajji's Bengali translation simply states that Mist called together notables from as far away as Calcutta and Dhaka to create a utopian village. Jai Krishna had come from Dhaka, and the Calcuttan might have been Rafeek Hai. In what does utopia consist? Education, justice, health, food, a spirit of cooperation, and the uninhibited worship of one's god. It was agreed that "worship" was restricted to Hinduism and Islam. Christians were barred from Mishtigunj, on the orders of Mist himself.

The nominal owner of Mishtigunj was the local nawab, Ghani Rehman Razak, but financial power was in the hands of the Hindu zamindar, Ashimlal Dutta. Together, with ample contributions from Mist himself, as well as taxes levied on foreign trade, they had kept the British out despite repeated overtures and forays. History has taught that what the British could not win by charm and concessions in India, they were accustomed to seizing by subterfuge.

In 1874, the year of the Tree Bride's birth, Mishtigunj poured two lakhs—two hundred thousand—of rupees into Razak's coffers. It is not written how the money was spent, merely that by 1877 Razak's indebtedness to Dutta and to creditors in Dhaka, Calcutta, and even London had reached five lakhs. An agreement was reached with the British authorities in Dhaka to take control of Mishtigunj town and the outlying district in return for wiping out the nawab's debts and paying him an extraordinarily generous annual stipend of one lakh until his death.

Ghani Rehman Razak died in 1902. His son, Abdul Mohammed Razak, was born in 1882 and died in 1949. Sometime in the 1930s he was allied with the independence movement in East Bengal; he is the Razak for whom Razakpur, the old Mishtigunj, is now named. I should tell Victoria Khanna it's not just a drop of blood that reveals the world. Any scrap of the historical record, the stalagmitic *drip-drip* of old newspapers, old letters, old bills and receipts, can do the same. You wonder sometimes how historians keep their sanity, or how the ironies of history do not sputter into absurd comedy. Hai saved Mist, but they died together. Hai's grandson sold me the *nama;* but perhaps it was his great-

great-grandson who tracked me to San Francisco and nearly killed us all. Mist and Hai were hanged by the British, who had been invited to enter because of Razak's debts; Razak's son, rich from British bribes, became history's darling, the man with his name on the map.

Part Three

1

"Six months and ticking," says Victoria Khanna.

"Ticking and kicking," I add. Sixteen years ago, with Rabi, I'd been sick for the whole nine months and ended up weighing less at delivery than I had at conception. I wore saris in those years and looked like a high school girl, so no one even guessed I was pregnant. I didn't get the perks, not that I was in any condition to enjoy them. I was a nineteen-year-old girl from a good Calcutta family, which meant I'd never been on intimate terms with any hidden part of my body. One day a virgin who'd never even looked in the mirror, three months later, vomiting twenty times a day.

"Don't worry, I won't let you go through that again." Victoria Khanna makes me feel like a wondrous survivor of primitive times. She won't prescribe anything except rubs and therapies, or, at most, acupuncture. This pregnancy is a dream. I could gain thirty pounds if I gave in to all my urges.

"I was wondering . . . when should we, you know, not indulge?"

"Never," she laughs. "Only when you're so big and round he might fall off."

During my first pregnancy, I felt I'd been ambushed, invaded by aliens. And, oh, how my body fought back! We're in this together, I pleaded, how can you be so cruel? I even surprised Susan Atkinson, my highly esteemed Stanford doctor. She was *so* happy to see me, she said. Indian women come from a baby-raising culture with strong families and good values. We didn't pose the high-maintenance problems of regular Americans. "Please pass the bucket," I said.

"Every time I see Indian women with their children, they seem so serene. They never shout, they never get rattled. I'm just struck by their incredible devotion." She was trying to compliment me. "And their children don't cry and throw tantrums, they just sit there like little angels." I used to sit like a little angel, and I never threw tantrums. Tantrums would have shamed my mother in the company of her in-laws. She would have been blamed for being a bad mother, another crime her mother-in-law could hold against her. In fact, many members of the family would have loved me to scream and misbehave. I learned to protect her when I was about two years old. So much for our family values.

I try to picture my daughter as a two-year-old. She sits on this very deck, maybe with a soap-and-bubbles game. When my sisters and I were little, we blew bubbles through wooden thread-holders. The maid would bring each of us a spool with its narrow hole through the center, and a tiny tin mug of water in which she had dropped a sliver of bath soap. We would sit for hours on the verandah, sending sandalwood-scented bubbles over the verandah railings.

Susan had given me a questionnaire. I was shocked. I assured her that yes, I actually knew the name of that shadowy presence called "the likely father." Indian girls didn't drink, smoke, or take drugs—at least not then—we didn't catch unmentionable diseases, we hadn't had multiple partners, and we had no convoluted histories of "high risk" behavior. We were young and innocent, with centuries of peasant wisdom and family structure to guide us. My vomiting frustrated Susan, for which I felt I should apologize. After all, if I truly loved my husband, if I truly loved babies, my body would adjust, no? Maybe it was the dark ages. "Well, then, this is your first body trauma. Maybe that's why you're sick all the time," she tried to joke. If I got sick, I was on my own, and all of it was my fault.

My mother remembered her three pregnancies as nine months' pure rapture, a reprieve from scrutiny and anxiety, when even her mother-in-law paid some grudging attention to her. Not to her exactly, of course, but to her as the proxy-carrier of Bhattacharjee family genes. Her little gift to the world was never "the baby" or "the pregnancy," but always "the boy." So, in those pre-amnio, pre-sono days, she enjoyed nine months' presumption of dutiful compliance. She remembered her three pregnancies as pamper-time with unquestioned permission, even an injunction, to fatten up. She got first pick of every food; "good for the boy," the servants would say, as they brought her the heads of carp, sweets, and bitter vegetables fried in special spices. "This is for the boy. Much-much vitamin," they would say, but the prayed-for "boy" never came. If any of the three embryonic daughters had caused her even a morning of discomfort, my father would have run out to the corner chemist's—India being the land of open drug-counters where every pill in existence is foil-wrapped and individually sold without prescription—and shouted till they coughed up a Western wonder drug like thalidomide.

"Remarkable!" that Stanford doctor had said when Rabi was delivered. Eight pounds, beaming with health. On my second night home I ate a catered ten-course meal that made my stitches hurt.

We've been seeing the Khannas on weekends. Yash visits Bish every Saturday morning, bringing him a sheaf of articles and the occasional book on advanced information design. It's May; Rabi took the second semester off from school in order to spend time with my parents, then join a Himalayan trek. Yash and Bish sit at the dinner table like boys with a new board game, spreading clean sheets of paper in front of them and calling for a box of colored pencils. "How about a nice new set of crayons, boys?" Victoria teases, and Yash answers, "only if you let us color outside the lines," and then we aging girls head off to the farmer's market for bread and cheese, and we drive out to Easy Come in Sausalito. The design, perched on a cliff, has won designs. The furnishings come from every country Yash and Victoria know and love. I'd seen it in Bay Area magazines long before putting myself, and my daughter, in her hands. Her life is close to one I used to have. It's a model for one I'd like to regain. Their back deck cantilevers over a harbor filled with houseboats. The chatter from a dozen deck parties rises from the water.

No wine for me these days, but out on the deck, I could sit for hours with iced tea, she with her Pinot, and we talk of everything except the baby, "the ripening seed." That's for the office visit. Here, she's interested in India.

"Have you dug into Vertie's papers yet?" she asks, and I tell her I've just finished with the *Mist-nama*, the oldest and most exciting material, and I'm about to start with what she gave me. I'm all the way up to 1832 and poor blood-soaked John Mist is just a boy in a stagecoach galloping into an unknown future. He hasn't even got to Mishtigunj yet. There is no Mishtigunj yet, and Vertie doesn't arrive there for another hundred years. At least I know why he was sent there. It was all about the Tree Bride's gold and her gift to Gandhi. A hundred years must pass between Mist's murders in Garden Reach and the arrival of Vertie Tread-well in the town he built.

"I have to control my personal feelings," I say.

"No, you don't, my dear. Personally, I find my grandfather, which is what he is, god help me, a reprehensible little prick," and then she cuts loose with a hearty, woman-of-the-world, honk-ing laugh.

"All right. If I don't control my feelings and let myself be as judgmental as I please, I'd say that if you were setting out to cre-ate a model for adult dysfunction you could do worse than copy child-rearing patterns of the British Raj."

"Precisely my point," she says. "Assembly-line prick produc-tion."

"On the other hand, if you are setting out to create a cadre of clerks and petty administrators—let's say, an army of anal-retentive assholes—you should bottle the formula because it's never been done better."

I never say "asshole" in quite that context. I'll have to use it more often, since Victoria nearly chokes on her wine.

Whenever I think I have a grip on Treadwell's character, something new turns up. Not that he's terribly complicated, or that he led a life of constant adventure like John Mist. Things just turn up in Treadwell's life, odds and ends, like the contents of an unsorted closet or a desk stuffed with papers, that make me think for a day or two: maybe I got him wrong. It's like finding odd tickets or a love letter in your son's pocket. You know confronting him is out of the question. It's something you shouldn't have found, but dammit, it's something he should have hidden better. You just adjust your thinking. This boy of mine, or this Treadwell, isn't what I think he is. I need a *Treadwell-nama,* but Vertie Treadwell lived at arm's length from his inner self. He thought to keep only two brief notices about himself, both of which he wrote himself, both of them rigorously plain. Perhaps there was no inner self. Something vital had failed to be implanted. T. S. Eliot must have met dozens of Vertie Treadwells in his London bank-clerk years. He could have been a model for the Hollow Man, alas.

"A man like Vertie lived without women," Victoria says. "It's a pathology of misogyny. They lived without love. It's the tragedy of the Raj."

There are statistics to dispute that, but I hold back. Charm-free Vertie, oddly, was quite a magnet for certain kinds of women. The Raj marriages I've read about seem as calculated for material and bureaucratic advancement as anything out of the ruling houses of Renaissance Europe. Marriage was extension of empire by different means, a progenerating institution for the denial of intimacy, tenderness, or any crack in the façade of icy self-control. I'm sure there were exceptions; they've simply eluded my reach.

"Most were married," I say.

"Married," she snorts. "Do the math, Tara. Their wives spent a year or two in Bombay or Calcutta at the beginning of their careers. They had two or three children in two or three years—that's if she didn't die in the process. When it came time to educate the little beasts—the boys, I mean—she ripped them from the arms of their loving ayah and dropped them into those ghastly public schools. The girls could be tutored in the arts at home, the finest art being that of repression. That was the marriage, except for the reams of letters they wrote."

That was Vertie, except for the letters. From what I can tell, when his wife went back to England with their daughter—the legitimate one who ended up in New Zealand—he never wrote, and if she did, he didn't save them. And his wife seemed to have missed the lectures on repression, having taken off for New Zealand as well.

"He's lucky he didn't kill anyone."

"A slight exaggeration," I say. But it's true, I wouldn't have wanted to know him, and indisputably, there was violence in the man and maybe he did kill. But violence implies heat and rage, like the violence of John Mist. Mist had a woman in his life only briefly, but love for her inspired him to murder. The violence of Vertie Treadwell is cold and calculating, something very modern, a menacing, bureaucratic rage. "Those I fight I do not hate / those I serve I do not love."

He could have worked equally well inside the German or Russian bureaucracies, signing the same papers, laboring over the same point-perfect reports. Bish and I have pawed through the papers and I've found nothing specific that inspired the rage, or even restrained it. These days, when scholars speak of "a culture" of corruption inside an institution, or a culture of greed or arrogance, they could just as easily speak of a culture of spite and bitterness, along with the usual inflated self-regard, jingoism, race, and chauvinism inside the intricate mechanism of empire. In that sense, Vertie Treadwell was a man of deep Edwardian culture, which is to say, of a curdled and cynical Victorianism.

Officers of the Raj behaved like preachers, or imams, or rabbis in some small, closed, self-perpetuating sect. They married daughters of other officers, girls who'd grown up speaking kitchen Hindi to the servants. They'd been raised by ayahs, spoiled by servants. They were like army brats; they knew the drill, they dealt with long separations, frequent moves, the indignities and petty jealousies of rank. If their husbands got posted to the frontier or the interior, the wives did not follow. No facilities up there or down there for gentlewomen. Of course that left the men with their pick of cantonment women and their bibis, but those relationships were part of the historic bargain and constrained from the beginning. After a few years together, the women would drift back to England when it came time to educate the children. Maybe the men visited every few years, or they saw their sons again after they were grown, or their daughters after they got married—but only if they came out to India themselves.

"And those are the happy stories, when everything was working the way it was supposed to," Victoria charges, this time with passion. I think she feels, many years too late, the bitterness of her father, the bastard's rage. Vertie never saw his children again. He cared less for them than a street dog for its pups.

And then the men retired and came back "home" to an England that was as foreign to them as it had been to the Anglo-Indians of my childhood, those Christian Indian girls in my school named for English flowers, Poppy and Rosie and Camilla, with their Western clothes and talk of uncles and aunties in Battersea and Belsize.

"Are those tears, dear?" Victoria asks, and I say it must be hormones.

"Nonsense," she says, "you're thinking of Vertie's life, aren't you?"

Yes, I confess, I've been thinking of his life, the barrenness, the sterility, lives like a discarded tin can on a garbage heap. They'd been serving England all their lives but hadn't seen it in forty years.

"What a formula for disaster! What madman designed it?" Victoria asks. "Oh, have a little wine, it won't hurt. It's better than tears." We sit awhile longer on the deck. From the houseboats, a few men and women wave up to us and invite us down.

When we get back from Sausalito, the dining table is strewn with papers, littered like weather maps with grids and colored, wavy lines. When he's working on a problem, Bish is young again, his hair is mussed, white roots and all, and he hops around the table on his canes; you'd swear it was Yash who'd suffered the damage, the way he sits still, staring at the paper. While Victoria and I have been at Easy Come, they've gone through a packet of typing paper.

"Routers," says Yash. They haven't eaten, haven't drunk, turned on the radio or television. I can at least provide a bowl of hot Punjabi mix and beers. We'll probably end up across the street in the Thai place for dinner.

I'm reminded of our Stanford student apartment, when I'd bring Bish and Chet Yee bowls of food that in my sickness I couldn't even bear to look at. They designed the original CHATTY model in that apartment, on our dining table. The Sunday—at least it's famous in the information-design underground—when a 49ers game unlocked the secret of broadband technology. "That's it! Short passes in the flat!" Bish cried, and I didn't know what he was talking about. A few minutes later, Chet tried to explain. "You see, Tara, everyone's been trying to connect with long passes down the field." He drew a football grid. "In normal communications, you send two receivers deep and hope to connect. But look at the odds against it." He filled the space with a flood of X's. "But if you flood this area here with receivers"—he stuck in a bunch of O's off to the side—"there aren't enough X's to cover them, you follow? Easy connections, without interference. You don't need a super-transmitter or a super-receiver in order to connect."

"You need accuracy, not strength," Bish put in. "Joe Montana is a digital quarterback. He's small and he's accurate. He isn't fast and he isn't strong and he doesn't have to be. Everyone else is still analog."

Bish knew I'd never quite leaped the digital, or was it the analogical, divide. Chet had more patience. He said, "If we improve the chances of reception and cut down on the interference and if we can do it without huge new transmitters and receptors, we've just redesigned communications for the twentieth century." His voice was firm, but his hands were shaking.

"And we don't have to huddle up after every call," said Bish. "It's all happening at the speed of light."

I remember looking at that page, a football field with a few X's and O's connected with dotted lines. It started an industry, it launched a revolution. It belongs in the Smithsonian, but in my zealous housekeeping, I probably threw it out that night. Hormones. Clean, cook, vomit. Then I ran to the bathroom.

⸴ ⸴ ⸴

Our post-bombing life, the enforced and premature middle age of doctors and therapies and the caution that comes with the proof that you're a special target and that life is a diminishing commodity, has settled upon us with the gay solemnity of a second marriage. We haven't actually remarried, but we know something we didn't know back then; we're capable of making grave mistakes.

The fairy-dust world of CHATTY, the billions of dollars that flowed from the application of that Sunday morning idea, the empire it built, the importance attached to every pronouncement from the Sage of Atherton, are gone. The Bay Area Bachelor to Die For came too close to death, as did the Rani of Rivoli. These days, the Sage wonders if he should start on the Atkins diet since he can't do his accustomed exercises, and the Rani slips new pages she's written onto the table and asks for suggestions. He reads the Bangla *Mist-nama,* translating as he goes. He paws through the Treadwell box, trying as I do to find a center to the man. I have enough faith in his genius to believe that if it's there, he'll find it. He never had time for novels, now it's a passion.

After the Thai dinner is delivered and the last Singhas drunk, the Khannas are gone and maybe Rabi has found a phone to call us from, or a Nepalese Internet café from which to launch a computer chat, and then we make our slow way to bed. We used to be night owls; now sleep hits at ten o'clock. Maybe in our forties we'll recover our youth.

We were legends, once. Now we shuffle to bed, willing but slowed, holding tightly to each other for safety and comfort.

2

EAST ANGLIA, 1948

A recently planted low hedge separated the footpath from the pitch. The old man paused to watch the St. Alban's boys practicing, and lit a fresh cigarette off the smoldering ash. Thick white hair flared from under his short-visored cap. A colorfully embroidered woolen shawl lay over his shoulders and gathered at his throat. He always paused for cricket. Cricket brought back nothing but pleasant memories. The boy at long-off stood twenty feet away, slapping his spindly legs every few seconds to keep them warm. None of those lads were strong enough to reach the boundary with a sixer, but still, it sent a useful message of aspiration. There will always be an England however dull and squalid, it said, so long as boys in short pants play cricket in the cold.

It was a spring day, at least in theory and according to the calendar, in the East Anglia village of Brynnsmere. Even without cigarette smoke his breath condensed, as did everyone else's walking past. His shawl seemed riotously out of place against the shabby tweed jacket and knitted blue vest. The sky was gray, the branches satiny black, topped with unopened buds. New grass had failed to rise. The boys were playing on tufts of brown.

Now that Britain had embraced the drab and tattered as a matter of state policy, color looked out of place anywhere. The shawl with its fanciful embroidery sent a signal that its wearer had once proudly served the greatest empire the world had ever seen and not this rump thing called the United Kingdom. The afternoon outing to the tobacconist's followed by a pint or two at the Painted Lion could wait a bit. St. Alban's had been his school. Cricket said something about the tradition of the gentleman. It spoke of continuity. He remembered playing on this same pitch in the same short pants and magenta cap, when? Sixty-six years ago? It would have been 1882, a fine year to be eight years old, a boy, and British. We owned the world, and we knew it. What would this lot have to look forward to? A dreary post in a dreary ministry.

In those distant years, the month of May, which this allegedly was, had offered the foretaste of summer. The last few weeks of school assignments seemed less serious, and the masters made even the Latin and Greek translations turn a bit fanciful. The masters would ease up on the battle scenes and political orations and select sylvan passages which were infinitely more difficult to translate. "Good God, man, look out the window!" old Rutledge would exhort. "You can do better than *'the sun shone bright on the nascent leaf.'* What color do you *see* when the poet writes 'nascent'?"

Fresh, sir?

"'Fresh' is not a color, you incapacitated imbecile."

Newborn? Tender and green?

"Green? The leaf is green? Oh, I *am* impressed! Gentlemen!" he'd harrumph. "We are going out into nature and we are going to look at nascent leaves in the sunshine and we shan't return until one of you incompetent scribes can render a nascent leaf with such precision and perfection that even your blind, bedridden grandmother can see it and start running around her bedroom in bedlammed delight. Have I made myself clear? *Jaldi, jaldi,* gentlemen, fast, fast."

He remembered it all to this day, and the confidence it permitted him to slip Greek and Latin quotations into his reports and recommendations in the hope that some well-trained eye in Calcutta or New Delhi or even London might smile and mark his file for eventual promotion. *That chap Treadwell down in . . . where? The United Provinces, poor devil. Good head on his shoulders. Fine wit.* Not that it had ever happened, or would happen to anyone, again. With this clutch of Red Brick Labourites running the show, you'd draw more favorable attention making sly allusions to tonnages of Welsh coal and the eel-catch on the Mersey. They say for a British schoolboy, the greatest triumphs and deepest terrors in life all occur before the age of ten. His life, it seemed, could be submitted as evidence.

Like a mantis newly hatched/unfolding its wings on a blackened branch? Very fanciful, Mr. Treadwell. Rutledge turned the phrase over a few times. "Branch and hatched," he pronounced, "there's a nice little rhyme there. I can see it, I can feel it. The color of a newborn mantis is bright green, like a new leaf, but you might insert cicada for the sake of syllables. I am promoting you to class moron. Since ninety-nine percent of Englishmen are imbeciles, you are the proverbial one-eyed ruler, Mr. Treadwell."

How he loved his school days! Old Rutledge who never married and cautioned every boy against marriage's insane demands, was buried on the St. Alban's grounds. Treadwell often swung by the small cemetery, now impacted with Great War dead, for long chats. He'd already purchased his small plot, near enough to Octavius Rutledge (1832–1904) to make the inevitable less uninviting.

Could it be there'd be summer this year after all? In the fifteen minutes he'd been stalled behind the hedge, he felt a touch of warmth on his shoulders. He loosened the shawl about his throat. The sun was just a lighter smudge in the dingy sky, yet its rays had touched the sodden pitch, the muddy footpaths, and the branches. Not that nature could be entirely blamed for perpetual gray fog; it being the winter of Labour. Attlee and his cronies were creatures of the subterranean dark, the mist, and the cold. Coal miners dictated everything else, why not the seasons?

Mist was rising, as it did in warmer weather, not descending, as it had all winter and spring. He used to pay attention to the slightest change of wind and temperature. He'd got fairly good at predicting the weather, but since leaving India he'd grown dodgy on some of the principles. Perhaps it was the slant of light or a slight temperature differential. Cooler, drier air over warm, moist grasses. Or was it warmer, moister air over frost-bitten stalks? There hadn't been a strong temperature differential this year. The slide of winter into spring had been imperceptible, sleety gray to rainy gray, the buds retarded, no color anywhere, but today held, just briefly, a touch of magic.

Mist triggered a memory that kept recurring. At the Royal Turf Club in Cal, a syce pouring buckets of cool water over a race-horse after an early morning workout, the steam rising off every well-worked muscle. Because of the mist, he'd laid a pound on the beast and it had returned twenty-five. And he remembered forty years of early morning rides, when, if there had been rain or a heavy dew and no wind, the sun would strike each leaf, each blade of grass, each pond and freshet, and every leaf would send up its own diaphanous cloud and the mist would rise and lay undisturbed over the forest canopy.

There was nothing wrong with India. India lay just short of perfection. The heat, the dust, the monsoons, the flies and fevers, the mud; they were part of the natural abundance. You must not miss your food and exercise; do not expect to feel strong and healthy. He never failed to take new recruits aside and to lecture them on the splendors of India and their responsibility for preserving it. He warned against any complaint. If he heard any of his officers' whining about discomfort, he would immediately recommend banishment to a posting of supreme hardship. The only problem with India was the bloody Indians, God's test for Englishmen.

He was back in the jungle after a sudden, brief, leaf-glistening shower, turning every spike, every twig, every leaf into a jet of evaporation. Whole jungles he'd seen, canopies of steam released into air so humid you'd swear not a molecule more of vapor could be contained. Once on a hunt, his old shikari, Mohandass, had instructed him, "The tiger, sahib, he will be wet from fording the stream. We will not see him, but mark his path by the vapor trail." Only, he pronounced it "way-per"—"by the waypers, cloud of wayper clinging to him." Like the buffalo, the elephant, half in the river and half above, steaming as boys washed them and the sun dried them off. Those were the privileged views, the precious memories of India, when he might have been tempted to take up pastel chalks or to pen a poem, but who would see it, who would care? He always felt he had a poetic nature. The cicada newly hatched, it haunted his memory. He had a finer eye; he could endure those endless nights of native music and there was much in the charm and grace of India to appreciate, but too much involvement in the feminine side sent an improper message.

One day, out for his morning ride, he'd come upon a tiger prowling the river bank, perhaps for a *chital,* the steam rising from the magnificent cat as though it had been running for miles, and he had no gun with him and once his mare caught the scent there was no containing her.

He'd not remembered this simple phenomenon ever before in England, the rising of vapors from the ground, dissipating into the air, the cricket players looking as though they were about to burst into flame. A heavy mist must have fallen just before he'd left the flat and the temperature had risen—or had it fallen?

For the first time in months he felt positive warmth from under the shawl, the lightest and warmest and highest quality shawl spun from the wool of Himalayan wild goats. A fine shawl and an old tweed jacket over a knitted vest; a cap and knitted half-gloves that permitted smoking—what else does an Englishman need to survive the winter? Truth was, he didn't own a proper overcoat and on the pittance he received, couldn't afford to buy a decent one. Thelma prowled the church bins, humiliating him with leavings she'd found for a shilling or two. She had the pride of a scullery maid and he was sorry he'd given her a roof.

Wherever he'd been posted he had tried to introduce manly virtues—healthy competition, respect for rules, modesty in victory, dignity in defeat—in the form of cricket, always with predictable results. Communal riots, murders. At least when he was young he'd participated in the glory days of Bombay Gymkhana cricket, played on a pitch of perfect green. When he was too old to play he'd introduced it to Bengal, as far south as the Sunderbans. Never too early to get them started on team sports and a sense of competition and fair play and get them out of their Akha-ras where Lord knows what seditious nonsense was going on.

He decided it was a glorious triangulation of dew point, humidity, and temperature, some magic combination he might have noted in the old days with a special star, when everything, it seemed, mattered more and was more beautiful, or wondrous. There were those special days when the ride went well, the work load was manageable, favorite foods were fried to a turn, drinks were cold, and the woman came round and didn't try to stay. He'd trained his secretaries to get off their useless haunches and go out twice a day, sometimes more often, to gather a sheaf of meteoro-logical facts. Check the flytraps and mosquito strips, migratory bird sightings, fresh leopard or tiger kills, hyena burrows, river levels.

He assumed, they all assumed, the Crown would be there for-ever and it mattered, setting the meteorological clock as a base line of temperature, humidity, and wind direction, so that admin-istrators in centuries to come would have the authority of history behind them in drawing up their policies. Without a base line, there can be no valid trend line. Memory is discounted; simple facts are in disrepute. Degeneracy disguises itself, claiming unbroken continuity with the past. How else to know when the extraordinary is merely the delayed fulfillment of expectation? Labour wiped out British history. Little men vilify the achieve-ments of Empire and no one rises in Commons or on the radio or in the newssheets to object with passion and clarity. Winston Churchill, of course, the prophet in the wilderness, but no one else. Civilization plunges into anarchy.

It is the duty of a responsible commissioner to keep weather data, to know in at least three languages the names of every living

thing in his district, every fruit and flower and crawling and flying and swimming creature. Only through the Adamic naming
process can a conqueror be at ease and expect compliance from his
subjects. Three times a day for twenty years, entering observa-
tions, dry and wet, summer and winter. After he turned his
ledgers over, who would know or care about the date of first flow-
ering, the census of langurs, and the number of malaria deaths?
Bloody little brown bureaucrats probably ripped the pages out to
wrap their bidis.

He remembers the pleasures of walking to his water traps,
watching the slow, daily climb or fall of temperatures at five A.M.,
marking what passed for seasons when his mare would be brought
round. To think! The tweeds and the knitted vest used to signal
the onset of cool nights and bearable days of a subtropical winter.
Necessary on the morning ride, dispensable by first drink, back
on again by dinner. He'd been asked to donate them when he was
thrown out, damned if he'd will them to some file clerk suddenly
elevated to Deputy Commissioner. Good thing he hadn't; who'd
ever thought a tattered Indian wardrobe would stand between an
officer of the Crown and freezing to death?

The world reveals itself in tiny increments, statistically significant only when ingested over time. Could the onset of the monsoon, its duration and magnitude, be predicted weeks, even
months in advance? Decades of careful record-keeping might
reveal a pattern. Not that anyone bloody well cared anymore. All
those thousands of pages of ledgers he'd kept, the hour-by-hour,
day-by-day readings, all turned over on a final morning to a newly
elevated, uncomprehending native officer practically pissing his
pants in anticipation of sitting in the director's plush chair and
draining old bottles of whiskey abandoned in the sideboard. *You*

might give these ledgers some attention, Mr. Ismail, a few useful entries here and there.

Your car is waiting, Mr. Treadwell. Good day to you, sir. You are fortunate to have a home to return to. We here, we face misery and butchery. Misery and butchery, that is the legacy you have left us.

One day a message comes from London, relayed from New Delhi, and the structure and meaning of one's life is wiped out: *Gentlemen, the British Raj is ended. You will vacate your offices and surrender keys to your subordinate native staff. Expect a civil parting, but do not linger. Respect the men who replace you. It is understandable that bonds of affection and nostalgia might impede the smooth transfer of power. We trust you to exercise more than normal restraint. Bear in mind you are officers of the Crown, not of the Republic of India or Pakistan, and are expected to behave as such.*

Officials—one hesitates to call them men—who can wipe out three hundred years of glorious history and deny the sacrifice of thousands, and wipe out the achievement of the noblest members of the British race, are capable of the foulest treachery known to man.

He remembered cricket in Calcutta, trying to introduce that queen of English competition and being rebuffed. They didn't take to manly competition; it was as simple as that. Whatever physical training Bengalis undertook in their Akharas did not transfer to the competitive pitch. They did not see the moral advantage of testing oneself against one's fellow man. The entire structure of Hindu culture made intracaste competition impossible. No Brahmin would lift his hand in labor, nor permit himself to be caste-polluted in any way. He could not permit himself humiliation at the hand of a lower life form. Teamwork among Hindus entailed a fat Brahmin's sitting under a shade tree, direct-

ing the labor of sun-blackened coolies. It did not include diving
after a ball or receiving it still slippery with sweat from a lower
caste's brow. The confrontation between Hindu and Muslim was
life and death. Not may the better man win, but may the better
god, the higher order of existence, exterminate the other. Look at
the bloody mess they've made of their so-called Partition. At least
they made short work of Gandhi, so much for the apostle of peace
and forgiveness. We lacked the moral clarity to do it ourselves.
Gandhi, Nehru, Bose, the whole lot of them should have been
hanged or sent off to the Andamans. He harbored a special fantasy
of the Savile Row Pandit toiling in guano among the headhunters. If we'd done it when we had them in detention, if we'd
had the courage of our convictions, the moral clarity of our earlier
administrators, none of this would have happened. Premature liberation; they'd needed another hundred years. I'd still be there.
Ismail would bring me my files every morning. We'd chat over
tea and the morning post. He'd unroll his discreet little mat
somewhere off in a corner to pray, while I adjudicate. We knew
the secret of governance, but the Bolshies, lathered up with cant
calls to universal brotherhood, ignored three hundred years of history and took their instructions from a German Jew.

And now his reveries were pierced by a piping voice, "Please,
sir, our ball . . ." and across the hedge a scrawny lad with the
unmistakable face of India, framed in the hideous Public Health
glasses that all of them, English and Indian alike, would take to
their graves, stood with his hand outstretched like a bloody little
beggar. The ball had punched through the hedgerow and lay
practically at his feet. The cheeky little looter wouldn't get his
scheming hands on it, not so long as he drew breath. The ball settled comfortably in his hand and he took a few running steps in
the manner cricket had intended, rotating his arm like a propeller

blade and launching it. It skipped down the footpath a good twenty yards before striking a slab of protruding concrete and skittering toward Brynnsmere High Street.

Of all the things he'd not expected to see in the village of his upbringing was an Indian face. Had they not done enough damage to Britain and to himself? That girlish little face behind the round black glasses, those thin, girlish arms and legs, the high-pitched voice with a pure local accent—it sickened him. He could feel himself teetering and the footpath grow uneven. His knee gave way. And he was down, his cap rolling on its visor. He hadn't the opportunity to brace his fall, his nose had struck first and he knew immediately it was broken. His nose fairly gushed; his ghastly glasses lay broken and puddled in his blood. He prayed no blood had stained his shawl. A piping little voice drifted in and out of the roaring in his ears, "Sir? Sir? Do you require assistance?" He tried to swat the oversized tadpole head away with its insane spectacles bobbing over him.

"Keep your bloody hands to yourself," he commanded and the boy backed off, tears in his eyes.

He sat up with some effort and waited for his vision to clear. It was a new perspective for him, squatting in the middle of a public footpath like some bloody beggar with everything out of focus. No blood on the shawl, thank God, but it was still flowing from his aching, throbbing nose. He pinched it and winced; already the high, hawklike bridge of his nose was spongy to the touch. What a stupid thing, to trip, although now he saw what he had tripped over. One great broken slab of footpath concrete had heaved upward. No wonder he'd tripped. It might have happened to anyone who'd been walking and was distracted for a moment into watching a boys' cricket match.

A police vehicle slowed, then stopped and the window was

rolled down. "I say, Mr. Treadwell, took a tumble did you? Would you be needing a ride home or down to the Lion?" They knew his habits well, the cheeky bastards.

"It's this blasted footpath," he cried out. "Look at it! It's a bloody shame. I could have been killed."

"I reckon Town Council needs to send a leveling team, all right. No rides, then? Nothing broken? You might have them look at your nose. We can reach you to hospital."

"I said I'm perfectly all right." To prove it, he struggled to his feet and had to stagger forward a step before finding balance.

He'd wasted a lot of time. The others would be waiting, wondering where he'd gone.

He thought of touring cars, great steel beasts that settled immediately and eloquently questions of who ruled and who cleaned and drove. In 1937, as Mishtigunj DC, he'd put in for, and had had approved, a thumping grand sedan and driver. That was the car that drove him to the docks and off to Madras ahead of the killings, then back to England. Keeping a stable of horses had grown too expensive and responsible syces had left the remote mofussils of the Sunderbans for Dacca and Calcutta or any place they could earn a living near a racetrack.

Bloody Naseer Ahmed on this year's Honours List. Once he had a DC's sedan and driver he used to make special trips up to Dacca just to sit in on any trial where Naseer Ahmed and Sujit Lal Banerjee were to argue a case. All that was loquacious, mendacious, pedantic, allusive, melodramatic, bombastic, and seditious in the Bengali soul was on display, all couched in passable imitations of the King's English with meticulous attention to the niceties, and especially, the contradictions of British law. Here was the sad history of the British in India on public exhibit: we created these clever little Ariels and they used our own laws and language against us. Money was laid down. This was the kind of cricket Bengalis preferred; Muslim against Hindu Brahmin and no one even touched. There should have been posters outside the court, big fat Banerjee and snaky little Ahmed stripped down, fists up. Naseer Ahmed followed the British out of India, settling in London and minting money in litigation with all the Labour lackeys fawning over an Oriental. The galling Naseer Ahmed, K.C., O.B.E., W.O.G. After partition, Sujit Lal Banerjee fled to Calcutta.

What more could a drab and tattered country expect? Worse than tattered—Bolshie and dismembered—he and his friends had long decided. He fought it whenever and however he could, patronizing the Painted Lion where Teddy Rowan, a stout Ulsterman, kept the whining Catholics and Labourites at bay, and ripping down their posters wherever they sprouted. Fifty years ago any patriotic Englishman would have shown them a thing or two. Even fifteen years ago there was no tolerance for seditious sentiments. You spoke them, you acted on them, and you were hanged. Just five years ago he'd confronted sedition and he'd ended it. You wanted Socialism, you pathetic little mother's sons? Well, now you've got it, a systematic lowering of all that was noble and a raising to power the lowest variety of gutter slime.

"When should I expect you, Vertie?" Thelma had shouted down.

Slamming the door extra hard might give her an idea.

✦   ✦   ✦

The day that Vertie Treadwell died began like every other. Thelma had made his tea, as much for warming the hands as for the flat, insipid brew itself, which was never hot enough. A lifetime in India, he'd grant them that much, spoiled one for British tea, or such tea as a pensioner was able to afford on the pittance they paid. He'd read the daily outrages off the sheets—you could hardly call it a newspaper—and caught the morning dose of lies off the BBC, then bundled up for a walk to the Painted Lion and the familiar prospect of an afternoon stretching into an evening of pints with the boys. It rained a bit before he left. The sun struggled to assert itself. On the way, the fine mist lifted, he'd found the bonus cigarette in his jacket pocket, and he'd paused for cricket. The beastly little Indian boy unnerved him. He reminded him of the woman, as though she'd come back to haunt him.

He talked it over with Octavius Rutledge. "I feel it won't be long," he said. He'd been forced to hold the broken halves of his glasses, like lorgnettes. The bridge of his nose was puffy and painful to the touch. Rutledge always had trouble remembering him out of the thousands over a fifty-year career. "A cicada newly hatched," he said. Ah, on a blackened branch. Branch, hatched— a slant rhyme. You carried yourself well, Treadwell. Class moron, no? Whatever happened in your life?

"I tried to save the British Empire, sir," he said.

He would speak to Teddy today about changing the name. "Painted Tiger" would have majesty and a tie to Empire. Tigers had dignity. Lions were as mangy and moth-bitten as the country they symbolized on the coat of arms.

He'd been an average student though marked with extraordinary posture. According to Rutledge, Virgil Treadwell could intimidate his peers simply by standing still. He parted crowds with his eyes alone, he walked, according to one teacher, like a well-fed lion, patrolling the edges of a game-rich waterhole. Not about to pounce, just asserting his presence, maintaining his control.

The lion image pleased him at the time, as it might any English schoolboy, but the lion was not Vertie Treadwell's proper model. He reflected on his dissatisfaction with the lion serving as the national symbol of Britain in a contribution as a St. Alban's "Old Boy" some fifty years after his graduation. Lions hunt in pairs, or even in female packs of fours and fives. They crouch in the grass, pulling themselves closer to a herd of prey, and when they fall upon the fold they select the slowest reactor, the most confused, and close in relentlessly, ignoring hundreds of others in the pursuit of the weakest. There seemed to be nothing noble in their lives or practices. They certainly lacked beauty. In fact, he despised the lion, thinking it more properly the symbol of El-Mahdi and his gang of desert marauders. He thought too little of lions even to shoot them, when he'd had the opportunity on a trip to the Gir Forest, their last Indian refuge. His collection of more than one hundred tiger pelts testified to his great respect for that noblest of beasts.

Vertie Treadwell was a tiger. He hunted alone. No herds of prey paraded in front of him. He was absolute master of his territory, tolerating no other males, and he could personally manage any leopards and hyenas that impinged. He could climb, he could swim, and he could hide in broad daylight, standing tall in the play of light and shadow. Stealth and cunning tethered to a placid ferocity: that was Vertie Treadwell, at least in his self-image. Weight so well distributed, held like a bridge under so much tension, that even five hundred pounds of full-grown male tiger did not crush a leaf or break a twig. That was Vertie Treadwell.

In those postwar Attlee years they were still around, the old men feeling foolish in Nye Bevan glasses with shattered lenses, more often than not taped together, ashamed in their out-at-elbow, frayed-cuff tweed jackets over woolen vests, stoic in knitted half-gloves exposing yellowed fingers from which dangled the constant cigarette. They wore short-visored woolen caps more appropriate to lorry-drivers, atop uncut bristles of shock-white hair. Eyebrow-trimming was an art well beyond them. They shuffled along village footpaths, usually with a cane or walking stick. Curs and toddlers and in particular the erstwhile, off-white subjects of British rule seemed to find themselves helplessly entwined in their unsteady trajectory. They were best advised to take to the gutter or risk the business end of a shoe or cane. No village police would convict. In those sour times when the entire world seemed to have run off the cliff, the old colonial administrators constituted, to themselves at least, the last of a native aristocracy.

Cut them, and they bled imperial crimson. Listen to them and all you heard was a steady denunciation of the policies and politicians of the past fifty years, with the exception of Winston Churchill. They alone, however, had earned the right of bitter redress. These might be low times, but if anyone without their experience in the tropics dared express the same opinions, they would be well advised to prepare themselves for a tight slap across their ungrateful mouths, and no village policeman would dare arrest.

He found himself articulating all-embracing formulas for global understanding that normally began, "Anyone with the least understanding of the Indian character . . ." or "Anyone with even a passing acquaintance of colonial rule . . ." He'd become one of those Old Indja-Hands he used to mock: *In Indja, we used to give the filthy beggars fifty lashes and be done with it. . . .* How many letters to the editor extrapolated from success in India to failure in Britain? "In administering backward areas in India, if we entertained for a moment the folly of proportional or representative . . ." "Colonial experience gathered over a half century teaches one fact above all others, and that is . . ." "Successful rule in an Indian state vastly more populous than Great Britain . . ."

"The one way to treat the pestilence that has settled over our country is to . . ." "As a magistrate of thirty years standing, I know that one rotten apple, one bad egg, a cancerous growth, bacterium . . . the time comes when the swamp must be drained . . ." He'd read those letters in the morning *Times* and wanted to respond, but the writers had usually chosen *noms d'exile,* like "Simplicissmus," or "Nestor" with addresses like "The Rectory, Wessex" or "Blue Door Cottage" in the Dordogne.

Well, Mr. Simplicissmus, your all-embracing formula is simpleminded. Here is my forty-five-year observation. India was presented to Britain as a laboratory to work out British, not Indian destiny, and Britain has failed the test. India could have taught the British about how to live with the obligations and benefits of the greatest empire the world had ever seen and the noblest traditions in human history. Instead, Britain got tangled up in trying to raise pestilential hordes to a semblance of humanity, to eradicate the most intractable ignorance and superstition on the face of the earth and to reason with the most pig-headed malefactors in existence. An inferior culture has succeeded in bringing a noble one down to its level.

That the lone success India could muster was the likes of Pandit Nehru and his Congress Party gangsters is a compliment to Britain, of sorts. Two hundred years of slaving away, two centuries of selfless sacrifice and untold thousands of deaths have created one stupendously flawed human being in the English mold.

Congratulations, Dr. Frankenstein. It's a Pandit.

"Please, sir, the ball!" Cheeky little monkey.

When he'd played cricket sixty years ago, there had been an Indian boy on the team. His name was Arvind Thacker, and everyone made sure he'd have an easy time of it. In those years, an Indian in England was a curiosity. His schoolmates called him Irving

Tucker. His father was a medical doctor of some sort, sent out to do research on tropical diseases. A servant showed up at lunchtime with Arvind's tiffin, since he was religiously prohibited from eating English food. "Arvind will go to Hell if he eats a tongue sandwich. The rest of you lot have no excuses," the headmaster joked. As he remembered it, everyone had turned out to teach him cricket and to cheer his every half-hearted effort. They forgave him for never quite getting the hang of practicing, training, strategy, effort, running, throwing, discipline, teamwork, and sacrifice.

Whatever happens to the Arvind Thackers? he wondered now. Wherever he ended up, he damned well better feel gratitude to England, not that gratitude was part of an Indian's makeup. Just see how he'd prosper under the Dutch or the Portuguese with his superior attitudes and daily tiffin. The history of Indians coming to England to polish their education is a story of knife-in-the-back.

The founding principles of Empire had been sound: educate and elevate a native aristocracy, rather than crush it in the manner of other colonizers. British hearts weren't in the slaughter. A hundred years ago they thought they could lift the Indians up, even when ninety-nine percent lived in the Stone Age and wanted to stay there. But once you'd created this native aristocracy, where could they go? What could they do but cause mischief and end up on the Honours List while seceding from the Empire, when those who'd try to stop them, who'd seen their careers and reputations ruined, were left off?

Case in point, one strutting little popinjay by the name of Pandit Jawaharlal Nehru. A pretty fair imitation of a British gentleman, at least when he was misbehaving in England. Bolshie to the core and a shameless philanderer, but we're too well bred to be scandalized! Bolshie in public to please his Labour friends, but only so long as it didn't soil his suits and silks. In the laboratory of Indian colonialism, we created first-class hypocrites, something India hadn't known before we came. India was chockablock with black-guards and tyrants and the greediest despots in the modern world, but they'd always operated in the open and everyone knew who and what they were. They were like British royalty. They could do pretty much what they damn well pleased. We taught them to hide their thievery under plummy accents or dirty homespun.

Case in point, the late Great Soul, Mohandas K. Gandhi. You can criticize Nehru all you like and he'll throw it back at you because he's a Cambridge debater. Every inch the Indian lawyer; he would have been worth a drive to Dacca if he'd tangled with Ahmed or Banerjee. But if you criticize Gandhi, people ask how dare you, he's a saint and a martyr. To hear our besotted Bolshies tell it, he's Christ returned and his death at the hands of his own people seals it. Never mind he was a wily lawyer, the sneakiest dev-il we ever trained. Just because he discovered there was more power in a filthy dhoti than Savile Row tailoring doesn't mean he doesn't know us through and through and hate our guts. Oh, he can charm us, and everyone's taken in by his little act. If he were Irish or German we would have seen through it and hanged him for what he is. My God, the man demands more tribute than the Nizam of Hyderabad, and we think he lives like a monk.

There are women who've turned over fortunes in gold so he could go on marches. I've met them; I've interrogated them. Not that anyone believes me, not that anyone cares. Tell that in polite society and you're scorned for a fascist.

⸴　⸴　⸴

Roundtree was first in that day. He brought his pint over to the cor-ner table that was theirs by right of seniority and patronage. "Ver-tie, what the hell happened? Humpty Dumpty took a great fall?"

"Damned City Council footpath. Take your eye off it for one step and down you go." Roundtree seemed to be calculating the veracity of Treadwell's account. He asked where it had happened, then when. "You might check in at St. Crispin's. Looks to me you've cracked more than your glasses." It was Roundtree who called Teddy Rowan over and asked if he had a plaster for Vertie's broken specs. Finally they clanked glasses and Roundtree offered the first toast, "The king."

"The king."

"Did you read they're diverting city funds for a May Day parade?"

"Joe Stalin out in front?"

"Who needs Uncle Joe when you've got Nye?"

Stafford Roundtree was a good egg, retired in '47 like everyone, but from a higher shelf than Vertie and the usual run of District Commissioners. He'd been private secretary to the viceroy in Colombo. He was rumored to be in line for the Honours List, but was too outspoken a Tory for the current lot. Roundtree was a Falstaffian sort, heavy and jolly-looking at first glance, with merry cheeks and twinkling eyes, but very little got by him. He'd been invited by the Ceylonese to stay on their planning board and even by the British in their new High Commission. There was no Mrs. Roundtree keeping him here or pushing him out.

Vertie always wished he'd been posted in Ceylon, preferably on a white sand beach under a row of swaying palms. It was a damned sight more civilized than India, smaller and tidier. How it could survive on its own was anyone's guess. Coconuts? Coconut oil? Coir? What else did Ceylon have to offer? Roundtree was sanguine, it had a better chance than most Asian countries. Russians were poking around already. There was a Bolshie underbelly. It had their backward elements, Hindus in the north, but by and large, universal literacy, good health care, and the promise of stability under well-trained leaders should see them through.

Roundtree succeeded because he knew how to keep his ledger clean; forty years in Ceylon and nary a reprimand. He despised the cushioned aristocracy in the Colonial Office as deeply as Vertie, but somehow his hatred didn't seep through. Roundtree had cultivated the Ceylonese underground; he'd kept informants, something Vertie hadn't the stomach for. Vertie hated the police presence in his district, preferring to combine the roles of investigator, enforcer, and magistrate in himself, whenever possible. After 1930, he was saddled with a police inspector.

"I don't trust a single one of them," said Vertie, "especially if they were trained in our Bolshie schools."

"Oh, they can be reasoned with." He made the universal sliding motion of his thumb and fingertips. "We can leave it for the Americans now."

Plimps entered, Bascomb Plimpton. "I say, Treadwell, you're looking ghastly."

He could hear their voices, but had trouble summoning a response.

In 1930, on his accession to the post of District Commissioner for the Sunderbans, he wrote the following sketch, in answer to a request for a thumbnail autobiography:

Virgil Ernest Reginald Treadwell was born in the Laying-In (English) Hospital of Ootycomund in the late fall of 1874, the 30th of November, to be exact. It is of passing interest that he was born on the same day of the same year as the former head of the Colonial Office, the Hon. Winston Churchill. Treadwell obviously does not claim a comparable range of gifts and accomplishments, but the coincidental nature of their births might account for their congruent views, in particular, the important role of Britain's far-flung colonial Empire in forming a united defence in a world of deepening peril.

Treadwell's mother was a Canning, a name well known in Anglo-Indian as well as British circles, although her exact place within its hierarchy has never been fully established. Tragically, she was carried off by fevers two years later, following the birth of a second child, her daughter Canning. Her husband, Fleming Treadwell, an officer in the Indian Army then on manoeuvres along the Coromandel coast, sent the infant daughter and her brother back to Brynnsmere, the ancestral East Anglia village inhabited by Treadwells for the past five centuries. The daughter was subsequently sent to an aunt in South Africa, never to see her brother again. The boy would never know his father, but for the exemplary standards he set. He perished in the Sudan in 1884, in military action against the Mahdi.

The boy counts himself fortunate indeed to have been looked after by his uncles, dedicated town constables from whom he learned the value and dignity of maintaining social order. He received his education at St. Alban's, the local public school, and eventually, St John's College, Oxford. He joined the Indian Civil Service in 1896 and has served in Bombay, the United Provinces, and Orissa before assuming what promises to be a new and challenging post.

In olden days, when the Mughal emperors wished to show their displeasure with a town or a state, they expressed their rage in time-honored fashion. Perhaps they deprived a city of water, or burned its crops and killed its livestock; at other times, they burned the city, tortured its men, slaughtered its children, and carried off its younger wives and daughters for rape and enslavement. Heroic times called for epic displays. The tortures were exquisite, the killings artful, the suffering on a scale to rattle the gates of paradise.

In 1930, however, on the day of Vertie Treadwell's inauguration as DC, the mandated eleven-gun salute was clipped to ten when one rifle jammed. He knew it immediately, having attended innumerable installations of other commissioners as well as three of his own. He stood and saluted and never brought it up to the Sikh sergeant-major decked out in his plumed turban with culgee. He simply went back to his ledger book and noted that hereafter, Mishtigunj shall have one eleventh of its annual rice allotment held back, each year of his term.

When he was fifty years old in 1924, and feeling thwarted in his Indian career, he decided to write an autobiography.

"I had a proper English childhood and do not regret any element of it. Following the death of my mother, my care was entrusted to my paternal uncles, hard-working and disciplined men charged with the task of preserving order and the law. They were town constables, and as a result of that early training, I grew to manhood respecting social order above all other human benefits. I might even say I am loath to embrace the slightest deviance from what I consider the norms of an ordered society. My uncles understood I was instinctively one of society's enforcers; therefore I can say I was never punished unjustly. I was denied nothing I absolutely required. Those who complain of their cruel and impoverished childhood might as well complain of unjust weather or brutal water."

Alas, it is no *Mist-nama,* or perhaps I should say that not every life is cut from the epic mold. I found no other pages, yet he never ceased to believe in his poetic gift. He was poetic in his fanciful moments, his love of tigers, and his memories of the rising mist. And of course, one is free to doubt the sincerity of any autobiography. Perhaps, as he'd begun to write, Vertie did love his uncles and perhaps their only limitation was a constipated sense of virtue. Why, then, did he stop the account so soon? As he thought about them, did his opinion change?

More pertinently, why did Vertie Treadwell fight so passionately against the colonial police, whom he considered ineffectual enforcers of colonial policy? Throughout the Empire but especially in India, the police detachments were becoming a force of growing power. In some districts they ran the show. It is inevitable when an occupying force loses its sense of mission but is still determined to hold on to power. The Indian independence movement had its political and militant wings. Gandhi was someone the Treadwells could handle; he and Nehru seemed to gather prestige from all their time in jail. But when it came to real, armed threats like Subhas Bose and his Indian National Army, you had to meet force with force. The Japanese Empire was openly challenging British power in Asia and no one knew when, and how, the external and internal threats would some day join.

He'd grown up on stories of India, the Straits, and East Africa and on tales of the glorious mission: subduing the ungrateful and recalcitrant, bringing order and dignity to lives of unimaginable ignorance, defending the British garrison. Each new tale threw his shoulders back, tightened the belly, straightened that famous spine and hardened that jaw just a little more. He sought models of exercise, push-ups, squats, sit-ups, weights, jumping jacks, sprints, undertaken on the coldest days in the briefest clothing, on the hottest days swaddled in wool cap and muffler.

Roundtree was talking, but he couldn't make out the words. His head was ringing. He recognized Staffy's face, and Plimpton's, and now both of them shaking him rather roughly. Roundtree looked positively Churchillian today, jowly and distinguished.

"Vertie, you're looking positively dreadful! We're getting

Teddy to drive you to hospital." They had to pluck him from his chair and lift him, using their hands like crutches under his arms.

"Gentlemen," he said, "I give you the king."

"Hear, hear. The king."

"God bless the king."

There were six of them in Mrs. Harpenny's. He had the two front rooms, and there were O'Day and Muggsy in another pair, and three singles downstairs for the junior clerks. She was a widowed Yorkshire woman with unmarried daughters, meaning she was always keen on letting rooms to each year's new recruits.

"Christ, I thought the fat old cow would never die."

"Now you know how Bertie feels."

"It does seem absurd. Sixty years old and fat as a German boar, and still a prince."

"Gentlemen, I give you princes everywhere, every age."

"Princely."

"I say, you reckon the champagne is chilled?"

"The last thing you need is champagne, Vertie. Try walking with us, one foot out, that's a good man, next foot. Christ, it's not the drink, is it?"

"The ice is melted, but the melt's not yet warm."

"Open the bleedin' bottle, Vertie."

He had a study with a bed pushed to one side and a presentable drawing room. All three on the upper floor shared the facilities, the usual Indian-style foul-smelling hole in the floor with footpads on either side, or buckets of still water for bathing. Pestilence breeds and indolence flourishes in all that heat. That which would not be tolerated a minute in England is allowed to fester in the tropics, rampant disorder of the most basic and correctable kind. And so, unable to modify the heat, one looks for accommodation.

A proper architectural axis was a beginning, avoid the south and west exposures. Wide eaves, trees to block the afternoon sun, perhaps a pond and marble floors to cool the raw assault of the air as it passed into the house. Mrs. Harpenny or more likely her late husband knew the local conditions and had studied the available models. They had intended to stay after his commission ran out or until their daughters were married, and they never foresaw the day when the wife might have to take in boarders and the daughters would have to shift for themselves and not be sent back to England for proper marriages.

The daughters proved themselves enthusiastic apprentice brides. Probably their parents never foresaw the possibility of their ripening, and fading, in the glare of Bombay. In waiting for marriage they'd become right smart little tarts, building their trousseaux off nickered goods from trading ships.

It occurred to him suddenly that he'd got it all wrong. It was in '97, in Bombay, during the Golden Jubilee, that they'd toasted the queen with champagne. That was the year the old crone's youngest daughter—Agnes?—had gotten herself in a spot of trouble. It was disturbing and quite unlike him to confuse the Empress of India's Diamond Jubilee with her death in '01; the high spirits of '97, the Bombay cricket, the races, the fine political edge honed in the gymkhana with veteran officers, with forty-six years of loutish company in brutish postings. Where was Muggsy, where was O'Day? The night of the old sow's death he'd been drinking in the Meerut cantonment. A telegram had come in. "The Queen is dead, long live the King!" A few old officers were glum and crying and started a dreary chorus of "God Save the King," but it sounded strange to their ears and they quickly changed it to "Queen." Everyone else was running about, clinking glasses to the new king. Everyone under fifty was tired of being Victorian.

O'Day as usual was holding forth, showing off for the benefit of the Harpenny daughters. Little did they know it was sober old Treadwell who got the predawn visits.

"That mob in the colonial office never could figure why we come out. All that bloody hectoring on reports and maintaining order and respect for the Crown—"

"It's the sex, hot and heavy."

"Reckon they felt we could put two and two together."

"Two and two? Never seen a two. It's pure one and aught if you ask me."

"One goes into zero and it always comes out zero. Multiply by it, divide by it, it's always zero."

"As long as my one slips into her aught, I don't care."

"I find the quickest way is just to drop your eyes directly to her bosom. Stare at them as you talk. Never look up. Undress her with your eyes. I guarantee you she'll stop around that night saying she forgot something or needs a favor for a friend. As soon as she can get away from her bloody brothers and father and maybe a husband. That's your sign, man. Pounce!"

"In the night you'll find they have their little charms. Quite surprising, some are. Wonder where they learn it."

"Brothers and fathers, doubtless."

Treadwell opined that looking at their breasts doesn't seem manly. Much better to address the woman directly, express an interest, establish a price, set an appointment time and be done with it.

"Manly?" Muggsy asked. "Vertie, good God, man, we're not talking about manly things. We're talking about princely things. In the vernacular, of boffing a nigger."

They never guessed about Agnes Harpenny and why she took the trip to the hills that summer. A boy, he'd heard, and Mrs.

Harpenny turned from lovey-dovey granny and aspiring mother-in-law to petitioner before the court. Boffing a Yorkshire strumpet was a damned sight more perilous than reaching an orderly arrangement with a sensible native girl. Bombay was crawling with English girls begging to get out any way they could. A few, of course, made it. Others only claimed full British status, but look in their eyes and you'd see the mongrel traces. They were desperate enough, you'd think, to show a little gratitude rather than ruin a man's career over a spot of fun in the night.

Yes, he'd sorted it out. He wasn't in Bombay the night the old sow died. Bombay was the Jubilee. The night he ceased to be a Victorian he'd been drinking and smoking alone at a table in the gymkhana of the Meerut cantonment. He didn't know anyone in Meerut, since he'd been stashed in a primitive district a week's river-and-train passage away. The most pestilential district in all of India, an Oxford man among the grub-eaters and tree-worshipers with a literary rate of two percent and every disease known and unknown running rampant.

He'd found the table in the gymkhana, better to inspect the serving girls, while catching a view of the available women lounging about outside. Two months' abstinence in the jungle, one weekend of "consultations" in Meerut; it was the formula for a bachelor's long-term sanity. A young man could self-combust in the tropics. He preferred sitting alone, he wasn't the type to roam about the great hall with a pint of lager looking to cadge a fag from a bunch of strangers.

Bloody Meerut. Bloody United Provinces, Orissa, Bombay, Calcutta, Mishtigunj, a pox on the whole putrescent continent.

He and his sister, a girl in an ayah's arms whose face he sometimes recalled, unless he'd confused it with his daughter's, were born in Ootycomund. His dear children were born in India. India

194

was his country. His parents and grandparents were born, or had died, in India. His mother lies in the Anglican Cemetery of Mysore. She was a Canning, does that not count for something? When his father had fallen in the Sudan with Gordon Pasha, they'd found his last instructions stitched into his tunic: *Do not condemn me to a second English death. Bury me beside my wife in Mysore.*

And what did the future hold for him, unhoused by India, told he had no right to a plot of Indian soil? His son and daughter had abandoned him; he had no fool to accompany him, no blasted heath to walk upon. Thank the Lord he'd been able to secure that tiny St. Alban's slip next to the great ship Octavius Rutledge. They could converse all eternity in Greek and Latin and read Hopkins for light entertainment. Otherwise he'd moulder till the Resurrection beside two buggering uncles in East Anglia.

He remembered draining a "tank" down in the United Provinces, watching the fish trapped in the diminishing water-supply froth to the surface. Whoever guessed such big fish lived at the bottom of such a modest pool? He remembered their thick lips rising to the surface, gulping air. It is India, he'd thought, the surging population, diminished space and resources. Now, he realized, it is England, too. Elevation of the brutish bottom-feeders, survival of the leeches and reptiles. Rapid death of the light-seeking, the surface-skimming.

He thought of a mantis, newly hatched, crawling to the end of a blackened branch. The mantis swiveled her head and stared back at him.

3

He heard words he couldn't understand. "Cascading event," in a grotesque accent he couldn't quite place. He was on his back looking into a focused beam of sharp light with a nigger's face behind it.

"Meestah Treadwell," the voice was saying, "cahn you hear me? You have suffered a cranial event. A stroke. Cahn you undastand?" He tried to answer, *Of course I can hear you, you bloody idiot,* but the words clotted in his throat and he flayed his hands, reaching for the nigger's white coat but only brushing against a stethoscope.

"Your friends have called your wife. She will be here presently."

Will you stop your infernal interference you beastly little sweeper? He could imagine how she'd take the news, especially if delivered by Muggsy or the coppers. *Passed out in the pub, did he? I reckon he could use a night in hospital to sober up.*

"I must ask, how long ago did this happen? Your friends said you arrived at the pub with these abrasions."

There was an elusive figure dancing just out of sight. Certainly she was here, enjoying every minute of his distress. He could just make her out, the gray hair, her face darting in and out of view from behind the doctor. You dare to ask me how long ago this happened? I want to sleep, he tried to say. And get that bloody light out of my eyes.

He tried to reach out again, but his arms wouldn't move. *How long ago did this happen?* Cheeky devil has no right of inquiry, no standing in this court. How long ago did what happen, exactly? Fifty years, plus or minus.

He could make out their voices but not the meaning. If they spoke English instead of their vile patois it might help. But of course nothing in England exists these days for the comfort of the patient, unless he's been crushed in a coal mine by a capitalist trolley or run over by his drunken lordship in a Bentley. Then they'd rush to comfort him, oh, yes; he'd be a front-page victim of class brutality! He heard the words "very distinguished" and what might be Roundtree's reassuring voice. Staffy Roundtree will set them straight who they're dealing with. Roundtree on the Honours List, where I will be next year. Places on the Honours List, with a few exceptions, are reserved these days for Bolshie lackeys, those who can prove their treachery to the Crown.

Bloody Naseer Ahmed, K.C., O.B.E.

He had written his notice many times. He inserted it into the papers every day. A modest headline, lower left corner of the front page, details within. As he walked to the Lion he often rehearsed the proper signs of modesty. A stoop, a smile, a tip of the cap. "Long overdue" was certainly appropriate, but unseemly coming from his lips. "So many are worthy," he would say. "It was perhaps inevitable, after all, I have served king and country for nearly half a century, but such recognition is never predictable. . . . Yes, yes, distinguished company, to be sure. . . . I shine brighter in their glory." The boys in the Lion would be standing, and there would be a bucket of champagne cooling on the counter, opened by Teddy Rowan precisely at the moment of his arrival.

Hear, hear, Vertie! Hip, hip. For he's a jolly good fellow.

His public acknowledgment, simple but poetic, went: *Virgil Treadwell and Winston Churchill are cast from the same historic mold, born in the same year, 1874, and on the same day, November 30, and were taught similar values, exposed to the same pride and shame at the same age and through the same eyes. Neither, until today, has received the honours owing them for their long and selfless service to the Crown.*

That Winston Churchill had not been knighted galled him almost as much as his own absence from the Honours List. How to explain it but through conspiracy?

Many's the time he had taken up his pen to express his commiseration with the great man, then withdrawn, thinking it perhaps immodest to intrude on his retirement. It was understood that after a lifetime's service, he was writing. And not just his memoirs, but those of the entire English-speaking peoples. *Half a century we have toiled in the service of our Empire,* he once began. *My brave and brilliant mentor: The ingratitude of our subjects is to be expected. It is that of our masters that turns our heart to stone.* Interesting to see if he included any Indians among the English-speaking peoples.

English-speaking peoples: There's a jab there. Welsh and Irish and Australians and Americans are all fundamentally English. There's a huge difference between speaking it and actually being it. Jamaicans, Trinidadians, and the bloody Bengalis mimic a decent English, even Chinese out of Singapore and Hong Kong can do a fair job of copying the standard accent, if only to use our language against us, like bloody Naseer Ahmed of the Honours List. There were quite a number of things he might have done differently, had he occupied Churchill's high position, but the faults, like the differences between them, were small and of little consequence.

Virgil Treadwell understood the great man and sympathized with every agonized step along his road to defeat. He grieved with him for the collapse of the Empire. They had fought the same wars against the same debased savages—not just the Boers and the Huns—but the Gadarenes who ruled, the parliamentary blockheads and a brutish opposition, detestable viceroys and mischievous district commissioners. He'd been spared the discomforts, the indignities. It was Churchill himself, when the great man served as colonial secretary, for whom Vertie had spiced up his reports, throwing in the sly Greek and Latin references, not that they ever rose above the district desk in Meerut or, with luck, New Delhi.

It was indescribably decent of the man to help him celebrate now. "Virgil Treadwell," he said, "of course!" And with the King, a surprise; it was all a little grand.

"If I may, your majesty, I should like to address the British public on this most auspicious moment of my life."

"By all means, my dear fellow. We are most interested."

Like his friend Churchill, Treadwell was given to oracular pronouncements. He had been raised with the insights that come from experiencing the same events at the same age, the same theater, the same songs, the same sporting events, the same historic moments and unspoken agreements and identical frustrations. They could play the "Where were you when . . . ?" game.

"Hear, hear."

If what I am about to say seems harsh, it is only because we've grown accustomed to cringing before uniformed opinion. The King edged forward; Churchill beamed.

I shall not hold back. I am one of the India-born. Fully ninety percent of my life has been spent in India. I have probably spent a greater percentage of my life in India than Mr. Nehru has, and certainly more than the late Mr. Gandhi has. I have participated in many of India's greatest moments. I have endeavored, from love, to keep India free of modern contaminants. The indisputable truth, however they twist it, is that we built their country, and we saved them from their own bloodsucking tyrants, their ignorance, their indescribable filth and superstition. Yet they have the gall to serve notice on families that have known no reality but India's for two hundred years, loved nothing but Indians, served nothing but India's needs, and buried untold thousands of their children and wives in that malodorous, malarial muck, that steaming bog of vile licentiousness. My own mother and father are buried there.

"We are so terribly sorry, my dear man. Such dramatic service to one's country comes at a cost that is too infrequently expressed." The King offered a mild but sincere nod, then toddled off.

Churchill clipped the tip of a fresh cigar. "His heart is in the right place, poor fellow. If I am not mistaken, Treadwell, you tried to save the Empire."

"That I did. My only crime, if I say so myself."

"Let us sit here in the dark. I too am partially obscured these past few years. Fortunately, when the sword is in its scabbard, the pen comes out to slash and parry. Let us have a brandy, and why don't you tell me the full story. We're in no hurry. Perhaps I can put the word out, get your name on the proper registers. Perhaps you'll tell me a thing or two I can use in my History. True heroes are a vanishing breed, but I need not tell you, of all people. I hold you in the highest esteem, Treadwell."

—Where to begin? Treadwells have held positions of rank and responsibility in East Anglia for over half a millennium. Too grand, perhaps, too sweeping. The first Treadwell came out to India in 1743. My mother is a Canning. Father died in the Sudan with Gordon Pasha. The glories, the indignities, the grim, daily rounds of stewardship. The predawn rides, the tiger-trails, the hundred and twenty-five tiger pelts, and a hundred volumes of meteorological data. All of that and volumes more need recounting, simply to understand the background of the last Treadwell to serve the Crown in India. For thirty years without complaint I served among some of the most backward people of India. Stone Age people, tribal people, grub-eaters, and tree-worshipers. The literacy rate in my district was under two percent. Every disease imaginable, rampant.

—Bestial conditions, Churchill remarked.

I begged the colonial office for civilized help. A teacher, a doctor, someone with whom I could hold a decent British conversation.

In 1930, I was appointed District Commissioner in Mishtigunj, a port in the Sunderbans. Seditious elements were already at work down there. You are of course fully aware of the role played by Subhas Bose and the Indian National Army.

—Bloody Nazi, bloody Jap sympathizer. I'd have strung him up.

Precisely my sentiments. We had him in jail many times. There are many ways to stage a death in prison. There would be no official inquiry. We could weather the predictable outrage. In my estimation, we lack the taste for enlightened extermination. If we'd eliminated half a dozen of those beggars, the Empire would still rule the world.

Mr. Churchill was not quite finished with the subject.—I hate Indians. They are a beastly people with a beastly religion. Your African, on the other hand, is a stout fellow. Proud, loyal to a fault, a regular Gurkha. What do you say, Treadwell?

Having had fifty years' experience living intimately with them, sir, I would not be quite so categorical, or quite so harsh. More often than not they were misguided children, but shown the proper authority rationally administered the vast majority very quickly adjusted their attitudes. I would draw your attention to that Austrian charlatan—

—Dr. Freud, I presume?

The same. Do I surprise you with my casual erudition, Mr. Churchill? Given the postings I've endured, Blackwell's has been my only companion. His Majesty's several governments have not sufficiently moved the masses of India from libidinous superstition into a mature ego structure.

—Translated, you mean Indians are stuck in childhood and we are expecting too much of them?

And, therefore, too much of ourselves.

—Three hundred million of them, dumped in our care, said Churchill.

Except, of course, the Bengalis and especially the brahmins. He didn't know Africans or even the Gurkhas. He couldn't bring himself to raise an objection to Winston Churchill, savior of the nation, not in public.

Indeed, he heard himself agreeing. And all of Kipling, gets it right every time. The man's a wonder. Uncanny gift.

The manly aroma of cigar smoke and brandy filled the room,

that, and old leather—the eau de cologne of Empire—the click of
billiard balls, the rustle of fresh-off-the-boat London papers, the
thunking of ice-cubes tonged into a glass, the coughs, the wheez-
ing snores, the gymkhana at peace, in control. A Kipling mood.
Kipling sounds. He couldn't see Churchill now in the dark, but it
was reassuring just knowing he was out there and would be carrying his name forward at the highest levels.

He'd been told there was a certain lady in that Sunderbans
town whom he had to meet. Meet, that is, with an eye to cultivation. Her name was Gangooly; naturally, a brahmin. He thought
very little of it at first but her name kept recurring with the most
extraordinary tales attached to it.

—Mr. Treadwell? Please respond. Do you hear me?

What sort of tales? I hardly know where to begin. Indeed,
there are too many openings. You must know about that woman
but also about the village and about the founder of the village and
the history of the Sunderbans and maybe even about my parents
and my uncles in Brynnsmere. They all have a bearing, and how
many opportunities will I have to sit down with such an admired
figure as yourself and discuss them all? My uncles, sir, were the
most stalwart defenders of propriety the world has ever seen.
They were sticklers for regulations and details and I learned a
great deal from them that has proved helpful in my career as a
colonial administrator.

—But they buggered each other up the arse, isn't that what
you're saying, Mr. Treadwell? Incestuous sodomy, brothers in pan-
syhood. One rarely encounters such depraved behavior, even
among members of that sordid fraternity. You're not Irish, I take it.

I was never a witness to any such, sir. And I am English,
with a touch of Lowland Scot three generations back. On the
maternal side.

—How many bedrooms were there in the cottage?

Only one, sir. I slept on a pile of bedclothes in the parlor.

—Well, that's settled, then, is it not? Tell me more about this woman.

How had Churchill so easily guessed his deepest shame? The man's brilliance was uncanny. The secret of his uncles' oddity was the last thing he would ever divulge, and he never had. It was an article of faith with Vertie Treadwell that if references to his uncles ever arose they should be couched only in the most reverential of terms.

—I warn you, sir, I am reasonably well read in terms of human behavior and motivation and I will not be trifled with. Even great men at times need to be set aright.

An extra-thick cloud of smoke was sent his way.

She had been married to a tree—yes, you heard me correctly—and that's just the beginning. It seems incredible but if you know the Hindu mind and that backward region as I perforce do you can believe just about anything. The town itself was founded by a rather typical exemplum of the last century's excess, the sort of Sunderbans cutthroat attracted to the pestiferous jungles by the absence of British authority. To be attracted to the absence of legitimacy tells you a great deal right there.

In this case he was an escaped murderer by the name of John Mist. I think it is safe to say he saw himself as the Napoleon Bonaparte of the Bengal forests, a tyrant and a dictator with pretensions to omnipotence. He had gone totally native, didn't speak a word of English, forged an alliance between Mussalmans and Hindus and insinuated some money into schools and whatnot. Illiterate as the day he was born but a self-styled scientist. I'm speaking only of his legacy. The town schools did turn out a rather high number of scholars who went on to Dacca and even

Calcutta for advanced training. We are indebted to him for having established a very reliable guide to local flora and fauna as well as a meticulous record of tides and winds and rainfall, onset and vigor of monsoons, et cetera. Autodidacts, oddly enough, are quite often the most faithful of record keepers.

—It's not odd at all, Treadwell. All genius is self-taught.

You can imagine this fellow's surprise when the first act of the Crown was to arrest him for heinous crimes committed in Calcutta fifty years earlier. He was a common thief and sexual pervert, you understand, a bloodthirsty grotesque with only one eye. He had ravished a company wife on her voyage out to Calcutta, then fomented a mutiny to cover his crime. He and a confederate escaped from the Black Hole and made their way into the director's mansion where a meeting was underway. Guns blazing, they fell upon the innocent civilians and in the ensuing slaughter murdered perhaps half a dozen, women and children included.

If this Mist chap had been your typical Sunderbans escapee, they might well have left him be. But the Crown thought it necessary to set an example. If we didn't hang him and his Mohammedan accomplice in public, the credulous beggars would think he might come back. They say he smiled when they put the noose around his neck. Cheeky bastard even inspected it before he allowed it to be slipped on. According to legend his final words were *"Chalo. Kajey hat lagao,"* which means roughly, "Let's get on with it." You still hear those words on the streets. I must salute my unnamed predecessor in the collector's bungalow who exhibited unaccustomed steadfastness. Hanged the blackguards within the week.

—Treadwell, Treadwell, you were speaking of the woman.

The woman was a hardened case in many ways. I have never met an Indian woman more obdurate than Miss Gangooly. We knew she had been financing Gandhi and then she broke with him and started supporting this Subhas Bose. She seemed to have abandoned the rational and, I might say, containable, course of nonviolence for some sort of alliance with the devil himself.

—Odious chap. There's a man to hang on the spot.

We knew her house was a veritable printing press and munitions factory for seditious elements. Somehow or other every arrest we made throughout the district got reported to her first and if any detainee happened to meet with an unfortunate outcome in colonial custody she'd be the first to announce it. She probably maintained a network of informants in every village and there were over two hundred stations in the district, most of which I had never visited myself. And you must remember, sir, that she never set foot outside her compound. At least, according to rumors.

I paid my first visit to her house back in '31. Townsfolk called it Mist Mahal, for the original builder. It had been well-designed, rather like the two-storied Garden Reach mansions in Calcutta. She was most gracious, as these brahmins often are. They might not tolerate the shadow of a lower-caste Hindu but they cozy up to a white face very well. You and I, sir, and this latter woman, are of the same age, all of us born in 1874. You and I, in case I had not already mentioned it, share a coincidental birth date of November thirtieth, in fact. I never inquired as to her actual birth date.

—I find very little significance in raw coincidence, Treadwell. I'm sure we share the thirtieth of November with hosts of beggars and scoundrels.

Whatever you say, sir. The upshot is, she was a woman of fifty-three years when we first met. She wore her hair short in a bob but I don't think fashion was her purpose. It was practical, and since she didn't have to please a husband she could wear it any way that suited her. It had turned gray. She was a handsome woman, but

not initially attractive in a womanly way. Her face was too strong
and her eyebrows too assertive. She had taught herself to read and
write very forceful English, which was most uncommon for
women in that time and place, but she'd had little opportunity to
practice speaking it so that her speech was fluent but very difficult to decipher. I wouldn't even call it an Indian accent. I would
just say it was a rendition of English known only to her. It took
me the better part of that first visit before I got the hang of what
she was trying to say.

—And what is it, in your rendition, that she was trying to say?

She asked me an extraordinary question. She asked if I was
familiar with the work of a certain young British author named
George Orwell. In 1931, even well-read men had not heard of Mr.
Orwell. She mentioned hearing of a piece of his called "A Hanging." She said, I am told he is a most extraordinary author. I confessed to her that I had never heard of Mr. Orwell. I assumed he
might be some sort of romance writer whom Indian women are
fond of reading, especially those in isolated circumstances. I
began to understand the purpose of her question much later, only
after I had read some of his filthy tracts on the colonial administration in Upper Burma.

—You believe she was testing your sentiments, is that it? Had
you expressed an opinion on Mr. Orwell at that time, one way or
another, she would have known what kind of friend or foe you
were? Or was she arrogantly parading her own sentiments?

The former, I think. On the first visit I was protected by my
ignorance of that obscure hack. But I used Mr. Orwell to my
advantage later on, as you are perhaps aware.

—Protected by ignorance? You're rather proud of your gift for
the phrase, are you not, Treadwell? But I shouldn't get overly
attached to that means of defense.

I believe she was organizing an infamous attack on me. It is quite clear to me that she aimed at nothing less than my assassination. Just a fortnight after that initial visit I was attacked by a small army of her defenders as I quite innocently made my way down a lane near the Mist Mahal. They left me for dead. But had I made a full report, including my suspicions as to the origins and intent of the attack, we might have faced an insurrection that we were ill prepared to suppress.

—How very brave and calculating of you, Treadwell.

You see, I had managed to find a copy of that piece of trash she'd inquired about and arrange to have it delivered to her house as a gift. It concerns a case of swift justice meted out to a Bengali terrorist, actually. You now grasp the intent of her question, do you not? I believe she knew the case or was seeking to learn more about it and to circulate it among her confederates. If you've had a chance to study the warrant for her arrest in '42, you will find that possession of proscribed literature is near the top of the list. It names two pieces of writing, one being the magazine containing "A Hanging" and the other a reprehensible novel called *Burmese Days*. I knew she possessed them, because I had been their purveyor.

As I mentioned, she was most gracious on that first meeting, offering tea and biscuits although I would have preferred a stiff drink. She even inquired as to my opinion on an article dealing with that odious chap Subhas Bose, something in the *Times* which had not yet been received in the gymkhana. How she might have received it, considering that she never left her compound, I cannot begin to fathom.

—I should think she was indicating that she had contacts of slightly higher rank than yourself, Treadwell.

As she in fact did, sir. You are referring of course to that Bolshie in Calcutta, Coughlin, are you not? He had not yet been exposed for the double-dealer he was. In fact, he tried to make himself useful to me by sending items of incidental intelligence whenever I asked for them. I had no idea that Bolshies had risen so high in the colonial administration. Of course, now they run the government. My intent on that first visit was merely to communicate to her the fact that His Majesty's government would not tolerate any real or apparent support of Subhas Bose. I said to her that we wished to work cooperatively with all native elements, especially those in leadership positions. I suggested that since she occupied a revered place in the community, we expected greater signs of cooperation from her than we did from ordinary folk.

—A prudent position, Treadwell. You had praised her and warned her at the same time.

Her answer was most unsatisfactory. She said the only government she recognized was that of the Congress Party of India through its Bengal chairman, Subhas Bose.

—A most difficult situation. I sympathize. We had the whole lot of them in prison, Gandhi, Nehru, Bose. They should never have released them.

In truth, Miss Gangooly was revered as a god. Hindus are prone to excessive forms of idolatry. There are more than three hundred and fifty million Indians and someone once calculated that there are more than three hundred million named gods. A god for everyone and everything. A god for the sun, a god for rain, a god for the tree, for the leaves on the tree, for the fruit on the branch, the worm in the fruit, the bird that eats the worm, the bat that eats the fruit, the monkey that eats them all . . .

—Three hundred million backward people entrusted to our care, it boggles the mind. It hardens the heart as well. Gods and administrators don't mix, Churchill observed.

That reminds me, sir, of rather a comic encounter from an earlier posting. This goes back many years to the United Provinces. I once gave a shouting to Raman, my Tamilian secretary, who spent fifteen minutes of every day in his bloody midday prayers. He would rig up a kind of Hindu altar on the porch with brass pots and flowers—the commissioner's porch, mind you—and squat before them with a big smear of orange curd on his forehead. Well, I stormed out of my study and kicked the bloody pot all the way to Timbuktu. *There'll be none of that on my porch,* I said.

And in what, you might rightly ask, does such a profound act of piety, such a ritual of devotion consist? It consisted of Raman squatting rather noisily on my porch, rattling off the names of every god from a blade of grass up to the vultures circling overhead. *Where the hell does all this end?* That's what I demanded. He would have sat there all day, all year, if I hadn't hauled him back to the ledger books by his scruffy little neck. It's what I mean by childish behavior. This is what we saved them from!

He looked up at me with new respect, let me tell you. He was truly terrified. That's how you have to treat them. *Sahib, it does not ever end.* There's his wisdom, for you. That's all he could say.

—I believe I have already stated that I find Indians a beastly people with a beastly religion behind them, said Mr. Churchill.

Well, she was another one of them. She'd managed to take the curse of virginity—the worst thing a woman can be in that country—and elevate it into something worthy of a Catholic saint. Not that I believed for a moment that she was a virgin or anything close to it. Her house was seething with young men and she was surrounded by a virtual army of goondahs. Violent men, wanted men. Most of them ended up in prison.

Mr. Churchill? Winston?

He heard only a distant response. —I must be going soon.
Don't stop now.

In her youth she'd trained all her servants to read and write
and then she'd sent them out into the villages to teach five others.
Every day there'd be a knot of women sitting outside her door
praying to Tara-Ma. Praying for children, if you can believe it,
praying for sons, praying for healthy sons, praying for a husband,
for a sober husband—she who knew nothing of husbands and
children.

That's one reason it's so bloody hard to govern. How would you
like to maintain colonial control over a bunch of literate savages
that reserve the right to second-guess your every decision? I had
the sense there was always someone looking over my shoulder. An
uneasy feeling, is it not? Beastly people, as you have rightly said.

Winston?

Having had thirty years' experience in the most desperate
backwaters of the United Provinces and fifteen years in the jungles of Bengal, I can say I should much prefer to govern a tribe of
headhunters than a collection of disputatious Bengalis. A wise
man whose name escapes me now once called me a natural ruler, a
lion among men, much like yourself—although I rather prefer
the tiger, among major predators. In the kingdom of the blind,
you understand, he had determined that I had one good eye. In
the case of the Bengalis, a man-eating tiger would not be misplaced as a symbol of authority.

Churchill shifted in his armchair. He said, A wise man whose
name also seems to have escaped you once stated that to trade
with civilized men is infinitely more profitable than to govern
savages. It's been instructive, Treadwell, but I must be on my way.

"Winston!" he cried.

—I am here, she said.

He knew that voice and mangled accent. I knew you would come back.

—You will soon know what death is like, Mr. Treadwell. There are no more secrets. There is time only for your confessions, if you wish.

I want you to know I had nothing to do with any of that unfortunate business with the police. You brought it on yourself with your illegal activities and unsavory associates. I warned you but you refused my protection. Terrible things happen in wartime, why couldn't you understand? The hands of civilian administrators are tied. And there was the matter of Bose. Why did you not repudiate him?

—You perhaps have heard the story of my marriage when I was five years old. Yes, it was to a tree, for which I am grateful. My father was a visionary and marriage saved me from a life of widowhood. You probably have heard that I never left Mist Mahal until the night your Sergeant Mackenzie came calling, but that is not true—

I knew it!

—It is not what you imagine. When I was a married woman of six years, the British marched into Mishtigunj and took immediate possession of the compound. On that night, my father and I, and Mr. Mist and Mr. Hai, were seated on a mat. They were drinking tea. Musicians had been called in. It was to be a regular mela for the entire town. But the soldiers arrived with their rifles out and bayonets drawn and proceeded to tie up Mr. Mist and Mr. Hai, the two most noble gentlemen I have ever known, and march them out the gates onto a waiting bullock cart. They were thrown into the cart like bundles of trash. The guests had just started to arrive. My father had been a famous pleader in Dhaka, so he was not to be silenced. He immediately began an oration outside the collector's bungalow where the poor men had been thrown onto the ground and dragged into their cells. A very young British officer slapped my father across the face and told him he would be shot on the spot for leading an insurrection should he open his mouth for another word. He was a very young, very junior soldier, with pink cheeks and bright blue eyes.

—A week later I was witness to the twin hangings of Mr. Hai and Mr. Mist. I was six years and five months old and I stood with my father eight hours at the base of the gallows. I can still hear him crying out, *Chalo. Kajey hat lagao.* And then my father started the chant Ram, Ram, Ram, and it was picked up by the entire village, even our Muslim brothers. I can hear that louder and clearer than any words of Mr. Gandhi or Mr. Nehru or even of Sergeant Mackenzie during his attempted interrogation. Everyone worshipped John Mist. He was our father and our mother. We named the village for him after he died.

He was a filthy murderer, Miss Gangooly, do not shed tears over the likes of him. The word I have is that he cold-bloodedly slaughtered an entire houseful of innocent women and children.

—On the contrary, Mr. Treadwell. He was but a child when he killed to protect a lady's honor.

East is East, Miss Gangooly. Persist in your fantasies. Blame the past if you will, but it was the arrival of a police detachment in 1931 that made administration, as I had known it, impossible. With Gandhi's popularity outside of Bengal and Bose's fanatical following inside it, the police role kept expanding. I had successfully blocked the attachment of a police contingent to my posting in the United Provinces. I share some of the characteristics of the tiger. No other male dare intrude upon my territory. I am not referring to the native police, the various subinspectors, *deoghars,* and what have you. Native police are a necessary irritant, but they have contacts and the means to extract valuable information. It goes without saying they are corrupt and at times needlessly aggressive. But it is important to have someone with his ear to the ground who is also entirely under the thumb of a civil authority. It is also true that without them, fully three quarters of the crimes committed in any district would go unpunished. When I arrived in Mishtigunj, however, I found the police contingent practically waiting at my door.

—Had you not been complaining of your loneliness, Mr. Treadwell? I should think you would welcome a colleague.

I had imagined a different sort, madam. Older, perhaps a doctor, a teacher, or even a missionary. I'll have you know, I am a well-read man. I had looked forward to refined company as I rose through the civil service. That, apparently, was not to be my fate. I believe I can achieve the same results as the police without alienating the local populace. It is still my intention to write a tract on noncoercive intelligence gathering. It is true I had been asking for companionship for thirty years, and even begged for it in a number of humbling circumstances, but when they finally sent me someone, I found myself totally incapable of communication. His suitability for the post was all too perfect, like a hyena's in a hen house.

The man to whom you refer is Dominick Mackenzie. That's with an "a." Scotch by name, Irish by upbringing, but entirely English from his schooling and accent. I always took Dominick for a Catholic name but he swore up and down that he was Orange to his bones. That odd background always made me feel uneasy in his presence. I had no confidence that my vast experience in India and his rather short posting were in any way complementary. My aim was always the preservation of British rule through the cooperation of enlightened native elites. Win over the elites and the rabble will follow. His methods, in my opinion, guaranteed the precise opposite, which, I am sad to say, the record has borne out. When he drew upon precedent, it was likely to be from a textbook, or Nigeria, where the nature of common criminality has no Indian parallel. On the other hand, Indian involvement in seditious activity and their subtle mastery of the arts of subterfuge are infinitely more nefarious than anything he had ever encountered, except perhaps in Ireland.

I want you to know I had nothing to do with Mackenzie's activities, or his methods. We were on nonparallel tracks, destined to collide. I tried to protect you. Shortly after our first interview, I made an effort to find the work to which you had alluded, Mr. Orwell's little trifle entitled "A Hanging." I'd met a chap in Calcutta, Nigel Coughlin, a well-placed sodomite, secretary to the Eastern Army general staff. Orwell was just the sort of Bolshie intriguer a sympathizer like Coughlin would have in his library, which he did.

—Mr. Treadwell, if I may, I think you fail to give sufficient credit to Mr. Coughlin. It is true he was a man of divided political loyalties. Of sexual practices between British men, whatever their form and nature, I keep my own counsel, but I have every reason to believe he was a sincere friend of India.

And of Russia, and of Subhas Bose. Sodomites have no sense of loyalty, Miss Gangooly. On this topic, I happen to be well-informed. It was clear to me where Orwell's sympathies lay, despite his infiltration of the colonial police, and the virus he could unleash if given widespread dissemination.

—You are unaware, Mr. Treadwell, that Mr. Coughlin made many secret trips to Mishtigunj to keep me informed of British troop movements. I loved listening to him! I asked him once where one procures such an extravagant accent and he said Liverpool Irish underlying a Cambridge scholarship. Merseybridge, he called it.

Miss Gangooly, it pains me to inform you that after Coughlin's secret meetings with you he went promptly to the police *thana* and divulged the contents of your most private discussions directly to Dominick Mackenzie.

—Ah, but you do not know what he divulged to the police. He was a communist, as you say, therefore most critical of Subhas Bose's cultivation of German and Japanese fascists to force an earlier withdrawal of British interests. He was equally opposed to the continuation of British rule in India. It placed him in an awkward position. He was a most isolated figure. Almost tragic, some would say, was he not, Mr. Treadwell? Vertie, isn't it?

It is. It would give me great pleasure if you addressed me as Vertie. And if I may call you Tara Lata.

—Why not, Vertie, we are both of us well beyond the ceremonial threshold, are we not? If what you say of Mr. Mackenzie is true, why did you capitulate before his allegations? You calumnied me and my people, you sanctioned the deaths of thousands, and now it is time for you to prove your allegations.

My allegations were proven in court. They are now called undisputed facts.

—Not in court. To me. Your so-called undisputed facts murdered me, Vertie. You have me conspiring in the overthrow of the British Empire in India. Had I been permitted a day in court, I could have disproved all of your allegations. You bring up the name of Subhas Bose to defend your every action, but you do not mention the famine, caused by your shortsighted practices. Thanks to Mister Coughlin, we know you withheld several thousand tons of rice from our district, purely from spite. You carefully catalog every book and periodical in my possession, but not ten thousand tons of rice and pulses in your godown. You burned them, Vertie. You burned tons of rice rather than see them distributed to starving villagers.

That was Mackenzie's affair. I too found it needlessly harsh and counterproductive and I wrote him up in precisely those words. In their heart of hearts I am convinced that the Bengali people were exceedingly supportive of British rule. The average Bengali was prepared to wait a hundred years if necessary for a peaceful transfer of power.

—You are mistaken, as usual. I believe I know the sentiments of my people more accurately than any foreigner. I share the sentiments of one hundred percent of Bengalis. I admit only to having in my possession the eyewitness accounts of atrocities committed by British troops and police against unarmed villagers in the district of Mishtigunj.

Madam, I do not want to hear the name of that odious settlement one more time.

—Mishtigunj, she said.

Miss Gangooly? All was black, and silent. Tara Lata?

He remembered a small aspect of Mr. Orwell's writing on Burma that he had found sympathetic. It was called *Burmese Days* and there were moments in it that had brought him close to tears. The wretch had managed to animate quite convincingly the loneliness and isolation of colonial administration, the intolerable workload, the ingratitude from local, national, and London authorities. The futility, the myriad small humiliations. Raman and his brass pots, but afterward, deliberate misspellings and mislaid files. In that squalid village of Mishtigunj, someone had managed to push a long bamboo pole with a hook attached to the end through the bars of his bungalow window and lift his dentures from the glass on his nightstand. It was a political theft.

They could have lifted his purse, his briefcase, his silk jacket, but the bloody beggars knew how to strike at the heart of colonial authority, forcing the cancellation of all appearances and the suspension of court sessions until a reasonable facsimile could be fashioned and sent from London.

If you think I'm leaving Bombay with our daughter for that bloody jungle outpost in the back of beyond you're absolutely mad, Vertie!

Iris! Irene!

Never to enjoy the company of an upright British woman, to be condemned to the counterfeit embrace of paid or coerced consorts.

He remembered how oddly striking Miss Gangooly had appeared to him on that first visit, with her short, graying hair and assertive features, and he thought that since he possessed the piece of Orwell trash about the hanging of a Bengali anarchist that she'd requested, perhaps he could deliver it to her personally. Why should he deprive himself of companionship just because the government had seen fit to isolate him in a corner of nowhere? She would be happy to see him. Had he not felt intimations of interest from her, signs of a not unwelcoming nature? During their first interview he had dropped his gaze to her bosom and she had not colored or squirmed in discomfort. Indeed, she seemed to have dropped her gaze impudently onto his lap despite his steady crossing and uncrossing of his legs. At the very least, these were indications that he should press his case. We can drop the pretense of her virginity, with her house and compound practically bristling with a small army of virile young men, her steady gaze and brazen confidence, even in the company of males and superiors. He was willing to overlook their unequal status. They were simply an unattached man and woman, finding themselves in a negotiable posture.

The more he thought about it the more daring it seemed, and

the more daring, the more inevitable. Not only would an adult relationship be a palliative to his appalling loneliness, but a significant assault on the fortress of brahmin rectitude. He could also defend their lovemaking out of administrative advantage. He would be a spy within the very heart of the enemy camp. Noncoercive intelligence gathering, indeed!

He set out at dusk in casual clothes, carrying the magazine containing the piece of seditious trash. Before fifteen minutes had elapsed, the subtropical skies had darkened, and he found himself walking like a blind man along a broken footpath in the dark, with only the moon's reflection off white street dogs guiding him. Occasionally a rickshaw passed, its old man straining hard to pull a fat brahmin on a high bench, the lantern swinging from the passenger's canopy, and he wondered how they did not shank a leg with every outing in the dark.

There is no emptiness to compare with an Indian night, at least in the unelectrified small towns and villages. It is all enveloping, trousers and shoes are invisible unless one wears khadi under a full moon. And on moonless nights the skies are glorious with stars. He was something of an amateur in those matters, but he did possess a small telescope and made it his practice to note for posterity certain periodicities. It would be useful for his successors to have a reliable date book of first risings of constellations, first flowerings, onset and duration of monsoons, et cetera. They could be called the Treadwell Tables.

He is feeling once again the terror of a black, Indian night. That swinging lantern seems suddenly so ominous. The huts are dark, because families still live by the natural rhythms. He could drop into a twenty-foot hole, like an open grave, with any step. That seems to sum up his entire Indian experience. A giant hole in the dark that could swallow him and every valuable thing he'd ever done, without warning.

Mist Mahal is equipped with oil lamps and he can see it faintly behind a high, glass-topped wall. He makes his way slowly, as though plowing through mire or water, ignoring the open grave at his feet. The usual knot of pilgrims outside the gate has fallen asleep. A small fire sputters to its acrid, cow-dung coals. He pushes on the iron bars and it swings loudly on rusted hinges, waking the old chowkidar.

Sahib, no angrezi, but the chowkidar's upraised hand is so diaphanous he's able to sweep it aside like a spider's web. He's inside. The house is lit, the doors open. It appears at a distance that a meeting is taking place and he picks up his pace, curious to know the identity of her conspirators, but suddenly he sprawls and a primitive alarm of stone-filled tin cans tied to a jute cord rattles in the yard like a ten-gun salute. From the bushes her private army rises up and circles him, kicking his head and face as he tries to rise. He curls his body and they descend upon him in a rain of boots and lathis. The pain in his head builds to a series of explosions. In the distance, a woman claps her hands and he hears the slapping of sandals in retreat.

4

ish and Yash Khanna are sitting at the dining room
table designing communications for the twenty-first
century.

"Where's Joe Montana when you need him?" I joke.

Yash takes me seriously. "I believe he is retired."

When Victoria and I leave them in the apartment the calculations have spread to three pages, the Giants game is on television,
and cold Thai food is in the fridge. It's hard for me to cook these
days. We're learning to survive on deliveries and take-out.

It's July and I don't know how much longer I can keep carrying the baby. Every hour feels like an eternity, and I still have a
month to go. My grandmother's stories about transmigrations
keep coming back. I caress my domed stomach and wonder when
and how a troubled soul decided to settle here, in my womb.
Someone or some spirit has been guiding me through those dis-

tant times and places that I am writing about. Bish has a different take on pregnancy. He talks of the fetus as a starter-kit for every technology ever invented, just waiting for assembly. To me, I tell him, our unborn baby feels like a toolbox.

Climbing the hundred-and-fifty-foot narrow road up to Easy Come nearly did me in. Just below us a small armada of house-boats, some with satellite dishes, bobs like toys in a crowded tub. Caterers' vans line the dockside. Their decks and parties are open to our spying. We can hear their music, the occasional hearty laugh and expensive shrieks of pure delight. Fog-free summer days in the Bay Area mean glorious light, especially in Sausalito, which used to be an artist's colony. Today is particularly clear, the bay seems swimmable all the way across to Berkeley. But summer doesn't bring heat. I'm wearing a jacket and drinking warm tea, not iced.

Because I've been living inside Vertie Treadwell's head for the better part of two months, I'm both glad to leave and reluctant to let go. Victoria asks what impressed me most about him, since I am now the reigning expert on her origins, and I have to say it's his murderous love of tigers, admiring them enough to kill them almost to the point of slaughter. The doublethink behind it eludes me (being a child of these sensitive years) but it seems a bridge into something I must try harder to understand. As Bish would say, there's a term still missing in this equation. To kill is to possess for all time—I can get that, I'm a well-read person, too—but the follow-on is equally obvious: To kill is to lose the desirable quali-ties that attract you in the first place. Early hunters killed to possess the spirit of the animal, his heart, his sexuality, like Tom Crabbe's Amazon cannibals. Treadwell could have been one of them.

Tyger, Tyger, burning bright, in the forests of the night. By their "way-pers" you shall know them, Treadwell's old hunting-guide, Mohandass, had said. By the vapors rising from a tiger's body as he shakes off the night's river-crossing he reveals himself; *In what distant deeps or skies / Burst the fire of thine eyes?* The weight of a tiger, that fearful symmetry, is so artfully distributed that it crushes not even a leaf, yet a swipe of its paw can crack a chital's back. There's something tantalizing there about communication theory (I should be saying to Bish) that the tiger dies, the pelts disappear, but the vapors linger. A hundred and twenty-five pelts! The dead weight of a pelt without the bones and musculature must have felt heavier than the cat itself. I have pawed through every scrap of paper in that brimming banker's box and there's no mention in any of his papers of their fate, if he sold them, abandoned them to his successor, Mr. Ismail, or burned them. Or if Ismail impounded them for his own profit. Each pelt must have told a story of a hunt, a location, and the reason why. Ten dozen tiger pelts, an epic of a flawed, despotic life, his unread, untraced autobiography. I give up, it doesn't make sense.

"Perhaps," Victoria says, when I admit my defeat, "he was trying to kill Vertie Treadwell. Or something in himself. Given his identification with tigers, that is."

All his rage is directed inward? Of course, I think—she's right. It's so obvious. She has the distance to see through all his defenses. It wasn't India he hated—that long résumé of bitterness—but England. Those uncles of his and the shadow of infamy they cast on the family name set the pattern for a lifetime's shame and denial.

I wonder if he hauled those tiger pelts and the crates of books from one posting to the next, if he displayed them on the walls, the floors, and the beds? One hundred and twenty-five tiger pelts constitute a formidable mountain of dead cats. Did he sleep on tiger skins like the old Mughal emperors, gripping the enormous fangs in their propped-open mouths? What did Vertie Treadwell do at night? Did he rub his back against tiger-covered walls and curl his toes in tiger-plush? I can't imagine Vertie Treadwell in any kind of seraglio, yet he was an Edwardian in the last years of the British Raj; in his mind, he might have fancied himself another Sir Richard Burton, or Lawrence of Arabia, as he certainly did another Churchill.

The local press obituary reported his last word, articulated with great force and clarity, to be "Winston!" Perhaps the press was Labour-tinted; the final account referred to his uncles' disgrace of half a century earlier, his burial next to his old Classics tutor, and closed with a "twilight of the gods" drum roll. Virgil Treadwell had been one of the last witnesses to the greatest chapter of British history, whatever the final judgment might be, and had come away with little to show for it. Thelma, his bride of six months, and a son in Canada survive him. A sister, Canning, last known to live in South Africa, had effectively disappeared.

Did he who made the Lamb make thee?

But three weeks later, Stafford Roundtree, he of the Honours List, contributed a different piece. It must have been clipped by Thelma and dropped into the famous duffel bag.

A TIGER IN TWEEDS

Virgil Ernest Reginald Treadwell

BORN, INDIA, 30 NOVEMBER 1874
DIED, BRYNNSMERE, 25 APRIL 1948

My friend "Vertie" Treadwell, who was born in India and spent forty honourable years in the ICS, passed away in Brynnsmere, April 25th last. His name will not burnish the Honours List, and there will be no monuments, no parks or roads to carry his name. Yet, I submit, it was the dedication of men like Vertie Treadwell, an East

Anglian, a St. Alban's boy, a Brynnsmere resident, who carried the very soul of the British people into the darkest corners of a savage world and brought the light of civilisation to races bound in servitude to ignorance and superstition. Historians will be writing of Vertie Treadwell, of his generation and men like him, fifty years from now when the names of Gandhi and Nehru are consigned to dusty dossiers.

Characteristically, as we understand from hospital staff, the act that cost him his life was a gesture of kindness to a St. Alban's lad, a boy of Indian origin, who had permitted the cricket ball to elude his fielding skills. Vertie, who often stood at the boundary, lost, he would say, in a reverie of his own school years, gave chase to the ball and in the act of capturing it fell and struck his head on the lamentably uneven footpath.

His friends, who sorely miss his wit and companionship, have prevailed upon our good publican, Toby Rowan, to honour his name and loyalty by changing the name of that celebrated High Street establishment to "The Painted Tiger."

After retirement to England, many of those old Raj administrators wrote memoirs of their Indian experiences. They'd kept diaries and copious notes; they were Victorians, after all. They believed in their mission, they felt their lives had contributed, somehow, to hope and progress. How much more interesting than any of them Treadwell's could have been! There's so much bitterness and rage, so many glimpses into a dark and unknowable world.

What the hammer? What the chain?
In what furnace was thy brain?

There should have been a *Treadwell-nama*. Treadwell came along after the game of Empire had been exposed and everyone from

London to New Delhi and Calcutta was fatigued with the masquerade. I wonder if Treadwell ever looked into his Indian life, perhaps in the years between the death of Tara Lata and Independence and thought about condemning the whole experience, and then backed away because of the outrage such a book was likely to stir up. Disloyalty on that scale would not be like him. He would have tried to write a self-justification for the Raj and his role within it, his own less-than-Churchillian *History of the English-Speaking Peoples Trapped in the United Provinces and Sunderbans*.

He aspired to be Churchill, or to be admired by the likes of Churchill, but he belongs inside Orwell, especially *Burmese Days,* which he called seditious trash. But he saw his life captured in that book, not as a tiger, but as a pathetic, frightened little wretch. He recognized the truth, however much he ran from it. He ran from women, he ran from England. He'd joined the colonial service because in his family Indian administration was expected; but in his case he always claimed the strongest of motives to get away from England and never return. It must have concerned the exposure and threatened prosecution of his uncles. They resigned their posts in Brynnsmere in 1890, while Vertie was away at university. His Indian career is one long résumé of bitterness.

Most of what we know about the British in India comes from a few self-satisfied memoirs by the retired administrators themselves, frolics and challenges from the high noon of colonial dominance. They were novelists manqué, gently amused, hopeful Victorians, marvelously observant but not very reflective. They didn't have to be. But Treadwell lived in their shadows, in the ashes, through the final years. He could have provided the definitive record of the fall. He had the jaundiced eye of a writer in the mode of Orwell himself; everywhere he looked he saw decline, sordidness, and dishonesty. And as he continually reminds us, he was not an ill-read man, which is one of the many surprises I came upon.

"You can throw those papers out, now," Victoria says.

But I've grown attached to them, and anyway, what possible repository apart from this book exists for the preservation of moldering scraps?

Victoria says she's been inspired by my example. She's been doing some research of her own on a possible New World *Treadwell-nama*. She wants to know the name of Vertie's first love, her Bombay grandmother. She'd grown up deprived of history or context and came from an arid background, an only child on an isolated farm with a taciturn father who reveled in his bastardy. She knew only that her father's half sister, the so-called legitimate one, had been named Irene and that Irene's mother, who had deserted Vertie in Bombay, was named Iris. Armed with a name and a few keystrokes, she uncovered the fate of her half aunt Irene.

After leaving India, the ex–Mrs. Vertie had remarried in Auckland in 1908. The husband's name was Alec Stone. She had three more children, the youngest of whom, Ian Stone, survives and has written back:

My dear Dr. Khanna. It is a pleasure to respond to your inquiry and to realize that like a note entrusted to a bottle and thrown out to sea, nothing in this world is ever lost or without consequence. It is a wonder even to an old man who has seen much in the world that news of our family should wash up in San Francisco, India, Canada, and Lord only knows where else! It is my impression, contrary to popular opinion, that the world was far more integrated in those years than it is now. I mean simply that members of a single family residing on the five continents and significant islands in between were not at that time considered out of the ordinary. Of course, I am an old man and speak with some authority only on matters pertaining to the British diaspora to the corners of its late Empire.

Let me first get our relationship straight. You are the granddaughter of Virgil Treadwell. I am the son of the aforementioned's ex-wife and second husband; hence your grandfather is of no blood relation to me, nor are we to each other. This, dear lady, in no way shadows my delight in making this very late contact. Your late father, however, was my late half sister's half brother. Fractions have come to haunt me in my old age! My half sister is your half aunt. I hope I am not disappointing you when I say I cannot remember my mother ever mentioning her first husband. India was a blank. Only her daughter emerged, rather brightly, from that permanent darkness.

My half sister, Irene Treadwell, was nearly a generation older than I, and I have very little first-hand recollections of her. Enclosed, however, you will find a picture of her, c. 1922, which addresses your questions more eloquently than a thousand of my own poor words. Yes, she was a rare beauty in a place that harboured little respect for anything in a woman but her capacity for work and child-bearing. Yes, she rode that bicycle everywhere, she bared her legs shamelessly, according to my grandmother, and she quite provocatively chose to be photographed with a cigarette in her fingers. Quite the saucy pose for 1922 New Zealand!

I believe she was born in India in 1903. I did not come along until 1920. My mother was over forty when she carried me, a considerable feat in those days in the North Island bush. Our mother died in a train-crossing accident in 1965, still robust at eighty-five.

Sad to relate, Irene has been dead these many, many years. She

*married a chap in 1925, against the advice of my father, or I should
say, in defiance of him, and our mother. He was a dark, conniving
sort, of suspect origins. The sort that one day announces he's marrying
your daughter and the next asks for money to pay for the licence. He
said he had a touch of Maori blood, which these days in NZ is very
fashionable, but in those days was anything but. Others said he was
Indian or perhaps Indonesian. I cannot say I have a memory of him,
or indeed of her, having been myself only four years of age, but I know
that losing Irene cut my mother deeply.*

*They ran off to the bright lights of Melbourne, which was always
her big ambition, and with her already pregnant. The fact is, he
murdered her, pure and simple, and savagely so. It was quite shocking
for its time. There may still be newspaper records of his trial and
execution in Melbourne and Auckland papers.*

*I am obliged to you for the effort you've made and the interest
you've expressed. It is good to know this curious family-line persists in
its dogged fashion across the world.*

Once you get started in these things, it's addictive. You wonder if
everyone and everything in the world is intimately related. You're
a time-traveler and suddenly the past is alive, the dead are walking, cracked walls gleam, the rivers run free. Those old newspaper
files are just a keystroke away and you're off on another search.
You pluck a thread and it leads to . . . everywhere. I'll leave it to
Bish and Yash to explain it. Is there a limit to relatedness? (Yes,
Bish'll say. Death.)

I'm sure Vertie Treadwell never knew the fate of Irene—her
name's mentioned only once in his papers—but I can't say he
didn't grieve for her loss. *"No fool to accompany me, no blasted heath
underfoot."* He saw himself as Lear. At another time he quotes
Mortimer to Hotspur, "as bountiful as mines of India," and won-

ders where exactly anything bountiful in India apart from plague and pestilence might be found. Even Shakespeare knew of India's fabled wealth. Self-pitying, self-deceiving—Vertie! I wanted to shout over the decades, *you're* the one who abandoned *them*—yet I truly don't know.

And so, on a gorgeous Sausalito Sunday afternoon, under a polished dome of the palest blue, two ladies chat and giggle on a deck overlooking the marina. What do two ladies sitting on Easy Come's thrusting deck on a sunny day in June know about the world? The answer is, everything. Vertie Treadwell was a man of a late, unspoken, unacted passion—who would have guessed it? He was in love with the Tree Bride. Victoria's grandfather and my distant aunt. *It's all too bizarre,* I was about to say, but instead I say, "It's inevitable."

"We'll leave it to the boys to try to explain," says Victoria.

The tragic tale of Vertie and the brahmin lady gives her some pleasure. Oh, the curse of coincidence, the spurious nobility of a shared birth date! How much fun we're having, playing with history and turning scraps of paper into stories. Yash and Bish are working on their all-embracing mathematics of communication. No, it's not six degrees of separation, he'll tell me some day—it's closer to four-point-eight or three-point-five. It's plottable on a grid: This much input, these many years, that many miles, correct for variables, and there it will be—the Khanna-Chatterjee protocol for Universal Data Retrieval. Nothing in the world is ever lost and everything in the world is somehow connected. Plug it in, hit the key, and names like Mist and Gangooly and Hai and Octavius Rutledge and thousands of others lost to us now will pop up instantly.

Just this morning, Victoria received a second letter from her aged New Zealand not-quite cousin-uncle.

. . . Your inquiries have dislodged, or restored, another memory that came to me after our latest exchange of letters. I believe I mentioned I was only four years old when my half sister, Irene, left for Melbourne with her murderous husband, but I remember "Auntie Agnes," as she asked us to call her. She was a plump, darkish figure whom my mother engaged as nurse to us younger children. She was from Bombay, my mother said, but certifiably blood-British, which seemed very much to matter. I've searched through family documents and discovered her full name: Agnes Harpenny, in case that's a help in your researches. "Aunt Agnes" had tried numerous devices to get to England, she said, but failed in every endeavour. As I grew older, she told me of her heart being broken more times than she could count, then of a fiancé's death in the Great War. She was quite the gifted tragedienne.

I mention this because I am quite confident that she and my mother shared some connection from India that they never divulged. Later events showed her to be, may God forgive me, an evil woman, base in all intents, and especially vindictive to our family. I believe she manoeuvred our sister into meeting and eloping with her charming husband. . . .

" 'Harpenny,' what a strange name," Victoria says. " 'Agnes.' Is there an uglier name in the world?"

She must have been called *Ha'penny Agnes, the landlady's daughter*. There must have been songs, ditties, and little poems passed on from tenant to tenant about Mrs. Harpenny and her lovely daughter. Every young British officer who let a room in Mrs. Harpenny's or half a dozen other boardinghouses like it run by genteel widows of suspect pedigree probably took a swipe at the ever-hopeful, ever-available Agnes, or girls just like her. Anglo-

Indians, almost certainly, too English for the Indians, too Indian for ever settling in England. The late Yorkshire husband and father a convenient fiction, which means Victoria Treadwell Khanna has a deeper relationship to India than a mere second marriage. A drop of her blood represents more of the world than a drop of mine. Newly discovered sisters of color, we sit on her porch and I deliver the news. I agree that Agnes Harpenny is a grating name, but not one so easily dismissed.

"Victoria—say hello to your grandmother." I stop myself from saying out loud, Your grandmother was—shall we say—a little bit whorish?

"And by the way," I add, "I think you're a little bit Indian."
Ma semblable, ma soeur.

"No!"

But it's an amused exclamation, not a denial. It's the way any of us might react to a phone call telling us we've won the Lotto. She slaps hands on thighs and starts nodding her head very slowly as though straining to hear a muted conversation or to accept a long-standing denial. Finally she says, "I lugged that duffel bag around the world for forty years and I *knew* there was something important inside it that I just couldn't face." She looks happy. "I always had this inexplicable attachment to India. Now I guess I can die in peace."

We sit quietly for a few moments contemplating the odd majesty of all that has just transpired. I tell her we share a history. Under different circumstances—far different circumstances—we might even have been of the same family. The Brits chose India; we didn't choose them, but the consequences are just the same. Information feels like the glue of the universe, one of those unimaginable calculations of time and distance, but one that restores a bit of human scale to the ungraspable proportions of space. But there are days, and this is one of them, when the trillion-trillion random particles actually seem reducible to a simple formula. Why not? A drop of blood reveals all of human history.

I also want to say there is evil in the world. Succubae are out there, looking for host-bodies. Agnes Harpenny went all the way to New Zealand to stalk Iris Treadwell and destroy her beloved daughter—that seems to be the message of Ian Stone—and she might have set in motion Irene's meeting with the man who killed her. In a wilder turn of the imagination—and nothing is closed to me now—she might have been related to that killer; Victoria might have an evil uncle as well as a whorish grand-mother. I could warn her: Don't research that ancient murder in Melbourne; you might find poor Irene's husband was part of Agnes's family, an uncle as distant to you as the Tree Bride is to me. Abbas Sattar Hai attached himself to our son as a way of bur-rowing into our family and destroying an Indian foothold in America—and both he and Agnes succeeded. I can imagine that Agnes Harpenny decided to destroy every sign of Vertie Tread-well except her own son, who was already safe in his English orphanage.

"If Agnes ever wrote to Vertie, he didn't keep a copy," I say. It doesn't mean that she didn't. He might have given her Iris's name and address in New Zealand. Maybe he put her up to it: *Here's the woman who trapped me in marriage, then deserted me. You're a spiteful lady; do your worst to her.* He might even have been an honorable man, after his fashion. Perhaps he paid Agnes some money to keep their boy in England. Or paid some institution or individual off the books. Somebody must have. With Vertie, anything was possible, even virtue.

Oh, for the simple heroics of John Mist!

"Did she ever get in touch with your father?"

Victoria's sharp laugh probably roused the partygoers on the houseboats below. She had never asked her father anything of his time in England, knowing the response it would provoke. "He'd have burned anything coming from England."

If nothing in history is ever lost, and if everything human is finally connected, gaps in the record are only temporary, they don't really matter. That's Bish's opinion. He'd say the universe of information is like the infinite capacity of the brain itself. Every event of every minute is somehow imprinted and stored. We just don't have the key for retrieving it. Vertie's baby sister, little Canning, the two-year-old who was supposedly sent to an aunt in South Africa and never heard from again—she isn't lost. Nor is the "aunt" or whoever it was who received her lost, in that world-conspiracy of secrets. Did Canning grow up adventurous and prowl the Southern Hemisphere, ending up in Australia or Argentina? Did she make her way back to England, or get to Canada or the United States? *Canning Treadwell:* Lady Canning Treadwell; it's a name out of British lending library fiction, author or heroine. It's exactly as Victoria had said that day in her office—a drop of blood is like a novel, it contains the world.

And thank god it's now Victoria's problem, a keystroke away if she wants to pursue it.

′ ′ ′

The day should have ended with all of us back in our apartment picking over cold Thai food, speculating over Ian Stone's letter and Victoria's discovery of a probable drop of Indian blood, refreshed from a perfect day in a perfect house with museum-quality furnishings. Maybe one of us would have dared to open the Irene Treadwell file, going to Melbourne archives, learning the name of her husband and killer. And our "boys" would wheel out their calculations and say it's all very simple, life and the universe are just a hologram, time and space an illusion. What started out perfect, ended . . . well, it still hasn't ended.

The baby inside me turned and kicked—she's going to be a tough little soccer player, and I'm going to end up a soccer mom, I thought—and this seems melodramatic, maybe I'm confusing the order of events—it seemed to me the blue sky darkened and the temperature dropped, not from fog or clouds, but as though a filter had been placed on the sun, as from a partial eclipse. Victoria noticed it, too, and went to get a wrap. I glanced down to the houseboats where the loud partying was still going on and teams of young Mexican men in white jackets were hustling out from the galleys, filling large glass bowls with food and drink. And then I noticed the bartender and the dip of his shoulder as he poured a drink, the tilt of his head as he made small talk. I knew that gesture. He wasn't Mexican; he was Indian.

"Victoria," I almost whispered, "do you have a pair of binocs?" She was nearly inside.

"I'm a birder, remember?"

"Can you bring them to me? Don't rush. Don't make a fuss."

She must have thought I'd spotted a rare bird.

"What do you see?" she asked. I retreated to the farthest corner of the deck, nearly out of sight line with the houseboats. They are powerful glasses. Happy, happy faces gamboling on the deck, like villagers in a frieze on Keats's Grecian Urn. What greater innocence could be imagined than a houseboat party on a sunny Sunday in the Sausalito marina? I focused on the bartender. His head was down as he poured vodka and tomato juice over a stalk of celery. He looked up and I started shaking. My voice cracked as I tried to speak. He might have been a quarter of a mile away, but I could only whisper.

"Victoria, please bring me my purse."

He looked directly into my eyes as though he were the one watching me, and smiled ever so slightly. I kept the glasses on him, hoping to hide my face.

"Please give me my cell phone," I said.

"Sweetie, you're shaking. Go inside and sit. Doctor's orders."

I did as she commanded, then speed-dialed Jack Sidhu. I'm on his caller ID. He answered as he always does, on the second ring. "Hello, Mrs. Chatterjee. How can I help today?"

I tried to speak but nothing came out.

"Tara?"

"He's here, Jack—I've just seen him. He's on a houseboat in the Sausalito marina. White jacket, bartender, catering." No need to say his name. I couldn't have uttered those words.

"Sausalito? Then you're up at Dr. Khanna's. I know the address." How he knows things I've never asked. "Close the drapes and do not leave. Did he see you?"

"Yes," I said. I was shivering. How to say: I think he sees everything and I don't think this little encounter is a wild coincidence? I thought I had my life back.

"Listen. I'm on two phones. I'm dispatching an officer. You'll be safe. Five minutes, Tara, and it will all be over. I'll call."

"It's too late, Jack."

"Listen to me, Tara. It's about to be over."

I don't bother to close the drapes. We can't see down to the houseboats from inside the living room and I'm not about to go out on the deck again. Victoria just stares at me with a "What the—?" frown. I'm afraid she'll turn me out and I can't blame her. "I'm sorry," I say. "We have to get out."

"What in the world?"

I hold up my hand, like a child. "Five minutes."

"Tara, for God's sake, you're acting crazy."

It comes to me suddenly. I see the outline of a threat, something approaching from the corner of my eye that I hadn't considered, had never considered.

"We can't stay!" I cry, and I grab her hand, practically jerking her out of the center of her own living room toward the front door. "We have to get out *now!*" and suddenly I'm screaming, "Move! Move!" She starts to resist but I'm stronger. *I'll explain, I'll explain,* I want to say, but first we've got to get out. It's going to blow. I don't care for myself and not even for Victoria. It's for my precious daughter. He won't take my baby.

Ten, twenty running steps and we're in the middle of the narrow, car-wide lane, looking downhill. No policeman is yet in sight, no sirens wail in the distance. Victoria looks back at Easy Come and leans toward it. Its million-dollar views have won prizes. We've left the front door open. Her purse is inside. I pull her away.

"It's going to blow!" This time I can say it. She squints, her lips form the word "what?" Now, faintly, I hear the sirens. We can't see the marina through the trees.

I say to her, "The man who bombed us is on a houseboat in a white jacket pouring Bloody Marys."

Her lips form *"No!"*

A great calm settles over me; an enormous truth has been revealed. So: Now I know. The target of Abbas Sattar Hai's bomb wasn't Bish or Indian money in Silicon Valley. It's *me* he wants to kill. It really is *all about me*. Maybe he caught a glint off the binocs, perhaps he was waiting for a sign that I'd seen him. He'd like that bit of premeditated terror. He must have followed me to Victoria's house and he knows I come here every Sunday and that we spend hours on the deck, heedless and exposed.

"Tara, really, what's the big deal here?" She must have kicked off her shoes inside; she's barefoot out here. "I'm getting cold, sweetie, let's just go back inside." It's the first time I've ever seen her confused about *anything*. Stay, go. She looks to me.

"He's down there. He's been following me."

Meaning, Don't you get it? *I'm* the one he's after. It's not safe being with *me*. He saw *me*, and he was waiting for *me* to see him. She still doesn't understand.

A police car threads slowly up the lane, its red and blue lights throbbing. It stops, but the officer stays inside, still talking on the phone. He gets out, smiling broadly. "Ladies, I'm Bob," he says, "and I thought you were told to stay inside."

Just shut up, I want to say.

"I'm on the line with Officer Sidhu."

"Jack," I say.

He squints at me. "Jack?" He holds out the phone. Jack says it's good news, bad news. Abbas Sattar Hai just melted away before the squad got there. But they got his backpack and a cell phone that was inside his white jacket.

That's when the full meaning clicked in, the second shoe dropped: *cell phone*. If there's one thing we've learned in the past year, cell phones are the most dangerous technology on the planet. Digital communication made Bish and Chet Yee famous, but from a block away it also triggered the bomb hidden inside a boom box that nearly destroyed our lives. Eventually, we learned to laugh about it, a little: *the mother of all boom boxes*.

I must have screamed, "No!," causing Officer Bob to drop the phone. I hear Jack through the static giving orders on another phone: *Don't touch that cell phone! Don't turn it on!* Victoria turns and takes half a step in the direction of the house.

But it's too late. An eager officer down on the houseboat, thinking he's stumbled upon an investigative shortcut, turns it on. I feel and smell the acid puff of a gentle breeze. I know that smell. Then comes the concussion as though all the earth has blown apart, followed by a mighty flash and a roar that knocks Victoria to her knees. Easy Come flings its shingles like a tiger shaking off beads of water. Glass and roof tiles hurl upward and outward and then the standing structure, in a vast inhalation, sucks itself flat.

Officer Bob is blown back, pinned against the windshield. Victoria gets to her feet immediately. In my bottom-heavy pregnancy, I'm still struggling to roll myself into a sitting position. A shock wave passes right over me, but its force staggers Victoria against the hood of the police car.

"Tara!" comes that staticky voice of Jack Sidhu. "Tara, please pick up!"

In a slow-motion collapse, tons of rubble teeter on the side of the cliff, balanced by the outthrust of the barren deck. Then the deck groans and the support beams buckle and everything tips, slowly at first, like a ship listing, then gathers speed as it sinks, like so much coal roaring down a scuttle. Victoria lowers her arms as though reaching down to lift me from a crib, and I reach up to her like a helpless baby, but ecstatic that I have saved her.

We will never complete that embrace. A flying object, a brick, a tile, a shard of glass, slams into her chest. Jack keeps shouting, "Tara, Tara, Mrs. Chatterjee, Tara!" Victoria smiles and looks down as though to flick it away, *you naughty thing, you!* then she coughs. It's just a little cough, but all the air in her lungs is squeezed through it. Blood seeps around the wound, but I can't see brick or glass or anything there, just a ragged, dark brown, rectangular hole.

She was conscious all the way to the hospital, telling me what I must avoid in the final month and which doctors I should contact in the event she might not be able to deliver my daughter. The EMS lady tried to quiet her. "They get excited. It's the shock," she said, but there was nothing she could give her. The object still lay embedded in the middle of her chest and if we tried to remove it, the open wound might start sucking air.

She worried about bomb insurance. She was certain they didn't have it, such a terrible pity, the house was their grand-child—everything had gone into its decoration and maintenance. Of course, what did it matter in light of this exciting new discovery? I'm Indian! She was talking to herself, or to some distant friend.

"I'm Indian, my dear, what do you think of that? He will be so amused. We won't tell him right away, will we?"

"Please, madam, try not to talk so much."

It was like having her old self back for a few more seconds.

"Just us five little Indians," Victoria tried to laugh. Then she fell asleep, and never awoke.

✓ ✓ ✓

Victoria died on the way to Marin General. Yash arrived a few minutes later, under police escort, directly from San Francisco. His first concern was Bish. "You must get back to your husband," he said. Bish would be all alone back in the apartment with just a police guard posted outside. He knows I am all right, but he doesn't know about Victoria. They had just put their calculations aside and were turning their attention to the cold Thai food when the knock on the door came. They'd assumed we were tied up in traffic and had forgotten, as usual, to turn on our cell phones. They'd called the Sausalito number, but the phone was always busy. When the knock came, they thought we'd lost our keys as well, and so they'd been laughing and getting ready to tease us. "Oh, I forgot where the door is!" Bish had shouted out, but it was two unsmiling police officers.

The police said, "There's been some trouble." They didn't know much themselves, they were responding to a report. Something about an accident in Sausalito. Yash could only think automobile accident, but Victoria is a very safe driver. Bish begged to come, but the officer saw that he couldn't walk, and time was precious.

Yash offered me his cell phone to call Bish, but I couldn't touch it. It seemed at that moment the source of all the evil in the world. Yash did the calling, assuring Bish that I was unhurt. Victoria was less fortunate, he said. I would be home soon.

´   ´   ´

"I don't know what I should do," Yash said. He's old-school Hindu; stoic, meticulous, dedicated to the observance of certain rituals, and far more religious than I'd ever suspected. Our old religious training kicks in. Yama comes calling and there is no warning, no delaying, only the proper respect to be shown. Death is a different state of being, that's all; the important thing is to hasten the soul to its next safe harbor and not impede it in any way. Yash's concerns—what he should do—were with the proper disposal of Victoria's remains, not with himself and his shattered life. He chanted in Sanskrit under his breath. At last he burst out, "Fremont!"

Fremont is a festive place. Every new Bollywood extravaganza plays in Fremont first, touring Indian singers are on stage nightly, it is shop-till-you-drop, eat-till-you-burst Indianness, a place to find a doctor, a dentist, a loan, a matchmaker, everything to reconnect you to the community you left behind. Bish and I were never Fremont types. We thought we'd left India behind.

"There's a Cremation Society in Fremont," he said. "I was pondering Presbyterian or Hindu, but I don't know any Presbyterians. I think a proper Hindu cremation would serve her better. I never thought I'd need one so soon."

I told him Victoria would be pleased. It is most appropriate; she was Indian by adoption, by marriage, wasn't she? I didn't go into more detail. I said that she and I had been discussing that very thing, just . . . just two hours ago. She'd expressed great tenderness for India. I recalled her final words: "five little Indians." Bish and I, Yash and she, and baby make five. She felt, finally, she belonged with Indians.

"Professor Veeraswamy in Electrical Engineering is a priest. I play squash with him. I'll call him."

Jack Sidhu came running in from the parking lot, in uniform, blue-turbaned, distraught. To look at them, you'd think the younger man had just suffered a grotesque tragedy. Thank God he has an older man, a father perhaps, to comfort him. And a consoling auntie. They're always pregnant, aren't they? And Yash *is* a comforter. Jack blames himself for everything. That damned cell phone, why didn't I think of it? I should have remembered last year. That bastard made the police do his dirty work. Jack broke into tears. Yash patted his shoulder.

"It is no one's fault, certainly not yours," said Yash. "When Yama comes, it cannot be averted. It was my dear wife's time. But I do have a request."

"Anything," said Jack.

"I would like to inspect that chap's cell phone. Perhaps we can disable any remote detonating capability."

"It's in evidence," he said.

"There's time," said Yash. And then he took an adjacent seat.

"Dr. Khanna's right," I said to Jack. "No one saw it coming."

Yash said suddenly, with his voice rising and words pouring out, perhaps in his own kind of delayed shock, "Actually, Dr. Chatterjee did see it. Just this afternoon we talked about the bombing of your house last year and he observed there was a hole in the information field. We concluded that Dr. Chatterjee could not possibly have been the intended target. His decision to stay at your house that night was impulsive and not knowable in advance. If his house in Atherton had been bombed, *then* there would have been no question. It may seem paradoxical, but his injury proves he was not the target. Probabilities therefore support two logical conclusions. First, the bomb was not intended for him. Second, it was intended for you, Mrs. Chatterjee."

By far less persuasive means but at approximately the same time I had come to the same conclusion. "When I saw him on the houseboat looking up at me, I knew I'd been the target all along."

Yash took out his cell phone and I heard, "Veeraswamy? Khanna here. There's been an accident."

Now it was Jack's turn. "If you remember, Mrs. Chatterjee, we discussed all that last year. We assumed your husband had been followed from the airport."

"Excuse me, Veeraswamy." Yash again turned to us. "That is of course possible, but less probable. It presupposes more than one—many more than one—perpetrator. There would have to have been worldwide, round-the-clock surveillance on Dr. Chat-

terjee. These people have not been seen, or identified. If you elim-
inate the possibility of randomness, you are forced to invent people who perhaps do not exist."

We had been seduced by the magnitude of Bish's standing in
the world. His stature proved his vulnerability. Who would look
to the invisible ex-wife?

I could see Jack Sidhu's rapid calculation. If Yash was right, the
loss of eight months' worth of investigation. Time spent tracking
down leads all over North America, Singapore, and Malaysia, time
checking visas and raiding sleazy motels. Time that could have
been spent, if Yash cared to push it in the courts, on locating a lone
suspect, Abbas Sattar Hai. Jack's career was heavily invested in the
notion of the Indian Mafia infiltrating the Bay Area and in Bish's
prominence being the trigger, his collapse their triumph. He
hadn't checked the underground economy of undocumented labor.
His Ethnic Squad didn't cross ethnic frontiers. I had never seen
Jack Sidhu look indecisive, not even for a minute. And then I saw
him make up his mind.

"What did you ever do to him?" he asked me.

"I'm sure I never did anything to him." But I know I had.
Maybe not this "I" named Tara and living in San Francisco, and
not even the distant "I" of Calcutta that seems like a different life
from centuries ago.

"This doesn't offer me much to go on."

I know that somewhere in the wire-web of history, our lines
have crossed. A Gangooly and a Hai have clashed, and as a result,
I am responsible for killing Victoria and I nearly killed Bish and
Rabi. I grew up insular and protected, indifferent to anything
that did not touch me personally. We all did, that was the defen-
sive posture of middle-class Calcutta. I grew up hearing the hundred, the thousand, ways an unmarried woman or a straying wife

brings unending catastrophe to those nearest to her, knowing they were funny because they could never apply to me.

There's money to be made off a son's piss; there's rope to hang a daughter with. A woman without a husband roams the streets like an untethered ox. She brings calamity wherever she strays.

Already, my mind is reeling backward. The Hais and the Gangoolys have history in Mishtigunj. It all seems so crazy. My copy of Hajji's *Mist-nama* was lost in the original explosion. The original has been lost, or more likely, sold to Germans for pennies to the page. With the early days, I've been working from memory. But with Treadwell and the Tree Bride, I have the papers.

Part Four

1

To stretch a point, I'm sitting on a relative of my great-great uncle, perhaps my uncle himself, as I write. He was a sundari—shoondari—tree, and the only piece of furniture Bish and I still have from our original marriage dowry is a sundari chair, c. 1880, taken from my parents' house in Calcutta. The legs are straight, sturdy, and uncarved. The unvarnished wood is purplish in cast and resistant to all known forms of rot and infestation. I have come back to where I began, to the little girl who married a tree on a December night in 1879. This is the family legend, the stuff I thought I knew all along.

In the years following her marriage, Tara Lata Gangooly took on treelike characteristics herself. She was rooted to her father's house. She was silent as a tree. The grave little girl became a somber young lady. Uvaria trees, with their dense foliage, were imported from Orissa to shade the mansion. She communed with those trees for the next sixty years. When Victorians dreamed, they dreamed of the future. Nothing distracted her from the dream of an independent India. When we dream, or perhaps I should limit such a broad declaration only to myself, I dream of the past.

She left her father's house on only three occasions. The first, to go to the forest on a cold winter night in 1879, to marry a tree. Had her intended boy-groom not died that same afternoon on his way to the wedding, her first exposure to the world might have been even more dramatic. Just a year later, her father bundled her up again to witness the hangings of John Mist and Rafeek Hai in front of the new British jail. And there was the third, from which she never returned, in 1943, prodded by British rifles. The outer world, understandably, held terror and mystery. Cause of death: *Heart Attack* reads the official dossier on her death. The witness line is signed by Dominick Mackenzie, Inspector of Police. A signature I've grown familiar with, V.E.R. Treadwell, D.C., appears on the bottom line. The signing physician's name is British. I traced him; he practiced in Calcutta until 1946; local doctors did not inspect the remains. Her body was never found, nor proper rites ever performed.

I suspect it joined the body-heap, the unquiet grave of empire, begun with the disposal of John Mist and Rafeek Hai. When she was arrested, she was keeping the records of atrocities committed far from those lurid wartime headlines: While American troops were hopscotching across the Pacific, outrages were occurring in the remotest villages of East Bengal—rapes, torture, and off-the-books executions. She was looking for an outlet, any newspaper anywhere in the world that would carry somewhere in its pages the notice that a nineteen-year-old housewife named Habeeba Shah and her three infant daughters had been burned alive in their hut because her husband had joined the Indian National Army and a newspaper photo had identified him, or that fifteen-year-old Kananbala Devi had been raped and tortured in front of her parents because her fugitive brother was accused of bombing a police station in a fog-shrouded village where half the population had already died in the famine and the other half had joined the INA with the aim of linking to the Japanese and accelerating the departure of the British in India ahead of their own leisurely, amendable, and perhaps retractable timetable.

The world had more urgent business to report in 1943. Even the millions dying of famine in Bengal went unreported *("India Famine Deaths Greatly Exaggerated"),* as Japanese troops captured Burma then marched into the easternmost towns of India. Calcuttans came out on the streets cheering as Japanese planes bombed the Kidderpore docks.

All that, of course, lay in the distant future. When Tara Lata Gangooly dreamed as a little girl, she had every reason to suppose a life of harmony, such as she enjoyed with her father's friend John Mist, Mist-*jethu*—paternal older uncle John—as she called him, and with Sameena, the cook's daughter, would develop into a rich and deep maturity. Hindu and Muslim would live harmoniously in a free and prosperous India. Britain would leave behind its good works, its investments and infrastructure, small compensation for the fortunes it had extracted.

She would be in the first generation of liberated Indians, her radically reborn father had promised; she would see India take its deserved place among the great nations of the world. What a glorious future awaited her! What is European history, compared to India? he would ask. At most, four hundred years of derivative science and tedious paintings paid for by imperial plunder. Indian science in the Vedic period had already invented airplanes, telephones, radios, and chariots faster than the newest cars. Hindu science had solved every known question of the universe while Europeans still lived in caves. What are China and Japan but upstarts? Malaya and Siam and the Dutch East Indies, Burma and Ceylon, but offshoots of the greater *Hindutva*? When India emerges in its full glory, the confused Buddhists and Muslims of once-Hindu lands will shed their false identities and cling to their Mother India.

, , ,

Behind the walls, which were smooth-topped, without the shards of broken glass favored by the British and wealthy Indians in larger cities, a wondrous transformation had taken place. Marry a five-year-old girl to an inert and unseen ninety-foot groom twenty times her age, relieve her from having to meet the insatiable demands and constant belittling of an Indian mother-in-law, add to it the strain of Bengali devotion in which love of husband equates to love of god, and consider that her husband had probably been used for a mast on some British man-o'-war and now lay at the bottom of the ocean or else sat proudly in the harbor of a distant port of call, making her at once bride, widow, or abandoned and you have the fundamental conditions for a calm and focused life.

Like Queen Victoria, Tara Lata was prodigally fertile, but as the missionaries taught, virginity had never precluded motherhood. Her father had brought shoots from the forest and planted them on the grounds. Her children took root. They stood in a regimental row forming a wall within the back of the compound, shielding the main house from a view of the river. When Tara Lata was not at her desk she could often be found seated on a bench in her arboretum, her "sacred forest" as she called it, reading and talking with the trees. The little girls she had once played with, like Sameena the cook's daughter, were now her servants. Her father, in his newfound orthodoxy, had banished Sameena's father from the brahmin's kitchen.

Teach her to read and to write the oppressor's tongue as well as her own. Convince her of the intractable evil of the British Raj. Very few little girls in India had ever been so well prepared to face the future.

Her life changed when she was fifty-four years old and first discovered human love. Because she was a virtuous married woman, or widow, no man in Mishtigunj had dared treat her as— or even consider her as—a possible object of desire. Respect dictated that she should be approached with reverence. Nor would she have recognized the signals of amorous intent. No man had seen her as anything but the virgin recluse of Mist Mahal, teacher of literacy, distributor of grains, and occasional oracle on subjects of Indian freedom and communal harmony. Her house was open to all. Through it came visitors from abroad, men and women descending from polished motor cars. Gradually, the people of Mishtigunj believed the evidence of their own eyes, which told them that Tara-Ma, as she was familiarly called, dwelled on a higher spiritual plane. Later, when word seeped out that she had donated her gold to Gandhi's Salt March, reverence turned to veneration. Years later, in the eyes of many, she had become a goddess, prayed to by unmarried women needing husbands and by wives seeking sons.

On the three occasions that I visited today's Mist Mahal in teeming Razakpur, there were no trees on the grounds, no gardens, nothing but stagnant puddles in the bare red clay where dogs and goats ran free. The peeling, rust-stained "mansion" had holes in its roof. Tin-and-cardboard lean-tos buttressed its sides and the silt-laden river spilled over its channel, only a few feet from the door. The Tree Bride's fanciful children—my great-aunts and great-uncles, I could say—had long since been chopped and burned.

,　,　,

On that cool morning that she was fifty-four, mists lingered over the river and paddy fields. The winter foggy season was approaching. She often thought of the appropriately named John Mist and of mists in general whenever she consulted his entries in the buckram-bound ledgers. John Mist was everywhere and nowhere, like a tiger or a god. In his ledgers he noted the time of mist's descent, the time of its lifting, its duration, the relative thickness of its cover, the hourly dew point, temperature, air pressure, and wind velocity. He noted minute variations of temperature correlated with dates that marked the onset of seasons. He must never have slept. He must have spent his nights prowling the periphery of the village silent as a leopard. He was a demon for observances, driven year by year to ever more extensive reckonings. Is there a limit to what our eyes and instruments can tell us, or could a man spend a lifetime making ever finer distinctions, down to the shifting of a grain of sand? And what would the ultimate distinctions disclose? The handwriting was not his, of course, being illiterate or at least posing as such, but those of students recruited from the Hindu and Muslim schools, identical hands in identical inks.

As the keeper of the visible legacy of John Mist, she alone could interpret the elaborate codes and abbreviations. In time, she promised herself, when other pressing matters were disposed of—when the Britishers sailed away, never to return—there would be time to decipher it and send it all to scholars in Calcutta. *John Mist's Meteorological Gazetteer of the Sunderbans 1835–1880.* With, of course, twenty-five additional years of updates. *Pertinence Paid by Sundry Hands to Local Flora and Fauna*. Her hands, and those of students and schoolmasters.

Perhaps the visitor from Calcutta would have a suggestion. She had decided to meet him in her father's office. She would be seated behind the carved desk with stacks of papers between them and the ranks of books behind. He would be offered a chair, and tea. She planned to make their business civil but short of cordial, in the manner honed over the decades between native elites and ICS officers. It would be conducted in the language of the visitor's choice. She could not remember the last time a white man had spoken to her in Bengali. She preferred the lack of ambiguity. And to be spared having to smile through their stumbling and compliment them on their extraordinary facility with such a difficult tongue.

It was a rule of Mist Mahal, established by her father in the years following Mist's execution, to receive all visitors graciously, especially the British. We must never give them cause to suspect our true feelings. They act on resentment, not on principle. Her father had said one could only learn the ways of a snake, or of a cyclone, by dispassionate inspection. Like criminals, they have nothing to teach us but self-defense. Jai Krishna himself had abandoned the mansion shortly after arranging Tara Lata's marriage, going off to Dhaka and other eastern Bengal cities to defend nationalists and to marry eight more times in the hope of fathering a male heir. It had been left to Tara Lata, her sisters, and her mother to enforce the rules of hospitality.

In her childhood, the front room with its restricted view of the protective wall and gate had served as her father's office. The shelves housed the law books he'd brought from Calcutta, where he'd graduated in 1857—the years in which he'd still believed in the majesty of British jurisprudence—then had taken down from Dhaka where he'd practiced twenty years before renouncing the courts and British law. He'd answered Mist's call for a well-trained lawyer, Hindu, to work with a Muslim colleague. And there the volumes rested under blankets of dust, their gilt letter-ing dull but still readable. His framed graduation photo, tinted by a local specialist and garlanded in the proper manner, beamed down upon her approvingly, she liked to think. There was no doubting the link between the young Jai Krishna Gangooly with his thin mustache and thick eyebrows, and the woman who had replaced him as an unofficial judge in every litigation. Her long, black, braided hair had begun to gray. She had the same assertive face, the straight bar of heavy eyebrows, the sharp, masculine fea-tures—inevitable, some said, in a life-long virgin.

Fortunately, Mishtigunj was free of a resident British presence. The district magistrate assigned to the Sunderbans, Morgan Wainwright, was an old man who rarely left his Chittagong estate, high in the hills among fierce warrior types, more Burmese than Indian, whom he sketched and painted while cross-breeding fruits and wild roses. The altitude of the Chittagong Hills, he liked to explain, conferred a certain Cornish quality to the vege-tation. He was another of those curious record-keepers, matching the meteorology of the Hills to identical readings in Europe, Africa, and North America. His sole official function was to dis-pose of cases likely to rise through the appeals process, unless squelched at the outset. Tara Lata saw that no more than one or two a year ever appeared.

′ ′ ′

The British year, which happened to be 1928, was hardly relevant in Mishtigunj, which kept only the Muslim and Hindu calendars.

It was the British month of November, only because of the impending visit by the official from Calcutta. His letter of introduction, written in chaste Bengali, declared his passionate attraction to Bengal and a rather remarkable independence of spirit, heightened with a trace of mockery of the Raj. She immediately doubted any Britisher capable of such linguistic dexterity; surely a local secretary with secret literary ambitions had been pressed into service.

She was nonetheless intrigued by his boldness and his exaggerated flattery of her town and its culture. He declared Mishtigunj to be the pearl of the Raj. He swore that the Bengali language was one of his many passions (First Class First, Cantab. Oriental Languages), along with the discovery, recovery, and identification of Bengal terra-cotta sculptures. Was she herself a devotee of the goddess Durga? Might she be aware of any isolated, jungle-bound temples where terra-cotta figurines might have been abandoned? He listed a number that he himself had unearthed. They were a treasure to be cataloged and saved, he wrote, for the very soul of a future—and let us hope, a not-too-distant future—independent India.

Unless she was mistaken, an ICS officer in expressing a desire for Indian independence had just committed an act of actionable sedition.

The effusions of the gentleman, Nigel Coughlin, struck her as excessive and perhaps even unbalanced. Apart from his indiscretions, she was curious and even warmly disposed to any Britisher who presented himself as a devotee of Bengal and not a strangulating parasite. In every way, his manner of introduction proved him to be respectful in the extreme. He would require no welcome, no private sleeping space ("I carry my bedding and prefer to sleep under the stars"), no special meals ("no meats, save the finny honorary vegetables swimming in the River George"). He lacked the formality that attended the visits of D. M. Wainwright. In a single letter under the guise of introducing himself, he had revealed more of himself, declared more of his unwieldy passions, and cast doubts on more British pretensions to power than anyone she'd ever read, with the possible exceptions of Subhas Bose or Mohandas Gandhi. Mr. Coughlin would arrive in Jessore by train and engage some sort of river ferry down to Mishtigunj. He stated he was on his way to Burma.

She was unprepared for his mode of arrival. She had expected the usual motorcar filling the lane outside her walls, with half the town following in its wake. Dust would fly, goats and chickens scatter, and like as not teenage boys would fire pebbles at the entourage in hopes of smashing a window. But her visitor, as he'd promised, was upon her without warning. He had hired a small boat upstream and landed directly at Mist Mahal's disused *ghat,* the very place where her own intended, the boy who'd been poisoned by a snake on the way to the marriage, had been carried ashore. She'd blanked the river from view ever since and allowed the stairs to the river to grow loose and mossy. Treacherous stairs, however, did not dissuade the embarking of Nigel Coughlin.

He was tall and extremely thin. He wore a traditional dhoti, handloomed from coarse native cotton in the style and manner approved by Mr. Gandhi, with a woolen scarf tossed loosely about the shoulders. The shyness, the awkwardness, so evident when the servants greeted him at the muddy ghat and helped him off the boat and then ran back to tell Tara-Ma, giggling (*You can't imagine, tall as a tree with yellow hair, thin as a vine, I don't think he can speak, he only stutters*), vanished the moment he entered the house. What had truly astonished the servants—and not in a positive manner—was his dhoti, not even a fine cotton dhoti, ironed, starched, and crimped at the hem in gila-kara style as a zamindar might wear, but a simple villager's khadi, a rag, muddy in places, food-stained in others, such as any of their fathers might wear. He'd allowed it to get wet, he'd dragged it in the mud.

The servants took their cues and much of their self-respect from the status of the visitors they served, and they did not appreciate the fact that now they would become the targets of taunts from those same stone-tossing lookers-on. Once inside, he righted himself and straightened the folds of his dhoti. Then he lighted a cigarette and swept into Tara Lata's study with a theatrical flourish.

"My dear woman, permit me to extend sincerest wishes for your continued good fortune, directly from His Majesty's most loyal servant." He kissed her hand. His voice was deep and sonorous, despite certain odd inflections.

No man had ever touched her hand nor grazed her fingers with his lips. "The viceroy? I have not had the honor."

"Did I say Baron Irwin? Good lord, no! I presume he's loyal, but I was referring to King Billy, his Irish setter. Ulster Irish, of course. Loyal as Sita in the flames."

Europeans in India generally ran to fat, although extreme emaciation was not unknown. Gauntness seemed to her a more credible reflection of sincere affection.

And so the badinage continued over tea and biscuits for several hours; all thoughts of a curt and proper interview lay abandoned among the pistachio shells and assorted savories. His ashtray gradually filled as they drifted in and out of English and Bengali and every now and then reached into Persian, which, lamentably, was no longer used in official life.

"You have a most remarkable accent, Mr. Coughlin. I don't believe I've heard it."

"It's a wee bit Irish, Miss Gangooly, mixed with Merseyside Liverpool. My parents were Irish, but I was born and spent my childhood in the hills near Darjeeling. They settled me in England when I was seven. I learned what they call the King's English in schools and have been unlearning it ever since." Unlarnin'. Charming.

They knew precisely when to change languages, when references to the other's world were more appropriate than from their own. It seemed to Tara Lata for the moment that communion between the two great cultures of the world, the English and the Bengali, was possible, as it had been in the time of Mist, Hai, and her father. They touched on terra-cotta sculptures and reported temple sites—of which Tara Lata knew very little—and on textual interpretations of certain prayers, of which she knew nothing at all, having never considered alternate interpretations from the literal. From time to time he dropped hints of his own political slant, and then alluded to raging disputes within the administration regarding the future of Bengal. This, she listened to.

"You are familiar with the magistrate for this region, the redoubtable Wainwright, are you not?" he asked.

"Morgan-sahib," she answered. "A very cultured gentleman."

"Really?" he questioned, arching an eyebrow. "So is brewer's yeast."

She quickly righted herself. "Twice a year he visits. Once, after the monsoons have retreated and again before the spring heat begins. He descends from his Bentley like a god, his gold brocaded slipper barely touching the soil—"

"To decide the fate of mortal men," Coughlin completed, in the original Sanskrit of the *Mahabharata*.

Extraordinary! she thought.

"He is considered a harmless old coot by the Home Office. Did you know he sends his wretched paintings to the viceroy in New

Delhi? And they're not of wild roses—we might have found wall space for them in a garage somewhere if they were of native flowers and the like. Tigers—we're very fond of tigers. But I cannot describe to you the rapturous wealth of detail the old bugger lavishes on the circumcision rites of Meo tribesmen! I hope I haven't offended you?"

In truth, she had very little idea of what he talking about, but she was carried away by his accent, his theatrical manner, and the fact that he could launch magnificently complex sentences without pausing for breath. She understood that circumcision was an ordeal *down there* undergone by Muslim boys, following which they harvested a lifetime's demand of female submission. She had a few of Morgan-sahib's gaudy and rather graphic paintings herself—he generally presented one or two on every visit—which necessitated finding them in their hiding places in time to display them prominently before his arrival.

British officials were normally tight-lipped and regimentally loyal. Whatever shameful outrage resulting in the deaths of hundreds, or millions, of Indians was being discussed, they might at most allow a certain "personal questioning" of an action or policy, or, more likely, its "failed implementation" (which allowed the blame to be spread more widely), but it had always occurred within a system they defended as progressive and well-intentioned. Medicine was their favorite analogy. It may taste horrible, it may even prick and cause a moment's discomfort, but it's for your own good. They might *conceivably* have done it differently (whatever the "it" had been), but the effect would, drearily, have come out the same. You see, no one is really to blame, unless it's India, or Indians themselves. Nigel Coughlin paid no such obsequies.

"We've all been made painfully aware of the old bugger's

predilections and the general feeling among the staff is that he does less harm in the hills than he might anywhere else. In any event, Wainwright's little headhunters seem quiescent and even willing to settle their grievances peaceably. No sedition to speak of and very little in the way of the casual butchery, which I fear is on the rise everywhere else on the subcontinent. All of that gets credited to his record. Personally, I find his obsessions mildly perverse but harmless, particularly in comparison to the mischief we casually inflict on India every day. The common run of ICS officers are frustrated souls who lash out at innocents for crimes they themselves are too compromised to commit. I've often made the observation that if we *consciously* staffed the Indian Civil Service with known perverts and permitted them unfettered opportunity to indulge in the most unseemly behavior, the Raj might be restored to its earlier vigor. It's these bottled-up wankers we should fear, not a full-bore pederast, wouldn't you agree, Miss Gangooly?"

She hesitated to offer an opinion.

"As it was in the Company era. As it was right up to the time of the redoubtable Mist. Extraordinary fellow! I've done as much research on him as our faulty record-keeping permits. I'll leave you a copy of my monograph for the Asiatic Society, *The True Crime and Infamous Execution of John Mist.* Poor chap, some local official felt the need for a scapegoat and so he sent a chit forward, *execute the swine,* and some bored superior initialed it and the wheels of Her Majesty's justice were set in motion. What an epic clash! A regular British *Mahabharata*—the Company against the Raj! Armies of ravenous greed facing off against the guardians of righteous plunder! In Mist's day, no one cared about Empire and uplift and all that rot."

"I witnessed that execution, Mr. Coughlin. So horrendous

was it, so much revered was Mr. Mist in this community, that his killing left an enduring stain on relations between our two peoples."

"I understand. But"—he stopped a moment to calculate—"you could not have been more than six years old!"

"I was," she said. "My father wished me to witness it along with the sons and grandchildren of Mr. Hai and with my sisters and relatives. My father said from that day forward the British were to be feared for their venom and treated like snakes. I have not stepped outside these gates since that day."

Nearly half a century after the event she could still hear, in her memory's ear, Mist's command—*Chalo. Kajey hat lagao*—and the creak of the trapdoor, the *whirr* of the tautening rope, and the tearing *snap*, the gasp of Mist-jethu as the deadweighted rope began its slow rotation. They had waited for Mist's body to drop before placing the hood on Rafeek-jethu's head, and he was permitted the beginnings of a prayer, which the Anglo-Indian policeman, not knowing the language and suspecting he was merely malingering, cut short with a sharp command. *Enough!* She remembered the doctors' having to crawl under the scaffold to collect the bodies and pronounce them dead. Mist had recruited them both from Dhaka, the Hindu and the Muslim, and each body was claimed by a member of his faith. Mist, who had banned all Christians from Mishtigunj (or George's Bight, as he originally named it), was named a special, caste-exempt Hindu.

And she remembered something else. She had witnessed the British police wresting the bodies from the doctors and grieving families, denying the opportunity for Rafeek Hai's wives and children or the townspeople in general to mourn their deaths or set the proper rites. Protocols were in place to cover such events, the policeman announced. Most important to avoid a riot and the creation of more martyrs, it was said.

But to the people of Mishtigunj—the name was coined that night and Mist's designation, George's Bight, disappeared—the immediate interpretation was also the most persuasive. The Britishers wanted to desecrate the bodies. They wanted to shift loyalties from two men to a fat lady on a distant throne. Some said the bodies were dumped in the river, downstream so they wouldn't wash up. John Mist and Rafeek Hai might have been eaten by garials or saltwater crocs. Thus they became ghosts, bent on vengeance.

For the rest of her life she encountered villagers who had seen John Mist at night, walking the streets, and Rafeek Hai calling out for his family.

"In truth," said Coughlin, "we *are* monsters. Very few Britishers out here in India do not yield to some coveted fancy. Mine runs to terra-cotta, others to birds or Mughal paintings and there's a chap I've heard of in the United Provinces who parades around in tiger pelts."

✐ ✐ ✐

Nigel Coughlin had been born, *"like many of my ilk,"* as he put it, in India, the fifth generation of his family with Indian ties. "And there shall be no more," he promised. Again, like many in that tribe of displaced Englishmen, he remembered his childhood in the Bengal hills as idyllic. His parents were distant at best, and the only love he'd known before starting school in England had come from his ayah and the families of various house and grounds servants who treated him not as the master's privileged son, but as something from *Kim*. All very predictable, he apologized. It's no wonder we grew up monsters, otherwise we'd bore ourselves to death.

Even today, he did not know the English words for most plants and trees, for foods and fruits, he had no idea of the equivalent English words for the birds and fish of Bengal, nothing he ate or drank or wore bore the least resemblance to the Bengali word that leaped first to his mind. *Shirt, trousers, shoes?* What, pray tell, are they?

To Tara Lata, he was the avatar in manner and sincerity of John Mist himself, he who claimed to have forgotten every word of English. After dealing for nearly half a century with a succession of British administrators who wore their contempt more proudly than their ribbons of office, Tara Lata found herself daring to imagine that she would live to see the day when Indians and Britishers could sit together, sharing only the best of their common foods and experiences. Until that night, she had not thought it possible.

He declared himself to be a Hindu in his heart, but—deprived of a caste designation—with no way of gaining admission short of being hanged as a local martyr. "Oh, you people are most cruel to supplicants such as myself," he moaned, theatrically, but with a touch of sincerity. "If there was a way I could trade this pale skin and these blue eyes and lank yellow hair for anything I see on the streets of India, I should do so in a flash." He lay outside the pale of brahminical civilization, a *mleccha,* not even an untouchable.

" 'White Hindu' is a pejorative term these days," he said, "but I cannot think of a finer etymological oxymoron." He then added, "You would be surprised how many of us there still are in India. A regular congregation."

He had endured a typically sadistic British childhood and elite public schooling whose only solace was that it instilled the rigorous preparation for writing the ICS exams that would return him to India. His Persian and Bengali tutorials were the only things that got him through the worst years, until he was free to declare aloud his love of India.

It did not seem believable to her that any Britisher should love India in a manner that was more profound than an Indian's own. What did it consist of, this love? She loved her village and she loved the Sunderbans and the Bengali language and of course she was a Hindu and she could not imagine the world outside of her religion. But "India" was an abstraction she could not grasp; she felt closer in spirit to England, whose language and history she at least knew, than she did to Maharashtra or Gujarat. She feared at times Indians might get the India they dreamed about, only to find its various parts indigestible. The lofty allusions of Gandhi and Nehru to a nation-in-waiting spreading from the Indus to the Brahmaputra left her vertiginous and unengaged. She wanted a free Bengal, and she wished the same for other parts of India. None of this could be expressed, except perhaps to another Bengali, like Netaji Subhas Bose.

In this sense, Coughlin was a better pan-Indian than she could ever be. "I am of the Church of England in India. I am a devotee of goddess Durga. All of my life I have been looking for a suitable faith, and I believe in India I have found it. In religion I am Indian. In political commitment: Russian. In personal aspects of my life, I follow the Greek ideal." He said he belonged to "the Church of England in India." Among our parishioners, he said, the name of Subhas Bose was not taken in vain.

To which she replied, "I know very little of European matters. You say you are in line with the Russian experiment. They have spoken forcefully against colonialism, and in this matter they are my friends. Any government that places the good of the many above the privileges of the few has the support of India."

"Well said."

But what had happened to the lovely boy? His face by lamp-light was grave, lit from below so that frowns and creases leaped out at her like the deep lines and bulges of a religious mask. Her loyalty was to the Congress Party, particularly on the state level. If Mahatma Gandhi was her father, Nehru her brother, then Sub-has Bose, the Calcutta chief, was something other. He was Bengali. He was Netaji, Leader of the Nation. Unlike the others, his speeches could fire the blood.

Coughlin understood her confusion. "Gandhiji is old and Nehru poses as a proper Englishman. I understand why they don't fire the blood. *Netaji* is a lover."

She blushed.

"Now, madam, we come to the reason for my visit. What I am about to say could send us both to the gallows. Shall I continue?"

She was still confused. Whenever an ICS officer spoke of the "real reason for his visit," disaster soon followed. British under-statement, she'd learned, contained its own form of overinterven-tion. Like the night John Mist and Rafeek Hai were abducted from this very house, this very room. *Gentlemen, come with us, please. There's a slight irregularity we'd like to see cleared up. No, no, please, don't show us to the door. Just Mr. Mist and Mr. Hai. No, no, Mr. Gangooly, your presence is not required. That's a good chap. You others, please continue your dining. Splendid-looking feast, absolutely splendid.* And they never saw their friends, the founders, again, except bound and on the gallows.

She put herself on guard with nothing but the ritual response. "It is not my intention to provide comfort of any sort to His Majesty's government. Nor do I wish to impede the fulfilling of its legal mandate. It is natural for a great people to seek their freedom."

"Indeed it is. Everything I live and breathe is about freedom." He was speaking ex cathedra, he said, but he wanted her to know that he considered himself a reluctant Gandhian—a pacifist only so long as pacifism gained results—and in religion, because of caste, a spurned Hindu. Thus the rationale for the Church of England in India, a little joke he'd started among a circle of old Cambridge friends, all of them India-born, all of them serving in some part of the Indian Civil Service, all of them devoted to the same politics and the same desire to rid India of the British even faster than the Congress Party thought possible. "Except perhaps *Netaji*. He shows the proper impatience."

She begged him to continue. Gallows or not.

"I have come this long way to offer you my services. I see no reason, no reason whatsoever, that the Indian people, who after all have the most to lose, should be kept in the dark about His Majesty's whims. From time to time I hear of policy shifts. I wish to impart some of that intelligence to you so that you might better brace yourself against all that is detestable in the attempt of one race to govern another. I find myself in possession of certain files, items of interest related to potential postings of new officials. Do you understand my meaning?"

"I have committed no illegal acts."

"But you shall, madam, you shall. That is the reason I have taken it upon myself to give fair warning. The definition of 'illegal acts' is about to change. I am aware of your sympathies and your name already appears in certain intelligence files. I have no way of knowing how they got there or who is providing it. Evidently you have enemies in Mishtigunj. I shall do everything in my power to expunge them from any official dossier."

"That is quite impossible," she said. "My people love me." But psychologically, the damage had been done.

"You must understand. To be charged with sedition has absolutely nothing to do with anything you might have done. To be charged means you have violated a new definition of what constitutes sedition. Change the definition, and the government immediately expands the ring of suspects."

Coughlin slept, as he had promised, wrapped in his bedclothes on the floor outside the servants' entrance. Tara Lata found herself unable to sleep for the first time in her life. She paced her bedroom, then lit a lamp and walked down the servants' stairs to gaze on her sleeping guest. He slept like an Indian peasant, with an arm crooked over his eyes as though he were napping in bright sunlight and not a moonless night. He looked like a British schoolboy from illustrated books she'd read, one of the good lads, the sensitive artist, not the footballer. But she couldn't tell for sure. He was ICS despite his other odd allegiances. He was British. In India, that made him the bully, the sadistic brute. She'd never met one who, eventually, wasn't.

She had gone through many lives that evening, but none of them corresponded to the role she was best known for, the graying saint, the sage of Mishtigunj, she who had transcended all earthly needs and joined her fate with the country itself. Outside, old Abdulhaq, the former cook, demoted to chowkidar, raised his stout *lathi* and pounded it twice on the footpath bricks, his sign that he was awake and vigilant. The clap of the sundari against the brick rang like metal and vibrated in the night air. She raised her lamp twice and lowered it, the sign to him that the mistress of Mist Mahal was herself up and restless and not to be disturbed.

And so, Tara Lata was inducted into the war of Indian independence. Nigel Coughlin had left her files, and names she could appeal to should she, or those she valued, fall into police custody. In the morning he would be off to Burma to see his old school chum Eric Blair. Here, he'd said, Eric is quite the writer. You might use your sources and see if there's a name attached to this hanging. She'd read the article; a Bengali had been hanged, probably for sedition but maybe for common criminality, but Mr. Blair was not concerned with the Indian's guilt or innocence. In the world outside the police barracks, he was innocent. His dog thought him innocent. He died with the words "Ram, Ram" on his lips, a prayer cut short by administrative impatience, the need to get back to the club for a stiff peg.

It ought not to be hard to learn his name. She had contacts in Upper Burma. It was the most, and the least, she could do.

Until that night, she had spoken of its inevitability, but had never seen it as a war against the British requiring intelligence and subterfuge. She'd seen it as moral struggle, a way of strengthening the resistance of the Bengali people, uniting their divided communities, and building hope for a better future. Until tonight, the British had been absent from the equation.

2

thought I knew everything about the Tree Bride from the little bits she'd written about herself and the struggle for independence and the pamphlets about her I'd discovered in my parents' house. I hadn't known about Nigel Coughlin, however, until I read Treadwell's papers and then I discovered Coughlin's own cache, written during his retirement years in, of all places, Calcutta. Nigel Coughlin had managed to stay on and even to become an Indian citizen, one of the first ex-Britishers to fully Indianize in 1947. He took a job in a wing of the Fine Arts Museum devoted to terra-cotta sculptures. He wrote many monographs, trained numerous Indian curators, and died in 1973. I wonder now if he'd been the Englishman I'd seen buried in the British cemetery that long ago day when my parents and sisters and I had "paid our respects." There are days when every coincidence in the universe seems mandated to occur.

He also left a legacy of scholarship from the 1920s: his mono-graph on "the true crimes and execution of John Mist," his 1950 book-length (but never published) celebration of the early life of Eric Blair, before his emergence as George Orwell; and late in his life a memoir of his friendship with the long-forgotten Tara-Ma of Mishtigunj.

The letters Coughlin preserved show Tara Lata neither shrink-ing from the task, nor capitulating before the threat of sedition. In 1928 she wrote:

> *You asked if you might be of assistance, and it certainly seems to me (if you are sincere) that the victim of a hanging in Burmah in Mr. Blair's piece deserves a name and an identity. Given the resources at your command, might you be able to provide it? (I do not believe the British have taken to random, anonymous hangings quite yet.) I have made inquiries and determined that his likely name was Subodh Basu, born in Upper Burmah, 1886. He was a teak worker, married with eight children. He was an educated man, not a violent drunk as I'm certain the authorities tried to paint him. He had contacts in a small liberation cell; this does not make him seditious. I, and I daresay you, have similar contacts. In this time and place it is inevitable.*

> *Yes, it is most probable that Mr. Basu murdered his supervisor, but under what provocation? The story as relayed to me is at odds with the official police report. My informants tell me he was "caught" reading a Congress tract and his supervisor put him on report to the British lumber mill owner. The supervisor he killed was Anglo-Indian, as were his jailers. I do not understand why Mr. Blair did not provide at least part of this information in context, since he professes, as do you, a sympathy for the Quit India movement.*

Identification of our enemies is simple; separation from our so-called friends is infinitely more difficult.

The teak workers were organizing themselves into a kind of labor union. Of course, their activities had to be secretive. Their contacts, per force, were with the more militant members of Bengal Congress. I am suggesting this was a political execution, not a judicial murder. Will you please determine the facts?

Coughlin's history of Mist Mahal is more revealing yet. The history of the house, Mist Mansion Number One, is buried inside the Mist monograph, the same article in which he revealed the trumped-up charges that led to Mist's execution.

I had not known that John Mist, in his indigo-planting years before settling in George's Bight and founding the village that would later bear his name, had been remitting funds to the offices of that "perfect Welsh egg," David Llewellyn Owens, his first lawyer. The money was destined for the support of one "Olivia Pereira" of Kidderpore. Coughlin knew nothing of the story and fate of Olivia Todd; nor of Mist's role in her disgrace. He assumed only that the remittances were to a long-lost lover or perhaps even an illegitimate daughter. "A debt of honour," he called it, true enough so far as it goes, as he built his case for the "true history" of John Mist.

In 1880, when she was six years old, Tara Lata's childhood friend and chief house servant, Sameena, was married to Shafiq Mohammed Hai, a student in the local school who was destined, according to his father, Rafeek Hai, for a career in medicine in Dhaka or Calcutta. He was a boy of nine, standing in the jail-house square with Tara Lata and the other Gangoolys, and with his father's wives, when Rafeek Hai was hanged and denied a proper burial. He and Sameena and the crowd led by Jai Krishna had clamored with the authorities to release the bodies, but Shafiq had been struck across the face by a British truncheon. Somehow, Shafiq made it through secondary school and gained admission to the medical faculty in Dhaka, while Sameena stayed back in Mist Mahal, serving the needs of Tara Lata.

He returned as a doctor seven years later, becoming Tara Lata's personal physician. By this time, he and Sameena were living as husband and first wife, and after many pregnancies that terminated in failure, when she was nearly forty years old, a son, Gul Mohammed, was born. In gratitude, Shafiq went off to Mecca, becoming Hajji; and in 1932, when he completed his Persian translation of the *Mist-nama,* he was honored with the title "Chowdhury" by the newly installed district commissioner, Virgil Treadwell.

Apart from learning of the connection between Sameena and the Hais, the story was not out of line with my earlier knowledge. Sameena's father, the cook Abdulhaq, after having been fired by the newly orthodox Hindu Jai Krishna for being too unclean to cook or serve his food, was installed as gatekeeper, or chowkidar, a reassignment that might be considered compassionate, or cruelly demeaning.

But this time I'm coming with different questions and looking for different answers. Tara Lata had an enemy, someone who fed her name to the British authorities in Calcutta. It is tempting to think of the two little girls, one Hindu from a leading family, the other Muslim from the serving class, as best friends skipping between the rows of uvaria trees. I wanted so much to think it, I somehow made it so. But the power of her family's indignity must have been burning. What possible reaction could she, and her father, have had to the fact that Jai Krishna, in his quest for spiritual purity, had summarily fired Abdulhaq for a condition he could not rectify? And the fact that Sameena, a cook-turned-chowkidar's daughter, would be able to marry the son of the town's leading Muslim—*that* seems to me improbable. In a Muslim-majority area there must have been many more suitable bride candidates than little Sameena. Abdulhaq would not have been able to afford the dowry expected by an educated doctor from a leading family. There must have been the promise of a delayed dowry. Sameena's dowry was the house she never owned.

That, in fact, was Coughlin's conclusion: Sameena and her husband, Tara Lata's personal physician, plotted to take possession of Mist Mahal, sooner or later. The political involvement of Tara Lata in the war years of the famine and the Indian National Army and the pending Japanese invasion and the increasingly desperate British hold on its "Empire" emboldened nearly every component of Bengali society to stake its claims on an uncertain future.

In 1943, following the death of Tara Lata Gangooly while in police custody, her house passed to Begum Sameena Chowdhury, widow of the late (Dr.) Hajji Shafiq Mohammed Chowdhury. She was the mother of Gul Mohammed Chowdhury, the old hajji I'd met in Mishtigunji on my second visit. I'd met Hajji's son, on leave from the New York restaurant while he pillaged his father's holdings, on my third visit. And of course, I've had dealings with Sameena's great-grandson, Abbas Sattar Hai, in San Francisco.

Nigel Coughlin's records cease in 1971, near the time of his death. Mist Mahal, as he'd written in a Dhaka newspaper under their "Old Days in the Distant Country" column, was still legally owned, or at least occupied, by the ninety-seven-year-old widow, Sameena Chowdhury, and the families of her son and grandson, their wives and children and assorted other relatives. Although no will or bill of sale had ever been presented, it was thought that the original owners, the Gangoolys, would have favored the present outcome. Effectively, until challenged, the house belonged to the Hai-Chowdhurys.

Toward the end of his life Coughlin saw it as part of the inevitable "Muslimisation" of East Bengal. The great zamindari estates of the once-powerful Hindu minority had, one by one, become "majoritised." He pointed out that even Jai Krishna Gangooly's original occupancy of Mist Mansion Number One, following the founder's execution, was (legally speaking) no less secure.

I have a different take. It means that Victoria's murderer, my would-be assassin, the crippler of my husband, and an indiscriminate killer in India and America, was born and possibly raised in my family's house. The house itself, if that money to Olivia Pereira was traced back to him, might have killed John Mist, Rafeek Hai, and, eventually, the Tree Bride. The magic of Mishti-gunj is black indeed.

3

What I'm about to relate may strike you, dear reader, as mumbo-jumbo. I'm reluctant even to share it, but (as they say) in the interest of full disclosure, I will admit to being a believing, ritual-observing Hindu. Our children, born here, will never gain or suffer from that status.

The Tree Bride visits me in the rented house on Beulah Street. I feel her presence; I hear her urgent whispers.

I am trapped in your world of mortals, she pleads. *Perform the rites.*

I carry on with my routines. I ease Bish's legs into the elastic leggings he has to wear as part of pressure therapy.

Set me free, Tara.

This time it's a command, but I ignore it. My baby is waiting for an auspicious moment. My husband needs my every minute. It shames him to be so helpless.

Ah, distracted from duty to me by pati-seva, the Tree Bride sneers.

The selfless Hindu wife dedicates herself to her husband's welfare. Even a divorced one. Even in America.

Once Bish is settled in bed with his cell phone and laptop, I move from room to room turning on the lights. It's an evening ritual I learned thirty-odd years ago from my paternal great-grandmother. She believed that twilight was the time that evil spirits were most potent and unhappy ghosts most eager to take over living bodies. Most ghosts were unhappy, she said, caught between worlds. Some were dangerous. As the day-lit sky blackened with subtropical suddenness, she drove them out with a cobra-headed sacred lamp fueled by clarified butter. What was sanctified rite for my great-grandmother is for me an unbreakable habit. As night falls, I flick every light switch on in whatever apartment or house in whichever city I happen to be living. But Tara Lata will not allow herself to be banished. She floats beside me, and settles across the kitchen table from me as I boil myself a saucepan of milky tea on the stove.

The Tree Bride, I know, is one of the dangerous ones.

Did you know that Mackenzie hanged me in a jail cell?

Yes, I say under my breath. Dominick Mackenzie hanged or strangled or shot many freedom fighters. He was on a mission to defend British India against the Japanese Empire, at least in his mind and in his ledgers. *You,* Tara Lata, *you* knew the names of those boys and girls too, you kept your own files, you passed them on to Nigel Coughlin in Calcutta and he saw that they were published. At least he said he did. I have not found them.

I knew from my paternal great-grandmother, who had come as a child-bride to Mishtigunj, that the Tree Bride had died in jail of a heart attack. Hers was a suicide by fasting, the District Commissioner in that area had claimed. I know him now as Vertie

Treadwell. The same District Commissioner had ordered that her body be cremated by the police, a man I know as Dominick Mackenzie. The D.C. had been afraid that nationalist-minded villagers—especially those few members of the Congress Party whom he hadn't yet found a way to jail—would turn her funeral procession into an anti-Raj, pro–Netaji Subhas Bose protest rally. The Union Jack would be dishonored, the Rising Sun would fly, briefly, over the Commissioner's cottage. He wanted no part in the circuslike making of an Indian martyr. She had to die, and her body had to vanish. Dust to dust, or mud to mud, under controlled circumstances.

They tossed my body over the prison wall into the sewage ditch. I hovered above my corpse. It lay submerged in filth. Vultures ripped chunks off with their beaks. Starving dogs chewed my bones. I had no body but I felt the pain, and the shame.

I pour myself a cup of tea. I set a second in front of her.

Help me, Tara.

My father made his fortune in tea. "Trust to tea," he would joke when my sisters and I were young. "It makes for calm nerves and cool heads. What do you think Nehru served Lord Mountbatten when they were negotiating India's sovereignty?" If the Tree Bride is going to reveal my mission to me, it should be over strong tea.

I have waited half a century to be liberated. Her voice is soft again, as soft and steady as the mist pressing against the panes of the kitchen window. *Your son is there, he can perform my rites. Please! He can send me on my way to the Abode of Ancestors. I am ready for the journey.*

So it isn't vengeance that she seeks. It isn't even justice. It is her soul's release.

In the morning Bish doesn't mock me for listening to ghosts. He's a scientist; he keeps an open mind. Living or dead or somewhere in between, it's all information, and it's obviously a kind of communication. He says instead, "When we're fit enough, we'll make a trip to Kashi. I've always wanted to see the Manikarnika."

Kashi is to Varanasi as Mishtigunj is to Razakpur. It is in, but not of, the cities that surround it. In the legends, Kashi exists on Shiva's trident, held above the earth altogether. The Manikarnika Ghat on the Ganga River is the holiest cremation site in Hinduism. India is the navel of the universe and Kashi the navel of India and the Manikarnika Ghat the navel of Kashi.

It doesn't matter to Bish whether the Tree Bride came to me as a dream-figure or a ghost. For every problem there is a cause and, more important, a solution, and Bish has made solving problems his mission in life. Tara Lata's spirit is restless because she suffered a bad death. Her spirit is stalled from starting on its yearlong journey to the Abode of Ancestors. A ceremonial cremation, conducted in accordance with funerary rituals laid down from ancient times, is necessary for its liberation. Until the rites are completed, she cannot acquire the in-between body she needs to go on her journey. Until then, she is doomed to remain a *preta,* a ghost, instead of a *pitr,* an ancestor. Bish proposes that we give her soul its rightful send-off from the holiest cremation ghat at the holiest point of the Ganga River in the holiest of cities. In this world, it makes sense. We need all the godly help we can get.

"I'm ready to go right now."

Abbas Sattar Hai has taught me not to defer duties and pleasures. I troll the Internet for round trip San Francisco–Varanasi airfares and hotel rates. "I mean it, Bish." In the days of the Raj, when foreign rulers with clumsy tongues and lazy pens named India's cities, Varanasi was known to the world as Benares.

"I don't think commercial airlines like to fly eight-and-a-half-months'-pregnant ladies." He tries to smile as he says it, but the skin graft around his mouth has contracted more than his doctors had hoped it would. In the eight and a half months since the fire-bombing, Bish has learned the varieties of burn pain and I have learned about STGs, FTSGs, skin flaps, and skin regeneration. His legs are a laboratory for innovative skin-growth and scar-reduction experiments.

"Then why not do the funeral ceremonies in Fremont?" We know it now. Victoria died because the pasts of Vertie Treadwell, Rafeek Hai, and Tara Lata Gangooly conspired to reconnect us, their ignorant descendants.

Bish has made up his mind, and there'll be no dissuading him. But I'm impatient to set her tormented spirit free. So I give it one more try. "I'll call Yash and get the phone number of that south Indian priest."

"Veeraswamy, electrical engineering," says my memory-man. "He's a good priest, that's why he'll say go to India." Behind it all, I hear: Ours is a special case. It's not the passing of a loved one on alien soil. We're the aliens now. The Tree Bride would not permit burial outside of India. We're trying to bury a phase of history itself.

"Yash will say it's not worth saving the money or the time. He'll say we must do it right or not do it at all. That's why he went to Varanasi on his own."

In Fremont, the funeral home staff had focused on dignifying death: the tasteful casket, the floral arrangements, the muted lighting, the melancholic Muzak. Victoria was cremated in an underground oven and returned to Yash in a brass pot. In a cremation ghat in Kashi, the corpse would have been laid out on a platform of flammable branches drenched in ghee and oil while around it more corpses on bamboo biers were unloaded, wood-sellers haggled over prices, the funeral barbers demanded bigger tips, truant schoolboys hurled pebbles at stray dogs, vendors listened to film music on boom boxes, and solemn brahmin priests chanted Sanskrit verses. In Kashi, death would not have signaled the end of life, but the soul's return to the Abode of Ancestors, in realms invisible to mortals, to be judged, and returned in time to a new existence.

I've always been a little frightened, just as an outwardly observant Christian or Jew might be: Sorry, you cursed. You didn't keep the Sabbath holy. You coveted your neighbor's oxen. A Hindu has even more prohibitions. What if Yama demands perfect ritual adherence to every aspect of one's caste duty? *I warned you! I commanded you!*

I have crossed the Black Waters and, by my tradition, at least, I have lost my caste. I have mingled with the casteless, I've eaten and grown fond of red and white meats. I've divorced, I've had lovers, and I've been drunk on some occasions. I'd be a little reluctant to join any club where a rigid brahmin like Jai Krishna Gangooly sets the standards. Otherwise, I have no complaints. Hinduism is very scientific, very mathematical. At the center of consciousness is a zero; at the extremities, infinity. The universe collapses and expands in fifty-two-billion-year cycles—which seems about right—and has been creating and destroying itself forever, life recomposing itself endlessly around the cores of collapsing stars.

"Okay, we'll go to Kashi," I concede.

Bish's cell phone goes off just then. "Take Me Out to the Ball Game." Rabi had programmed it as an in-joke between him and me. Bish is not into American spectator sports even though, with

CHATTY systems, he has changed the way and the speed with which America communicates.

"Aren't you going to answer it?"

"It's Yash," he says, without picking it up. "We're pretty close to a breakthrough."

I worry that it hurts Bish too much to speak toward the end of the day. He is on more painkillers than anyone I know. "Do you want me to tell Yash you'll call him back tomorrow?"

"No."

Verizon's digitalized voice comes on.

"We'll go to Kashi only if you agree to one condition," Bish says.

Yash sounds more excited on the answering tape than I've ever heard him. "You cracked it, Bish old chap! We've done it! Watch out world, here comes KhanJee Communications! Call me tomorrow! First thing!"

"What have you two cracked, Bish?"

"I'll go to Kashi only as a married man."

I remember my great-grandmother's story of god Shiva showing Kashi to his bride, Parvati. Kashi, the luminous city, where death holds no terror and no finality. "Are you proposing to me, Bish?"

"Do you think I am?"

And so we were married in a fifteen-minute ceremony in a lawyer's office above a bar on Haight Street exactly seven days and twenty-one minutes before Victoria Kallie, our daughter, was born.

Epilogue

In Varanasi the Ganga River flows from south to north or, as Daddy explains to Rabi and me, it flows away from the Domain of Death toward the Realm of Rebirth. Bish, Rabi, infant Victoria, Mummy, and I are clustered around Daddy on the front porch of Clark's Hotel. It is a sun-sharded January morning, crisp by the standards of local residents, many of whom are wearing wool caps and scarves as well as sweaters and shawls. Our group ranges in age from seventy down to eight weeks, and we have gathered in Kashi for the Tree Bride's cremation.

It's been eighteen years since my last stay at Clark's Hotel. When Daddy's late personal swamiji was living in an ashram here and Daddy was still the owner of tea estates, we would stay at Clark's whenever he needed spiritual guidance for making corporate decisions. He has stayed in touch with the older residents of the ashram and one of them has found a head funeral priest, an assistant priest, and hired the necessary wood-bearers and pyre-builders for the ceremony. Kanai, the servant who has looked after Mummy and him for more than thirty years, has made sure that the kitchen staff has our "picnic lunches" and bottles of chilled filtered water ready in time for us to leave for the ghat.

We'll all squeeze into a rented car. Kanai and Bish's motorized chair will follow in a scooter-version of a pickup truck. Kanai, ever loyal to my parents, has developed a proprietorial attitude to Bish's wheelchair on Mummy's behalf. Her Parkinson's disease is no longer responding to medication. For today's trek through the dusty, crowded, twisting alleys leading to the cremation ghat, the nephew of another ashram resident has promised to have a sedan chair and four porters to carry her. "Please to call as soon as your car is stationary," the young man had assured me early this morning when I'd called to make sure he remembered. "We all have mobiles, no? Varanasi is high-tech city." Why ruin his pride in owning a cell phone? Why tell him that the man he sees being pushed in the wheelchair is Mr. Cell Phone, and that whatever the cell phone confers in convenience can be wiped out in a second?

Mummy was desolate as she listened to the young man's assurances. She had hoped that the hiring of a sedan chair would fall through. She wants to walk to the banks of the holy river. She sent Kanai to the bazaar and had him buy a sturdy stick hewed from a tree limb, the kind that pilgrims use as they make the rounds of the five sacred sites in Varanasi. "You never know," she said when I discovered the cane in the closet of her hotel room. "What if you break a leg? Or worse still, your hip?" I scolded. In response, she held a fumbling hand out toward little Victoria, who was asleep in her bassinette. "In Kashi, miracles happen."

Rabi catches our slightest gestures on his videocam. His favorite English teacher at the progressive school he goes to in San

Francisco has asked him to keep a video diary for his "Visual Autobiography" class while he is visiting family for a year in India. Right now his lens is focused on Daddy and Bish.

Bish appears engrossed in Daddy's story of how, since moving to Rishikesh from Kolkata, he has controlled his hypertension by reciting Sanskrit chants. "Two full hours twice a day," my father advises my husband. "Morning and evening. Best therapy I know, and I tell you I have tried many."

Daddy is just warming up. "I tell you, results are fantastic! What does Mummy know about anything? Ask my doctor if you don't believe me. Medication plus meditation. M-squared. Unbeatable combination!"

Bish, ever the perfect son-in-law, promises to try medico-meditation therapy before alerting us that Kanai is beckoning to us from just outside the hotel's lounge. "Ready or not, it's time."

/ , ,

So we make our slow way in a procession from a parking lot to Manikarnika Ghat near the Manikarnika tank that Lord Vishnu dug and filled with the divine sweat of his labor from cosmic creation. Rabi captures our party of many—Bish in his wheelchair, Mummy wobbly in the sedan chair on the shoulders of four hard-breathing porters, Daddy swinging the newly bought pilgrim's cane and shuffling along, little Victoria riding high in the Baby-Björn I've strapped on, the young middleman and his ashram friends bicycling alongside us and behind, a line of wood-bearers, funeral barbers, temple guides, taxi touts hoping to be hired, fruit-hawkers, sweetmeat-sellers, religious-beads vendors convinced we need their wares, and urchins wanting to earn tips by slapping away stray cows and dogs. We inch past schoolboys jostling each other to be in the range of Rabi's videocam; we swerve around bodybuilders from wrestling schools locked in fierce holds; we duck plumes of red betel-leaf juice spat out by men lounging in front of cigarette-and-paan stalls; we turn away vendors, drop coins in the leprous palms of beggars, and step over supine bhang-smokers.

Just as I am enjoying the vitality of the City of the Dead, one of the young men from the ashram sidles up to me. "How do you do, madam? What do you want to know about Hindu ceremonies? I am graduate of Benares Hindu University. What for is education but sharing of informations, no? Mohan is my good name. Please to ask Mohan any questions, not bloody tour guide. They know zero. Don't be shy, madam, okay please?"

There's no thanking him and moving ahead in this crowded alley. "Your son is making documentary? Sometimes foreigners see our city through cataract-eyes. You want I explain Kashi to him?"

I tell him that Rabi's just working on a school project. He then begins a story that threatens to end in a moral. It's about a virtuous king, the testing of whose faith involved his losing his kingdom, his wife and son, and working at a burning ghat in Kashi as a lowly watchman. Polite small talk? Kashi-dwellers' chauvinism? My enlightenment?

Once upon a time a skeptical sage wanted to find out for himself if the Hindu king with the reputation of being the most virtuous of all kings was deserving of the awe people accorded him. So the sage, disguising himself as a brahmin beggar, appeared at the royal court and demanded that the king give him, as alms, his entire kingdom. The virtuous king handed the alms-gatherer his kingdom. But the sage wasn't yet satisfied with the testing. He demanded another donation. The king, having already given up all his material wealth, was forced to sell his wife and only son into slavery in order to raise money for the second donation. In order to survive, the virtuous king had to take the job of guarding corpses in the cremation grounds in Kashi, a job that is performed by untouchables. Meanwhile, the sage, not content with the havoc he had already caused, decided to test the ex-king further by killing his son by snakebite as the boy was plucking flowers for devotional offerings. The king's wife, haggard from years of brutalization and therefore at first unrecognized by the king, carried the son's corpse to the cremation ground where the king was working. He demanded of her the fee that has to be paid for each cremation. Even after recognizing the desolate woman as his wife and the dead boy as his son, he insisted he must turn away the grieving woman if she couldn't pay. It was his destiny, he explained, to end up as a funerary worker, and it was his duty to collect the fee set down for cremations. Having no possession of value other than a ring he had given her when he had still been king, she slipped it off her finger and gave it to him. But the rules required that the corpse be covered with a sheet. The desperate mourner began to unwrap her sari so it could serve as the bier's covering. That finally convinced the sage, who revealed his identity. He restored life to the dead son and the kingdom to the most virtuous of virtuous kings.

A tale from the time of dharma; duty above all.

The boy who recited the narrative, hoping for an appreciative tip from a wealthy, obviously foreign-based family, had no idea how close to home he had struck. I don't think I can stand up to any more testing.

Rows of bamboo biers are lined up on the cremation grounds as we arrive. The smoke, the flames, the heat, the soot, and the grease: They become part of Rabi's project. Some of the corpses are of men and women who were brought to Kashi to die, because to die here is to be saved instantaneously. "A hundred pyres, no waiting," Rabi quips. We have no corpse of the Tree Bride. Instead we have a raffia figure the head funeral priest's assistants have made as a proxy. A proxy-soul for a proxy-bride.

An assistant priest explains that after today's ceremony, we are expected to perform three more postcremation ceremonies. "First one is ten days after today. Second one is after another ten days. Last one is one year from today."

My face must have given away my reluctance to stay around for another twenty days. I want to give a ghost peace, not fulfill rituals to the letter. "We've arranged a shortcut for you, madam," the middleman-turned–tour guide explains to me. "Most overseas peoples are taking shortcut option. Yours is extra-different, so, madam . . . ," he pauses delicately.

Just in case I didn't get it, a friend of his rubs the thumb and forefinger of his right hand together. "This way you don't have to take a dip in the river. The water is very, very holy here but will make you sick, no? But you can buy bottled Ganga water to take back. Or, if you wish, I can ship to you."

Wood-bearers had erected the pyre before we got here. The logs and kindling are drenched with oils and ghee. Prayers are chanted, the raffia body of the Tree Bride is placed on the pyre, ghee drizzled on it, and all prelighting rites completed.

"Who will touch flaming torch to skull?" The assistant priest translates for the head priest's Sanskrit and waves a burning splinter.

Rabi hands me his videocam. It is his duty as the only living male blood relative present, the Tree Bride being a mother's side connection. He seizes the kindling and touches the raffia mouth of the Tree Bride. If it were a real corpse—as someday Bish and I will be, and when Rabi performs our ceremonies—the skull would explode and the soul escape its fleshly prison. On pyres all around us, as sons light the bodies of their mothers and fathers, heads are popping, bodies twitch and shrivel, family members erupt in joy and sadness, shreds of Sanskrit prayers and other languages escape their lips. The raffia sizzles as more ghee is added. And in the hiss of the burning raffia and wood, I hear a whispered exclamation. "Ram! Ram!"